Especially for those who love a child struggling with addiction. And for those who seek compassion, not condemnation, and knowledge, not contempt, to treat this chronic mental health disease.

CONTENTS

It is night and, as Mona walks, the streetlights go out and it is completely dark. The street is deserted, and she hears her footsteps loud on the pavement, then terror erupts at the sound of other quick footsteps behind her. She starts to run. The terror builds; she is about to give in to it, but, with an enormous effort of will, she turns around and shouts, "No!" The fear dissolves and she is filled with a power she's never imagined she could possess.

The shyness might be an act, Erica considers. He's more likely one of those kids her daughter hung out with in senior year, speeding around without their seatbelts on, while high on the incredibly long list of stuff kids now use and abuse, from marijuana-laced lip balm to bath salts, to something they squeeze on their eyeballs, plus whatever pills are on hand. Booze of course. And heroin. Kyle has golden-brown hair cut short. Gym-type muscles.

Eventually, they get talking about why he's at the shelter doing community service.

"Ah, it was just pot," he says, grimacing. "OK, I was stupid to have it on the seat when the cops stopped me. But, I mean, I wasn't, like, dealin'. There's serious addicts in this town, man. Why do they bother over a little marijuana?"

Erica can't help but agree with him. Almost. Of course, everyone in the recovery business says marijuana is a gateway drug, slowing down brain development for kids, as well as reflexes. It was—it had—back in her day. But Erica has seen so much worse, she's on Kyle's side. What's a little pot? Compared to hard drugs, nothing in her view.

"I guess they're afraid once you use anything that not's legal, it's a slippery slope. You know, all that other stuff that's out there. Oxycodone—Oxys? Even heroin."

"I wouldn't get into that shit," Kyle says fervently, then turns bright red. "Stuff," he mumbles. "I would never be a junkie."

Erica stops folding and regards him. There is certainly hope for this lad if he is ashamed of saying *shit* in front of her—her own child slings the *f* word around endlessly, although it's her tendency to call Erica *dude* that really upsets her. But she can't let the *j* word slip by. "They're somebody's children, you know," she says, shakily.

"What?"

"Addicts. Drug addicts."

Kyle shrugs. "Yeah? So anyway, why are *you* here folding animal blankets?"

"Me? Oh, tickets. Speeding. One too many. Dumb, like you! Always in a hurry. Well, not now." She has folded way more blankets than Kyle. Clearly, his mom has always done the laundry.

Two mutts who have the run of the ramshackle building trot over. Kyle, ignoring Ernestine Gasparino's warning about petting strange dogs, bends over to stroke the black one with funny white patches like spilled paint all over its back, and all of a sudden Erica is about to cry. This happens so often that she knows exactly what to do. She pinches her arm with expert cruelty. That and the recent meds help fend off a lot of her emotional bingeing, but not all. The pain—let's be real, the anger—has to go somewhere. And it tends to spill out of her in stinging drops. Kyle's thoughtless "junkie" has made her think of Dane, Mona's friend or more–than–friend, the winter of Mona's senior year in high school, John's last winter, when everything but his falling apart had seemed insubstantial to Erica. Except that now she has a clear memory of Dane gently petting Casho. Dane, who was nothing like Kyle except for being a teenager. Dane was pale and wan, a vegan drifter—she's certain Kyle lives on sausage pizza and contact sports—and, of course, there were Dane's track-riddled arms. She saw them the morning she came out of her bedroom just as Dane was scooting out of the little bathroom in the hall to disappear back into the rankness of her daughter's room. Skinny, scarred, scabby arms. Probably his whole body looked like that. She'd felt sick and angry: this hangdog, half-homeless, adolescent addict was in her home and not even in the spare room she'd insisted on. (Her daughter had pleaded, "Please Mom, he's been kicked out of his house, and it's winter. He has nowhere to go but the train station. We're not doing anything; he just needs a friend.") At the same time that Erica wanted to throw him out in the cold, she also wanted to feed this wretched boy. So, she made a stack of pancakes and fruit salad for Dane that day when the kids finally got up. She could only hope he hadn't broken her rule about no drugs in her house. Yeah, right. As she was always relearning, however, addicts always do drugs.

One night, about a month after the Dane incident, she'd woken up before dawn to find her daughter curled in a ball next to her, shaking and sobbing. One of the kids in the alternative senior-year program she and Dane and a bunch of other bright, creative, fucked-up kids were in had called her: Dane, who'd been let back in his house, had been found in his bed by his dad, dead of an overdose. Eighteen years old.

"He was so mixed up, but he was a good kid."

Erica held her so tightly both could barely breathe.

"Can I stay here at home with you today and skip school?" Mona pleaded.

Erica scanned the ceiling, as if looking for an answer. There were rarely answers.

"OK." Mona could be next. At any time. And Erica was a husk.

But then life had lurched on, Dane was not talked about much, and, now, all these months later, Erica is here at the animal shelter, watching Kyle hug a funny-looking dog. "Champ," he says. "That's what I'm going to call him."

"Champ?" It doesn't suit him. He's a lowly misfit, this dog. An outcast. But, well, he's also a survivor.

"It's a good name for him." Kyle stands up and looks around at the huge store of bedding. "There's so much of this sh . . . stuff, we'll never get it done."

Erica snaps a thin blanket, and it sails out. "We don't have to get it all done," she tells him. "Just put in our time." She folds it, remembering her mother pegging out laundry on the line in their boxy backyard. Mom. Kyle is censoring *shit* to *stuff*, because she is a mom. Absurdly, Erica wants to tell him there had been a time when she was a hot babe. That words like *shit* and *fuck* had been part of the standard lexicon back then, too. That she had once seduced a boy kind of like Kyle during a college trip in Mexico and discovered (because he told her) that he was a virgin. A boy with golden curls she'd had not-very-satisfactory sex with on a beach, sand biting into her body, both of them full of wine and hormones.

"Anyway, it's not a real job."

In her third and last week at the shelter, she's given the plum job of walking dogs in the gilded October woods across the street from the shelter. On Friday, her very last day, she walks a pit-mutt that she doesn't trust. It pulls her up and up the winding path to the top of a ridge where, at last, the sad, endless barking of the beasts below cannot be heard. The air is filled with the incense of autumn, and the pit-mutt happily ignores her, nosing through the mess of earth and leaves and probably dead little animals. She thinks about Casho, her creamy pudge of a Labrador, who does the same thing. John and Mona had gotten him together as a puppy, as a surprise, in her other lifetime. Casho has developed the habit of peeing on rugs ever since the nightmare began.

"Have you been through a crisis recently?" Ann the shelter director, with her sensible, blunt-cut hair and sturdy boots, had inquired when Erica ventured to ask her for advice about this peeing problem a few days before. "Cos dogs pick up on our emotions, you know."

Well, yeah. Hell, yeah. "Cris*es*," Erica said. "As in a bunch." Maybe she should crate Casho, but he'd hate that. Or find him a more emotionally stable home. But that's unacceptable. She and Casho are in this for the long haul. She'll just have to keep buying Nature's Miracle and roll up the rugs.

When she brings the pit back to the shelter, she sees Kyle at the gate, car keys in hand.

"You're leaving, Kyle?" *Without saying goodbye to me, Kyle?*

"Oh, hey, yeah. I'm finally done with this fu . . . friggin' place. You weren't around, so . . ."

"Well, good for you. And me. We're done here! So, what's next for you?" *Community college? A shit job? Pot dealer?*

"Mmm, I don't know." He has that frozen look they all get at his age, which she is sure she used to get, while contemplating the future. She should tell him it will be all right—he can use all of *this* to build something solid—but she doesn't, because he can't hear the drone of grown-up voices. She wants to tell him not to settle, to have adventures, leave this town, hook up with girls, or guys if that's your preference, get or don't get tattoos, be a bartender somewhere cool, backpack through a Third World country. That was what they did back in her day, for what it was worth. But he wouldn't hear her. Today's kids are saddled with a different vision of the future: one of student debt and no security. You probably needed so much money today even for backpacking.

She settles for "Good luck, Kyle. You're a great guy."

What she doesn't want to tell him is that she, Erica Mason, is a liar; she is impersonating someone else. Her incapacitated daughter. She's done community service for her daughter's crime. She has kept it a secret from everyone, but the echoes of the canine howls of protest have been an aural backdrop to her guilt about pretending to be Mona these last three weeks. In the woods, walking dogs this past week, she'd imagined herself as Mona, kicking a pile of leaves, sullen with moisture. Imagined herself on a log in the dappled sun, talking to the dog, as Mona. "Good dog, good dog." Though he didn't seem to want to be petted. Poor beast, living in a holding cell. "I love you," she'd said to this dog. She tried to imagine Mona saying it, but she could not. Erica says, "I love you," a lot in her head to Mona. Sometimes she suspects she's saying it because, so often, she does not love Mona; in fact, sometimes she hates her. And that *cannot be*. In the woods, she stood up and kicked some leaves, thinking about kicking Mona. Erica has had her heart broken very recently, of course, over John, but she has never experienced such unbearable pain as she does now for her teenaged blackmailer who relentlessly ups the ransom each time.

She doesn't hate Mona. She hates what Mona has become.

In the little office, Ernestine hands her the completed time sheet to mail to the court. Signed, Mona Grey. What would the judge do if he knew it was a forgery? How would Erica be penalized? Lectured about what a pathetic enabler she is? Made to serve more community service hours for her crime?

As she drives home, languid raindrops turn into steady rain. She dashes into her silent house, makes the reluctant Casho go outside to pee—he doesn't like to get wet—makes coffee, and sits down to read the local paper. She comes to an interview with a young woman about her brother's recent suicide. "I realized how self-centered grieving was, and I decided I would be different; I would not grieve." Erica flings the paper away as if it were on fire.

Erica hears a choking sound; it's her, gagging on the invisible smoke that clogs her air, the smog and sting of grief. John is dead, Mona is a drug addict, and guess what? You don't get to choose how to grieve; it has its own agenda. It is a shapeshifter, it bides its time, striking when it can. Noiselessly and efficiently. Oh, the girl in the newspaper will find this out.

Later, she calls Ronnie, ready to confess her crime. Her most trusted friend for many years, a gentle soul, can't hide her incredulity. "You what? Did three weeks of community service pretending you were Mona? But why, Erica? What were you thinking? After what she's put you through?"

"It had to be done."

"By her. Not you. It's not your responsibility."

"But she's in Brooklyn, in college; she'd have to drop out, and she'd be back in the old neighborhood. I couldn't risk it."

OK, she's a bad liar, and Ronnie knows her so well. And Erica knows herself well enough to know she's way off base. She gets the faulty reasoning and the codependency thing from decades of going to AA meetings. She's "enabling" Mona's disease yet again, cleaning up after her big-time. But she can't get around or through it: Mona is incapable of doing her time. Mona with the now-jutting bones, the permanent cold. She has shaved her head; lucky for her, she has a beautifully shaped one. Mona in that hole of a room in Greenpoint, probably just pretending to go to classes. Erica prays every day that she is going, doing her work. She suspects that Mona is still doing drugs.

After dinner on a tray (always on a tray now, even though there are three tables to choose from in this house: the round one in the kitchen, the polished, French country antique in the dining room, and the wicker one on the porch), Erica picks up one of the Scandinavian crime novels she reads as mindlessly as eating pistachios. This one features a detective who's also a recent widow. Imagine that. Hyperattentive to the real and imagined pathology of their shared status, Erica compares their symptoms. The Swede seems basically psychotic—the book says that "she existed outside all reality"—resigned to a lifetime of sustained, crushing loss, which seems plausible to Erica.

As she reads, she realizes she has picked up a lot about Nordic ways: their chronic crappy, gray, wet weather with virtually no sunshine for months, all that aquavit, and extreme introversion tied to a general, modern, European sense of there being no way out, the opposite of the can-do-ism of America (still!). A yellow brick road is not in these folks' lives. So it makes sense that the mourning detective expects to feel depleted for the rest of her life. Probing her own psyche, Erica wonders if she is that badly wounded. Because she can't imagine feeling like herself again. Take that, newspaper girl. She'd settle for being somewhere in the middle, between the young woman with the dead brother who refuses the reality of grief and the emotionally overwhelmed (though still crime-fighting) Swedish detective.

Sleep has been Erica's favorite drug since she gave up booze and mood-changing chemicals in the late seventies. In the last year or so, though, a couple of legal drugs have become part of her repertoire, too. These prescriptions carve out a semblance of normalcy, helping her, in her doctor's words, "to even out." But it all catches up with her at night. Erica's working theory is that the clutching mix of sorrow and terror, squashed now by these pills, finds an outlet in vivid, bad dreams. Her current lack of coherence and creativity during waking hours is counterbalanced by high-octane, visually arresting nightmares. Every night, prepped by a sleeping pill, an antianxiety pill, three pillows, a melancholy Scandinavian crime novel, and two squares of chocolate, Erica approaches sleep with, still, a shred of hope. Tonight could be the charm, the passage from the horrible to . . . well, anything less horrible. She longs for mundane, meandering dreams, the kind she had before John finally, mercifully, died last June, and Mona went off the rails.

She is often shoved awake by her own voice crying out and a heaving of the brain, the vivid recall of a dream that boiled up from the lava pit of her subconscious. Awake, she scribbles it down on a pad she keeps beside the bed or does a quick sketch, with an obscure, yet urgent, purpose in keeping track of her night mind.

Tonight she sees there is a fat autumn moon, hung outside the window where she has neglected to draw the curtains. The harvest moon. She rummages in the drawer of her bedside table, where she keeps, among eye drops, earplugs, and hand cream, a clutch of the Shakespeare passages that John had routinely

Erica has always found libraries, museums, and galleries to be sacred spaces, probably because she came from a large, cramped family and craved space and quiet. Libraries, of course, are no longer the hushed chapels of her childhood and youth. Cell phones bling, preschoolers run wild, and the clerks talk loudly to each other; once, they'd broken into song—the theme from *Gilligan's Island*—and they weren't bad either. But there is an expectation among adult patrons that they, at least, will behave. And so it is that, when Erica blurts, "No! You're shitting me!" upon seeing a particular title in the New Books section, nearby browsers turn and frown pointedly.

Years before, John had bought her something called *Apple for Dummies*, trying to be helpful as she wrestled her way into the new technology of the computer age. Then, she'd noticed an epidemic of *Dummies* and *Idiot's Guides* in the SELF-HELP section at bookstores. But *Grieving for Dummies* is over the top, surely? No, she immediately corrects herself, the endless possibilities of the marketplace must be filled! How about *Perversions for Dummies, Tax Evasion for Dummies, Achieving Nirvana for Dummies?* As a matter of fact, there has to be one on getting over death. That's what Americans are supposed to do. There's no excuse for hanging on to negative emotions in this country. And, certainly, there has to be a good market for *Grieving for Dummies*, an endless chorus line of the bereaved. She flips through the book, its bullet points, its briskly written pseudo empathy, its checklists for achieving closure. The hidden message: *Get over it. We will show you how.* The advice is pretty standard; it's the stuff they tell all the walking wounded, the people suffering from depression, cancer, eating disorders, what have you. Eat lots of fruit and vegetables. Get plenty of exercise and sleep. Drink alcohol sparingly. What about using drugs? (That's an editorial slipup.) Erica keeps her drugs—all nice and prescribed—for antianxiety, antidepression, and antisleeplessness, in her shoes these days, away from Mona's prying fingers. She never takes more than she should. Those years are long gone. But lots of folks do overindulge. The book goes on: *Attend a support group. Befriend your fellow mourners.*

"No," she says, loudly again, and drops the book to the table, to more frowns from her fellow booklovers. No to all of it, and especially, no, no, no, to any more support groups. Last spring, as John was slowly dying in his ever more potent fentanyl/morphine haze, she and Mona, neither of them happily, had attended the support group at Wings of Hope for teens in the outpatient program, along with their mostly shattered parents or whoever else was still willing to care for them. Mona's hair at the time was the color of seaweed, and she had regressed physically to her preteen state, Kate Moss-skinny and undeveloped, with bad skin and ricocheting emotions. Erica sat in the circle of the support group with other stunned, hopping-mad, and/or haggard adults, her mermaid-haired, seventeen-year-old child across the room with her compatriots, as far as they could get from the adults. Erica rarely spoke up, although she knew a lot about addiction, didn't she, from all her AA years. But Mona shared frequently, as articulate as the "facilitator" about the snares and pitfalls addicts must avoid. Oh, A+ performance, Mona! Erica, slumped in her chair, had so wanted to believe Mona, to believe in her again. Recalling this now at the library, to her horror she begins to blubber, and a woman reaching for a book nearby scoots protectively away from this unstable, sniffling woman staring unseeingly at *Grieving for Dummies.*

That useless family support group! That counselor who called himself a "facilitator" but who never facilitated squat. For example, she remembers he would never interrupt the small number of long-winded parents who spewed blame at the schools, the community, the police—everyone but themselves or their kids.

Or the parents who did the opposite, publicly flagellating them-selves. These were people who didn't know anything about addic-tion except what it left in its wake—anger, fear, blame, and guilt. Which Erica got. The first time she'd gone to an AA meeting and heard someone call himself an alcoholic, she'd felt intense, almost volcanic shame for the poor fellow. Now, of course, the word trips off her tongue. After hundreds, possibly thousands, of Twelve-Step meetings, she's fully inculcated the disease concept (now reinforced by the American medical establishment, unlike years ago, when she "came into the program"). But the family group for addicted teens was made up of civilians, presumably nonaddicted grown-ups with all the baggage of the uninitiated.

Yet, for all her exposure to the vampire ways of addiction and for all the firsthand evidence she had about the restoration of sanity that happens to people in recovery, she was basically in the same mental boat as these civilians. They were all wrestling with the monster that turned their children into wayward/insolent/troublemaking/heartbreaking/slothful/criminal/intensely self-involved addicts. And all the parents just wanted it to *stop*; life was too hard, too painful, too much, too everything. Occa-sionally, Erica and another parent, a guy she recognizes from the rooms of AA, managed to say something about the nature of addiction, about the hope of recovery, to the circle in agony, mostly Caucasians, but with sprinklings of African Ameri-cans, Latinos, Indians, Asians. Once Erica heard herself talking about how shame and blame are not only pointless but actually worsen the situation. But all the while, Erica knew she too was full of shame and blame and was as apt to act it out, despite what she knew and said. Because of Mona, her beloved child, her addict child.

Now, wiping her eyes and still staring at *Grieving for Dum-mies*, Erica feels suddenly insubstantial. As if she is skimming along the edge of the world, trying to stay upright. Kind of like her dim memory of being stoned. This has been happening to her, off and on, over the past year or so, these little breaks from reality. Her trance is broken by a teenage hulk who slumps down loudly in a chair nearby beside an earnest computer geek, probably a tutor, a math book between them on the table.

"Nope, I don't see it. Nope. Don't get precalc, never will, and don't care." The kid scrapes his chair back. "Screw it, I'm going outside to have a smoke."

"I'm with you there, brother," Erica mutters.

Last spring, when those weekly family meetings at The Wings of Hope Recovery Center were over, the parents would shamble off, stunned and weary, to their cars, while a good number of the teenagers took off in other cars. Including Mona. The kids were supposed to go home or stop at a coffee shop for healthy interaction, but were probably on their way to cop or score or whatever the slang verb was now. There was no way to rein her in; Erica had tried everything except jail and inpatient, including taking away the car keys. But Mona just found rides to the next drug high. The next step appeared to be having her put in inpatient at Wings or else waiting for jail again or a hospital. Mona just screamed and covered her ears when Erica brought up the topic of inpatient. And Erica, who had to conserve her strength for John as he lay dying in bits, had let the matter drop.

The tall library windows today frame a gray November sky, the trees bare but for a few stubborn, flame-colored maples. Erica flips to a chapter called "Give It a Year." This is interesting to her, as it's full of cautionary tales about the intemperate acts of the newly grieving. People, wild with grief, who give away large sums of money, sell their houses, get married again (to some psycho) without thinking it through. In short, they act like addicts.

Erica herself had behaved intemperately, giving away John's

beloved old BMW to the tree-cutting guy a week after he died. True, she wasn't about to learn to drive stick, but give it away? And she couldn't wait to do it. And that was just the start of her exorcism of John's possessions, still ongoing because there was so much; he was a saver, not a hoarder, but close. And it has only been four months since he died. What will she do next? Well, *Grieving for Dummies* has a lot of suggestions.

Enough of this, Erica thinks. She needs comfort. She'll go to the art section, *her* section. Yet the *Dummies* book holds her a little longer, impishly falling open to a list of support groups, including . . . really? The Modern Widows Club? Now, there's a name for a Julia Roberts movie. Or Meryl Streep. Yes, better— she can do crazy like falling off a log. A crazy new widow with a child shooting heroin. Modern Widows, yes! A niche market to be sure.

The imp gets hold of Erica. On a nearby computer, she finds the Modern Widows Club website and discovers she can get a T-shirt upon payment of modest dues. Why not a kitchen magnet? A cap? A bumper sticker. Caution: Modern Widow on Board. She speed-reads through the mission statement. Nothing eye-catching. A list, inevitably, of tips, including:

"Don't be afraid to vent your anger."

"Oh, I am not afraid of that!" Erica declares aloud. Again, heads swivel and eyebrows crease. She and her anger have spent many a sweaty hour recently, hacking at bushes and tree limbs and heaving trash bags full of mildewed collections of John's *True Detective* magazines. Erica logs off. She's flunking Grief 101; she has given away a BMW, albeit a rusty BMW. And why? Because it reminded her too much of happy times. One terrible afternoon in October, Wally the tree man drove past in the Beemer as Erica sat in the garden with Casho, who froze and then busted through his invisible fence, bellowing, running after the car. His master's car.

She pays no attention to eating right and has taken up smoking cigarillos. She needs a pill to get through the night and another to get through the day. More grief peccadilloes are sure to follow.

Well, let there be art. She mentally consigns *Grieving for Dummies* to the hell of poor sales and turns away, noticing as she does that the math-challenged teenager is back, staring at a worksheet. "I feel for you, buddy," she murmurs. In the art section, she finds a new biography about the great and seriously fucked-up Modigliani. That and a couple of sun-starved new Norwegian thrillers should hold her for a while.

Driving home, Erica pays little heed to the treacherously narrow, winding, old cart-roads. They are dark but deeply familiar. The gloomy copses of denuded trees seem to wait impatiently for snow to press upon them; the sun flirts ineptly with the gray sky, and she is stuck behind a crawling car with no head visible in the driver's seat, the sure sign of an elderly, feeble-sighted driver. But she doesn't care. She is free to brood and does. At least she hasn't done something monumentally dumb like fallen in love. The Modern Widows Club website had more or less repeated the *Dummies'* advice on that, which boils down to: don't do it! But anyway, it's the man who rushes into relationships after the wife dies. Can't do without a woman looking after him.

Erica is fairly certain she'll never have to worry about a man again. She's not old; she's not unattractive, but, since John died, she often feels like a tourist in a really foreign country—Yemen, say, or North Korea. She's tethered to new, as yet nonsensical, rules. This country—grief—has its own arcane strictures of the really foreign type: you must not pat babies on the head or you could steal their souls; don't photograph people for the same reason; never eat with your left hand. In grief country, you learn the rules and the language from scratch, never mind a guidebook like *Grieving for Dummies.* In grief country, you find out that tables and chairs aren't solid but are full of holes, like the physicists claim. That a wizard has been behind a screen all the time, conjuring the illusion you've always believed of the sureness of the senses. "Or maybe," Erica says aloud, suddenly laughing at herself. "I'm just a natural-born paranoid!"

She doesn't laugh long. Disaster survivors have a short supply of mirth. *I used to believe it when I said there are no guarantees. But I was fooling myself. I thought there was always an ace or two in the hole. I had no idea.* And here she has to brake sharply, as the tiny old person driving in front of her suddenly turns off the road without warning. Ah yes, no guarantees. That someone will use their turn signal, for example.

The sun is feebler still, the sky is a gray sheet, the day pulls in on itself, reminding her of winter around the corner. "Ah, help me," Erica says in a sigh, hardly hearing herself.

WALKING THE DOG

Groggy from anesthesia, Erica realizes she's lying on a metal table under hard, fluorescent lights. Has she had an operation? Why is she panting so hard? Why is her heart jumping? She needs help urgently, but she can't speak and nobody comes. Have the doctors and nurses forgotten her? Something presses on her arm, then a moist, soft sponge is placed over her mouth. She realizes the dog is licking her face and wakes up.

Get up already and feed me! Erica pushes Casho's large head and paws off the bed and squirms in the warm sheets, still in the panic of the dream.

Grief's toxicity is familiar now, suffering is her constant companion. She wants to lie in the bed as long as she can. But the powerfully built Labrador, no subservient canine, thrusts his upper body upon her again, making his simple requirements forcefully known. Food when the sun rises and sets, tussles with toys, and eager, sometimes frantic, walks. He is, of course, always grateful for extra scraps of food and praise, when Erica can muster the energy to remember them. But it's his basic needs that he demands, stalking her from room to room; she is used to the click of his nails, a crescendo of barked and whined rebukes if she lags. He, too, has lived through chronic turmoil, and this has made him peevish, restless to go out or come in, and likely to have accidents in the rooms of the house he doesn't frequent. Calling cards of distress.

But Erica loves and needs the dog, his clown nose and clanky brain, his perfect trust in her. He gives her a reason to get up; he forgives her, his new master, always. He accepts that she is not John, who would walk him for hours in forests. But she sticks to the neighborhood, which feels safe because it's familiar. Every day, or almost, they follow one of several familiar routes. They climb the steep hill past several lovely, old, large houses and the horse barn, stubbornly holding on in their shred of exurbia. Or they go down another hill, lined with more modest vinyl-sided houses, past the one Erica plans to paint someday, so shabby and glowering, its yard festooned with creepy plastic gnomes and a red car up on blocks with the front door open. It has been like that for as long as she can remember. One afternoon, she received an explanation: a young man, walking like Frankenstein, clutching steel braces, waves cheerfully at her from where he's fiddling with the car engine, and she remembers that he's the boy who survived the motorcycle accident and lives here. "Hey, big guy!" he calls out to Casho.

Casho is, of course, her entrée to the neighborhood. To the cyclists and the shy Guatemalan day laborers who live, packed together, in certain shabby houses at the far end of that road, who she often meets walking up or down the hill from the village below. And the elderly porch-sitters, the white-haired lady with dementia who screams at the dog, then smiles and says, "Hello." And the other dog-walkers, who often stop to talk. The sad-eyed rock drummer with the rescue shepherd mutt. One day, he breaks down, telling

Erica that his wife has left him and he gets few gigs anymore. Also, a couple with a rescue Rottweiler (who loves Casho but no other dogs, they tell her). Five minutes with them, and she figures out the jolly husband is also in AA from the programese he uses (often a sign of early sobriety): "It's a day at a time." "Easy does it."

"You must be a friend of Bill's?" Erica says, the corny code for members of their club. He nods, grinning wildly. "Me too," she says. Down at the bottom of the hill, before she and Casho turn around, is the cranky woman with the two poodles, who watches suspiciously in case Casho poops on her lawn. They all know that John has died, of course, such things are soon known in neighborhoods, but they don't bring it up except for the drummer, who'd met him. Death is a topic to be avoided; it's unseemly, even hostile territory for the uninitiated, she supposes. *Well, don't worry, we're all going there.*

Erica thinks she must look different since John died, marked in some way. She notices it's harder to move, as if John's death has added a thick, invisible padding around her. If grief is loss, it is also a heavy load to carry.

There are, though, bits of real pleasure in the interesting things she sees on these dog walks. She pictures the person (she is sure it's a woman) who regularly flings little airplane-size vodka bottles along the road; at least Erica is long free of that brand of desperation. She sees all kinds of animals. Deer, of course, the adorable fawns who will soon become monsters chewing up her garden. Once, she sees a huge snapping turtle, perched on a stone wall. How long had it taken to labor up from the river that lies half a mile down the hill, and why make the trip? A baby skunk sitting in the middle of the road, tail raised when Casho spots it. She needs all her strength to hold him back. Two hawks that she thinks are fighting, then realizes are mating, in bare, high limbs of a maple in March. A coyote, odd and ugly, a fox. Wildflowers marking the passing of the seasons. The heavenly scents of the earth after rain, the infinity of mysterious aromas of dung and animals teased or rooted out by Casho's nose, the serendipity of a bone nosed out of brush and crunched quickly before she can get it out of his jaws.

One afternoon, sensing something in a small, dense wood beside the hill, Casho jerks hard, and Erica is flung headfirst into a patch of poison ivy. She sits up slowly, feeling to see if anything is broken. Thankfully, no, and she is not too allergic to the plant that grows with abandon in the area, though she'll have to rush home and apply cream. Casho reappears with a flourish—in his jaws a squirrel, alive. A rare catch for him. And she begins to laugh. "Drop it!" she tells him, and he does.

There is, in fact, a good deal of cosmic humor in this grief thing, when she is in the mood to see it. The day after John died, she was at the Bendelli Funeral Home, a late Victorian pile, black oak and maroon, embossed wallpaper. She was there to complete what are called the "arrangements" with the director. Death means instant paperwork, bureaucracy, the clearing of the decks. And, of course, forking out money. He handed her forms.

The director, across from her at the dark oak table, looked at her solemnly, then suddenly began honking his nose repeatedly with a handkerchief. "Sorry, summer cold," he muttered. He handed her the death certificate with his non-nose-blowing hand.

"But this isn't his name!" Erica said, her voice almost disembodied. She pushed the paper at him. "It's 'Grey' with an *e* not 'Gray' with an *a*."

Gray, Grey, what's the difference? the honking director was probably thinking as he went away to produce a revised form. But it made all the difference to her. She heard the hum of a copy machine. He came back, discussed the fees for filing John Grey's death certificate, the cremation, the urn. She took out her checkbook. She was ready to get the hell out of there.

"Oh, *yes*. One more moment, please, Mrs. Grey."

"Ms. Mason," she said, but the director had left the room again. He came back holding a Ziploc bag, and her world cracked. All that was left of John was in this plastic baggie: smeared glasses, watch, gold wedding band.

"Sorry," the man said unapologetically. He sniffed loudly.

Speechless, Erica fled. Was that the sound of a crow cackling as she wrenched open her car door, she wondered?

Truisms have to be rediscovered by each person, endlessly. For example, people don't know what to do with widows after the first few weeks. Right up to and after the big event, of course, there are hugs, cards, too many phone calls, too many cakes, casseroles, flowers. Too many, "Call me anytime you need anything." Then she is left to her own devices. Is it a lingering, atavistic belief that widows are only good for the scrap heap? (Funeral pyres?) Ancient superstitions, yes, but such things die hard. And then there are the tenacious few who linger too long.

Erica called Ronnie, the one person she could bear to talk to at this point, and she ranted, because Ronnie always allowed her to rant, before steering her back on course. Miraculous! "They call to see how I'm doing. What am I supposed to say? The usual fine, good, great? I have no fucking idea how I'm doing most of the time. I don't feel anything. Or they peer at me when I run into them at the supermarket. I guess they want to see if I've completely lost it? Well, I have, you know. I've lost it."

"You haven't lost it. It's perfectly natural to feel the way you do."

Lost it. Yes. Erica had the sense that she'd been breaking certain unspoken rules about dealing with grief from the start. Take that morning, three days after John died, when she returned several overdue books to the library. Because libraries felt safe to her in a world that was not safe anymore.

"That'll be twelve thirty-five," the clerk, a round-faced woman with a bad overbite, told her.

Erica fished out a twenty. "My husband was reading these," she said. "Well, I was reading them to him."

"These all got good reviews. Did he like them?"

"I don't know. He died before I could finish them. We could finish them. On Wednesday. He died." Erica's voice caught on the terrible wonder of those two words. *He died.*

The clerk slid the twenty back as if it was on fire. "Oh! Well, you didn't have to bring them back *now*! We won't charge you a fine."

Better than "the dog ate my homework," Erica thought, but didn't say. John would have appreciated that sly, fumbling attempt at humor. A shred of sanity kept her from further shocking the buck-toothed clerk by actually saying it.

From the library, she had driven to the mall, or "maul," as she and Mona had always called it, joking about the way it sucked at their credit cards, back when she and Mona did things together, talked to each other. At home later, with a pizza and her newly purchased funeral wear, she called Morgan Lopez, another old friend who had pledged to do anything for Erica. "Morg, you wouldn't believe how long it took me to find one reasonable, black skirt for the funeral. Finally, I found one in the back on sale at Ann Taylor's. Everything seems to be micro-mini."

"You went shopping today?"

Erica was shuffling around in a kind of samba with the phone tight against her ear. She hadn't been able to stop moving for long since the day John died. Full of nervous energy, she could have been that woman she remembered reading about in the paper who lifted a car off her child who was pinned underneath. Filled with impossible strength.

"Morg, I'm not helpless."

"But I would have come, Erica. Why didn't you ask? You don't have to do these things alone."

"Who wants to wander around the mall unless they have to, unless you're fourteen?" She started to cry, a shuddering, ugly sound. Morg was one of the few she could cry around.

"Oh, *Erica*. Do you want me to come over and bring some food? We can sit outside."

Erica almost gasped and started to hiccup. At least she wasn't crying anymore. "Morg? Are you *serious*?" Morgan hadn't been to her house since the time one of the cats—Dim—had managed to pry open what she'd thought was the firmly shut bedroom door where they'd been put for the duration of Morgan's visit. The cat had stalked downstairs and stopped in front of Morgan, causing her friend, a six-foot-tall, dignified redhead, to leap up and crash out of the house, hyperventilating. "I've tried everything," Morgan had confessed. "Hypnosis, exposure therapy—nothing works for me." She was just deeply, completely, terrified of cats. Offering to come to Erica's house, even to sit on the patio outside, was a real sacrifice, an act of love.

"Or you could come over here."

"I will. Soon. Thank you for that, Morg. But today, I'm better by myself."

"Anything I can do, you'll let me know?"

Alone was what Erica wanted though, alone with mindless, sweaty tasks that she could check off. Haul out the ladder and clean the gutters, where little plants were sprouting from the leaf mold of several seasons. Weed, weed, weed, mop floors.

Thank God, no sitting Shiva or purdah for her. Her religion—where was it now? No soft comfort there. Say what they would about eternal life, etc., she wasn't buying it at the moment. No, her religion felt like the hard, wooden pillows that Chinese emperors put their heads on at night: it was holding her up relentlessly. The ceremonies. The memorial party and the funeral looming, the new black clothing, the people coming in from around the country. Religion but hardly faith at the moment.

Ken Ramos played the jazz tunes John had chosen, when he was still well enough, on the freshly tuned Steinway in the old white church. Unseen hands prepared food and did the flowers. Erica's sister Claire and their mother had answered the phone and did whatever needed doing before a funeral. Mona made cameo appearances, looking stoned and stricken. Erica, in the fresh early morning before the funeral, went to her neglected garden, attacking the tough weeds that flourished there before showering, putting on the new black skirt and a black linen blouse she'd fished out from the back of the closet. Then she took an antianxiety pill.

The truth was that Erica would remember little of the first weeks after John died. The memorial party in the church hall with the photomontage that Claire put together, comprising the various stages of his healthy life, was a blur. All those people coming and going, Ken playing his heart out for his friend. As a child, Erica was one of those kids who'd mask her eyes with her hands during scary bits on television programs, watching between her fingers. That's what she would have liked to do at the memorial party the night before the funeral. Peek through her fingers as people approached, forced her to listen to fond memories, insisted on a shared sense of loss. Really, John knew so many people—far more than she did—people who spread baked brie on bread rounds, scooped fruit salad from large glass bowls, downed glasses of wine (John would have liked that). Several women she didn't know smiled in her direction, the kind of scrunched-up smile directed at a child who's scraped her knee. Who were they? Old girlfriends, wives of friends, workmates? Had she met them before?

Erica moved down the hall from the party to the sanctuary of the church, dim and almost cool that hot summer night. People sat in the pews, listening to Ken's plangent, Bill Evans-ish compositions. At the funeral the next day, he'd play a set of the beautiful jazz tunes John had selected: Billy Strayhorn, Jimmy Rowles, a New Orleans strut in "Just a Closer Walk with Thee." The loud hum from the party was a fitting counterpoint to Ken, like being in a jazz club. Her first date with John had been in a jazz club, and one of the reasons she'd liked him so much was that they had similar tastes in music. She began to shiver, though it was hot, recalling the noisy, funky club—Small's, in the Village, she thinks it was—and that charged feeling of anticipation of going to bed, later, soon, with someone brand-new who excites you. She heard a burst of laughter. The noise these people were generating with their eating and drinking and talking and, yes, laughing. And, suddenly, her mood turned dark: the noise was brutal, and she could not make sense of it, not even Ken's sensitive playing. In the wings of her mind was a different music, something savage like Stravinsky's *Rite of Spring*. As if John had been a sacrifice to give heat and light to those who mingled here.

Erica seldom wanted her mother, but she wanted her now, and she wanted her sister Claire. She wanted Ronnie or Ginger or Morgan to come find her. Above all, she wanted Mona. But she couldn't think of her: that way lay total despair tonight. But when she left to go back to the party she bumped into her child, along with her pale shadow, the aptly named Misty, and, surprisingly, three uncomfortable-looking young guys who were clearly there to support Mona. She hugged her frail daughter for the seconds that Mona allowed her to do so. She never forgot what was wrong with Mona, never; she dragged it around like a clubfoot.

Mona was crying.

"I have to get out of here, Mom."

"Please. My darling girl, don't go."

"Mom."

They cried into each other's necks, and Erica whispered wildly, "It's going to be all right."

Mona reared back. "How can you say that?"

She and her entourage shuffled away.

Back at the party, Erica moved into a corner. Someone handed her a drink. Club soda.

"Eric."

He hugged her, long and softly. He was John's oldest friend. He pulled over a chair and sat in a way that blocked anyone from approaching.

"Eric, I know there are far worse things people have to live through. All these wars and plagues and famine . . ." She was sobbing.

"Right now," he said softly, "you can't imagine it, but there will come a time when you remember John as he really was."

She nodded, because Eric was in the club, having lost his wife to cancer years ago when he had three little kids to bring up alone. "It doesn't seem . . . possible," she said, willing herself to stop crying.

"I know. But you have Mona. You have to stay strong for her."

"Eric? How did you bear it?"

"I don't know," he said. "But you do."

HE'S NOT THERE

Mona skates with lazy grace around the rink in her body-hugging blue costume, while holding a glass of white wine high as if it were a trophy. She takes a drink and starts to choke on slivers of ice that have been secreted in the glass. Now, the ice rink too heaves up shards of ice. She thinks, What if I fall? I can't fall. And my throat, is it bleeding?

Mona gasped for breath as she woke up in the big, white sleigh bed her parents had given her for her birthday when she was twelve. She groaned and flopped to her side, glad to be away from the nightmare but not awake. She reached as usual for her phone. Surrounding her were the cats, Dim and Dimmer, empty Snapple bottles, an overflowing ashtray, and tiny packets of crushed-up Oxys stuffed into the crevices of the bedframe, where Mom never cleaned. She didn't want to get up, ever, except to pee and eventually see Misty, who she was texting now. And, of course, get more Oxys. It was the day after Dad's funeral, and she felt crushed by her monstrousness. She had left the funeral midway; she had abandoned her mother, the rest of the family staring at her, aghast, as she tapped out of the church on those stupid, six-inch heels. And for what? Misty had driven around aimlessly as she cried and cried. Then, they went to Misty's basement and snorted the Oxys and, at midnight, when Mom would be buried under an Ambien or two, Misty took her back to her house, and she snuck upstairs. Mona didn't want to do anything today, except score later. She just wanted to lie here. She let her thoughts swish around. Her dad was dead. She'd never see him again. But Dad had been dying for months, and she was actually kind of relieved. She picked at a scab on her arm without noticing the bloody trail it left on the sheet. She checked her phone: the usual, sketchy-type guys wanting to hang, nothing yet from Misty. Suddenly, Mona saw in her mind a close-up of her mom's face at the funeral when she whispered to her, "Sorry, but I gotta get out of here, Mom." She tried not to look at her mom, usually, because there was so much guilt-tripping going on, but she hadn't escaped it then. Her mother had looked . . . well, almost dead herself. Just out of it.

"Mona, don't go," she had rasped. Mona scrabbled around, remembering there were some shards left from her last hit last night, in the foil stuffed by the wall; there was barely enough to count, but it was enough to dim this crappy feeling. There, she felt better, hollower. But maybe not, because old, familiar scenes began playing in her head: The day she wouldn't go on a walk with Dad last fall when he could still just manage to hobble along. The time she said no to watching a movie with him when that was about all he could do anymore. Yeah, stealing his hydrocodone and then the oxycodone and, finally, the fentanyl patches—the gold standard of getting wasted; that was really bad, taking your father's cancer meds. But she had needed them. She did feel bad lying to Mom about going to visit him at the hospital and, later, the hospice. *I did go that one time!* she told herself. "I did go see him," she said aloud.

It was horrible; he was far more stoned than she has ever

been or even wants to be, his eyes glittering. His hospital bed was cranked up to a sitting position with all those blankets; it was like ninety degrees in his horrible-smelling room, and he was shivering. When he said her name, it sounded like a door creaking. "Mona." She sat next to him and held his hand and cried and told him she was sorry and fell on his chest. She felt his bones pressing sharply against her. When she looked up, his eyes were closed and his mouth gaping. He looked dead already. She didn't remember leaving, but, later, she sniffed some Dilaudid and had to slap herself so she wouldn't go under.

She fired up a Salem Light and swigged from a warm Snapple bottle, craving more Oxys. Her mind, that treacherous beast, went to her absolutely rock-bottom day with Dad, because the day at hospice, horrible as it was, wasn't the worst, since by then, she knew he was dying. No, it was the afternoon she had been home alone with him, months before. That hardly ever happened because Mom, the control freak, was always there, washing his disgusting catheter bags, doing laundry, making smoothies, or shutting herself in her studio when he was stoned out on fents. Mona never did that stuff for him, but she would have, she thought. If Mom had asked her. But Mom never asked. She and Misty, dissecting their mothers with their teenaged scalpels, agreed that Erica and Jean were classic helicopter parents. But this one day, Mom said she had to go out and get some stuff, so could Mona stay with him for an hour, two at the most? If he woke up, warm up some soup from the fridge or else scoop out some ice cream, if that's what he wanted. Of course, she also left a list of instructions for Mona on what to do if there was an emergency, as if Mona was a little kid but Dad just slept in his drug haze in that hospital bed set up in the living room, since he (runner of marathons, hiker, tennis player, chopper of firewood) couldn't do the stairs anymore. Dad was covered with about six quilts, because he could never get warm enough.

Mona told herself she was pissed about having to stay with him, as, of course, she had plans with Misty, but really, she knew she was afraid to be around him anymore. It hurt too much. She'd already sneaked downstairs in the middle of the night to locate Mom's wallet, which was stashed this time behind the shelf of cookbooks—what a joke, Mom thinking she could hide money from her! Mona knew how she thought and discovered each of Mom's new hiding places without much trouble. Under a pillow in her bedroom, inside a mixing bowl in a kitchen cabinet, at the bottom of the laundry basket. When Mona took cash from her wallet, she always flipped it open to look at the photo of Dad taken a few years before, that time they'd gone cross-country skiing in Vermont, in which he was kind of sexy in an older dude way. His thick, graying hair, a little long, the way Mom liked it and he didn't, poked out from under his knit cap, his brown eyes crinkling in the snow-dazzled sun. She thought about copping the picture also, but Mom would really freak, more than about the money. But it also actually freaked Mona, she realized, to be reminded of when he was a healthy, normal dad. She kind of froze for a while, just staring at the picture. Finally, she made herself shove the wallet back behind the Mexican cookbook. They used to have great meals out of that cookbook, stuff Mom had learned to cook when she was a hippie artist in Mexico. Plus the pasta, soups and pies Dad loved. Back when he could eat real food.

That day Mom left her alone with Dad, Mona eventually got up, went to the bathroom, and brought a bowl of cereal back to her room. She got out her sketchbook, snorted some stuff and worked on a self-portrait until she got bored and must have zoned out, because, all of a sudden, she heard this loud banging and groans from downstairs. Stumbling out of bed, she ran down to the living room. Somehow, Dad had gotten over the slats of the hospital bed, which were supposed to prevent him from falling. He was sprawled on the floor, and the creepiest thing was the way he was just staring, totally stoned. His robe had fallen open, and Mona saw, for the first time, his skeletal body and that horrible tube and the bag filled with piss. Mona was unable to move until Casho went into overdrive, whining and pushing at her with his wet snout. She dropped to the floor and held her dad's hands, telling him it would be OK. She wanted to feel like this was a movie about a girl and her dying father. But only for a moment. Kneeling, Mona began to cry so hard she thought she'd puke. Because, what the fuck? She was almost eighteen, she knew all about the important stuff in life, right, except that suddenly she felt she knew nothing. That her whole life up to then had been severed from her.

Once upon a time, her father had smelled of the city where he worked, and pipe tobacco, and a general, good *man* smell; now, he smelled of piss and decay. Her tears fell onto his white T-shirt as she bent over him. She was unable to let go of his hands, but her panic finally forced her to her feet. She dialed Mom's cellphone, again and again, a dozen times maybe, but Mom didn't pick up. Her friggin' phone must have been left off again. Then Mona called 911.

Things happened pretty fast, the ambulance with the lights flashing, a bunch of big men standing around the living room and bending over Dad, checking him out. Mona tried to answer their questions, but she had to keep saying, "I don't know, I don't know." Except for cancer and fentanyl, she didn't know much. Yes, her mom should be back any minute. Where the hell was she? And then she was there, that white, blank face, and soon she was climbing into the back of the ambulance where they'd put him. Her mother had done this several times already, had had to call the ambulance, but Mona hadn't been there to see it. She stood next to the living room window, watching, the blue lights making her crazy. Crazier. Then Mom was getting out of the ambulance and nodding at the EMT guys, and Mona heard one say, "Better stay with your daughter, ma'am. She seems pretty upset."

And that was it, the worst day she'd ever had. And Mona thought, *Yeah, OK, I need something now that doesn't cost a fucking fortune like Oxys. And everybody says it's the best high ever. I'm only gonna sniff it.*

Yeah, let's try heroin.

MY POOR NAME REHEARSE

Erica is staring in a mirror at her bearded self. She scrapes
at it furiously with a razor, but a wispy goatee remains.
Again and again, she pulls the razor across her chin, until
it is smooth. Smooth but wet: blood! As she comes awake,
she remembers the last bit of the dream. She was saying,
"The self is a leaky container."

The snug country church was built like a boat, with tall windows that let in the hard noon sun. In the first row of pews sat
Erica with her mother, then Tom, Erica's grown stepson and his
wife Sally, who had modest, semi-hippie jobs in a remote part of
Arizona that kept them from being able to travel East. Erica had
bought their plane tickets. Next to them sat Erica's sister Claire.
As the organ music rose and the service began, Mona edged in
beside Erica; Misty was firmly led to the other end of the row by
Claire. The packed rows behind Erica seemed to press in on her
like a stiff wind at her back. This space, this faith, had drawn them
in, she and John, to her continual surprise: she hadn't known she
wanted religion, or a faith community. They had first attended
St. Bart's for its concerts of baroque, jazz, and blues music, and,

slowly, the message of perfectly embodied love, of a new kind of serenity, delivered in a—mostly—literate and warm, liberal manner, drew them in. But mostly it was the people. It was a convivial group. Mona had been baptized, gone to Sunday school, sang in the junior choir, ran around the grounds and, finally, was confirmed at St. Bart's. And then she announced (as her mother had done before her) that she didn't believe in all that stuff anymore.

Erica heard the rustle of the packed sanctuary; all these people came for John, many of them here again after the previous night's memorial party. During the service, she rose, sat, listened, but it was all fragmentary. She was aware of a terrible need for Mona, who was next to her but as far away as the moon. In due time, when Father Locke held up the chalice for communion, Erica was led by her mother up the steps of the altar. Religion gave Erica no comfort on this day but all the people here did. Mona remained in her seat. As Erica descended the steps, everything was a blur except for that face, then, annoyingly, Misty sitting next to Mona. *What a time to wonder if they are a couple,* Erica chided herself. *Or going through some experimental phase.* She knew so little about her child. She stumbled. Her mother took her hand.

Now, despair leaked around the padding of the anxiety pill her kindly family doctor had told her to take "as needed."

She heard her mother murmur, "I'm here, dear," and the tears slithered down her face. Her sad, thirty-something stepson Tom was at the podium, telling the anecdote about John blowing his top at him when he got his ears pierced and put in dangling turquoise earrings; years later, gripping the podium, Tom could pass for a clipped Marine. She heard little choking sounds from Mona as Tom wrapped up. "My dad was a man who memorized poetry on his daily runs in Central Park," he said, and then, as she had asked him, he read several lines she'd picked from one of the poems John had kept in his pockets:

No longer mourn for me when I am dead . . .
  Do not so much as my poor name rehearse,
  But let your love even with my life decay,
  Lest the wise world should look into your moan,
  And mock you with me after I am gone.

Erica felt, rather than saw, Mona push herself out of the pew and totter out the back door of the church, with Misty in her wake. Then the service seemed to be over. Now, she thought, you go to the memorial garden and find his name etched on a brass plate in front of the niche with his ashes inside. She looked around, lost. Oh right: Mona had fled.

They all—all but Mona—sat inside her house, although it was a sunny afternoon. There was baked chicken, ham, casseroles, rolls, salads, cakes, and pies. No one was hungry, but Mrs. Mason set the dining room table that was only used for formal occasions with the good china (Grandma's) and called them in.

"Dear, let me stay with you tonight." The family was staying at a hotel suite nearby, but the house had a snug, little spare room.

I'd like that, Erica thought. *My mother taking care of* me.

Whatever their points of contention, her mom was a five-star caregiver (which was one of their points of contention!). But there was the problem of Mona. "Mom, thank you. I really appreciate that. But I'll be all right." Erica had been the problem child. Like Mona was hers. It had taken years for her and her mother to reknit their relationship. "I'll probably just go to bed soon." They all picked at the food a little more, cleared the table. At last, they hugged goodbye. Tom, tall and grown-up now, Sally his sweet shadow, Claire with her doe-eyed sister-love expression, her mother solemn. After they left, the cats padded in to retake their positions, and Casho heaved a windy sigh, no doubt exhausted by yet another confusing day.

There was nothing Erica wanted from any of her dear ones; there was nothing anyone could say or do. They all thought she was devastated because John had died. She made coffee, turned the TV on, put it on mute, and sat in the old armchair, Casho at her feet. When she awoke, it was nearly nine, still light. She had been startled by strange sounds. They were coming from her. The animals watched her, computing the time to the next feed.

"The thing is," she told them, wiping her face, "I'm relieved. No," she added, "that's not the right word. I am glad." *But I should have spent every hour with him, I should have been there up to the very last minute, like in the movies. Selflessly, endlessly. But I wasn't. I was always so glad to get away, I hated having to be there.*

Was this true? She didn't know. It was half-true. She was a half-fraud.

Erica prowled the small living room. She supposed she was in shock. She wasn't going to drown her sorrows because she was a recovered substance abuser, and she wouldn't overdo her current meds; she was wary of their rattlesnake aura. But she had to do something.

She'd weed. Wrestle primordially with the neglected garden, as generations of the women in her family had done. As she applied bug spray, crammed on her old sneakers, and unearthed the trowel—her weapon of choice—and the pruner in the shed, these women crowded her mind, a line of aunts, grandmothers, her mother, sister. Erica was on her knees in the vegetable patch as the sky darkened, attacking lush clots of crab grass and the devious creeping Charlie weed, its scent a puzzle: stinky yet comfortably earthy too. Granna Winifred's voice leaned into her. *I'll give you a quarter when you finish weeding this patch. And an ice cream.* This last was probably added grudgingly, with Granna watching austere and stiff-backed nearby, or whip-hoeing her prized daylily beds, with little Erica never daring to ask, *And if I won't? What will you do to me if I won't weed?*

Against this memory, Erica bowed into the thick stalk of a tomato plant, which bucked in protest, the surly leaves scratching her arm. But she didn't register the itch that resulted, the pungency of the weeds, the soft burrs of the bees and mosquitoes, the trills and squawks of birds, the howl of a neighbor's dog. She was in a senseless interstice, had been yanking out weeds for minutes or hours uselessly, this futile stab against the reality of nature. A pain in her wrist recalled her to herself. She abandoned the trowel and the pruner in the weeds, a cardinal sin among gardeners, for it could rain and then the tools would have rusted in the interim before she rescued them. Erica groaned, getting to her feet.

In the house, she checked Mona's empty room and called and called her, but Mona wasn't picking up her phone. Erica ended up screaming into the phone, "Where are you, Mona?" Because this dear one she did need.

Ginger stopped by the next day unannounced, bearing a trowel and a salmon-colored phlox in a pot. Erica was in the old Adirondack chair staring at a book.

"You're outside! I was just going to just plant this for you and leave," Ginger said.

"I'm not an invalid," Erica said mildly, after a hug. "I can do it."

"Really, I'd like to. Show me a spot."

"Iced tea or lemonade after?"

"Whatever's easier."

On the patio, where the phlox found a home near the untended roses in the plot where the gardening tools were still lying, Ginger pointed out a hummingbird frenetically feeding at the trumpet vine and then an albino squirrel perched in the ancient maple.

Thank God it's you, Ginger, Erica thought. The family had been over, leaving after lunch. They would return for dinner, which would be more of the donated dishes; Erica was to do nothing, they had made that clear. Her mother had brought up the subject of Mona's absence twice, Tom had wandered off— Erica suspected to smoke some pot—and Sally and Claire had fussed over her and offered to weed this very patio garden and do any other tasks Erica came up with. Loving them, Erica wanted nothing, was glad they'd gone back to the hotel or shopping or hiking. Whatever it was that normal people did. With Ginger, she could be as silent as she liked. *We're like two old married people.* She thought, *We don't have to say much; we know each other so well.* Ginger was a large, attractive person with sun-roughened skin, short, ruffled hair, and a take-charge personality, absolutely reliable. And though Ginger almost never talked about feelings, she had a sweet side to her. Erica found her reticence refreshing and never more so than now. If one more person asked her how she was feeling these blank, black days, she fantasized about turning on them like a wild animal, screaming. It was just a daydream, but grief contained a cauldron of rage in the gated, private property of Erica's head.

After a short while, Ginger heaved herself up. "Want to come over for dinner Saturday? Absolutely casual."

"Not really, Ginger. Thanks."

"Well, call me if you want to take a walk or change your mind."

"I will. The phlox is lovely."

Erica sat until Casho ordered dinner. Dim and Dimmer waited within streaking distance of their bowls, as she shook kibble into the dog's and refilled his water dish. The cats had no fear of the giant dog. When Dimmer was a kitten, he used

Casho's water bowl as a wading pool and flirted with the dog's paws, which were almost as big as his little body. Dim, on the other hand, preferred to ignore everything dog-related. After the feed, Erica cleaned out their litter box. *They have incredibly active bowels and bladders*, she thought, which inevitably led her to thoughts of John or, rather, thoughts of taking care of him at the end. You get used to anything—the volcanic messes, the wiping, the disinfecting, the washing, the dryer on at all hours. You get hardened to it because you have to. She stood behind him, on guard, when he could still turtle up the steps to the second floor; once, she clocked him at twenty-five minutes to make the climb, so the next day she ordered the hospital bed for the ground floor. Even when nothing happened to him—no falls, digestive explosions, or sudden infections—her time was taken up by his care—changing sheets, tubes, basins, counting out pills, making special food. And, of course, all the doctors' appointments: first, all the specialists who couldn't figure out why his back was in agony, then, the chemo, and, finally, the falling apart. Wrapping him in thick sweaters and robes and heating pads and blankets as he shivered in the new La-Z-Boy, when he could no longer bear to sit in the old armchair.

Thank God Claire was coming with the others. Dear Claire had come before, all the way from California for a week, to help out during John's decline. She'd pureed soups and frozen them in small containers; she'd inventoried the laundry, helped pick out the best La-Z-Boy, read to John, devised a handy system to keep track of the pills and the symptoms, went with them to the oncologist to be, as she put it, Erica's "eyes and ears." And, finally, sitting down with a groan and a glass of Chardonnay (part of John's store), she'd had "the Talk" with Erica.

Erica was the older sister by two years, so they were bound together firmly and forever; furthermore, it had been Claire and only Claire who'd had the guts to confront Erica all those years ago, back in their late twenties, about Erica's drinking problem. Not that Claire had been a saint. One time, they had dropped acid together, and Claire had decided to take a bubble bath. Erica heard her yelling from the bathroom of her apartment. "They're moving, they're moving!"

Pin-eyed, Erica had gone in to her. "Moving?" she'd said. "Everything's moving!" she added, which was literally true when you were on LSD. But Claire had insisted there was something moving on her besides the bubbles and the universe and, somehow, the two of them deduced that the frenetic dots swarming over her stomach and crotch were "cooties." The next sober day, Claire had gone to a pharmacy for lice shampoo. Ever since, if one of them said, "they're moving, they're moving!" the other would have to laugh. Crucially, though, Claire had soon after left the drug scene behind and gone about the business of growing up. She did not have an addictive personality.

It was deep winter during her visit, and Erica had lent Claire, long unaccustomed to real cold, a thick red sweater in which Claire, a tiny-boned woman, sat hunched with her glass of wine. "You know you can't go on like this," Claire said. She finished the glass. "I mean not with John and certainly not with Mona. Where is she, by the way?"

How strange, Erica thought. *She said the same thing to me about my drinking. "You can't go on like this."*

"At her friend Misty's."

"That Misty girl is quite strange, isn't she? She jiggered all through the funeral."

"Yes, she's ADD or ADHD or OCD." All Erica wanted was to take her sleeping pill. Many of her AA compatriots would have warned her she was playing with fire with these pills, disrupting her brain in a way that could lead her back to drinking, but Erica didn't believe so or, more to the point, didn't care. "And I've tried everything I can think of with Mona, I know she's . . . well, you know. She's not a bad kid, Claire!"

"No, of course she's not." Claire heaved a long sigh. "Please, don't get defensive, Erica, I'm just so worried for her . . . and you."

This was always Claire, trying to help. "Now, I'm not being defensive, but, really, I have no energy to get into a long discussion about what to do about Mona. None."

"I know, I know, it's just, she's like a lost puppy. Whatever drugs she's using . . . Neither of you can go on like this."

"Well, she's in the gifted and troubled program at her high school. She sees this highly recommended therapist every week. I take away privileges; I talk and talk to her." Erica stood. "I don't know what else to do. And I'm going to bed now."

"I knew you'd get angry with me."

"Don't, Claire. I have to take care of him, I have to take care of her, and, when I can sleep, that's all I want to do. I'm not angry."

"Erica . . . look, you sleep in tomorrow. I'll take care of John in the morning. You need a break, that's why I'm here."

When Erica got up at the gloriously late hour of nine thirty, Claire had done everything: medicated, fed, cleaned, and changed John, fed and watered the animals and the plants, folded a stack of laundry, and even roused Mona, who didn't have to be at school until noon that day. The two of them sat with deceptive coziness in the kitchen, drinking coffee.

Erica wished she felt more grateful. And Claire's helpfulness extended throughout her visit. She wouldn't let Erica do any chores—"Read a book, watch TV, go to your studio," she suggested, folding yet another pile of laundry as chicken soup simmered on the stove. One evening, when Mona got home promptly after classes were finished, which almost never happened when Erica was in charge, Claire enlisted her to give her father his meal (soup) and read to him while she and Erica went out for a quick dinner. The following day, Claire came with them to the oncologist's office and, while John had his infusions (in that horrible room with the La-Z-Boys lined up in rows filled with patients), she ran a lot of questions by the oncologist, things Erica hadn't thought to ask.

Claire was leaving the next day. She'd insisted on booking an airport limo, so Erica wouldn't have to drive. Half-packed, she drifted into what was now Erica's bedroom, where Erica sat in bed, trying to read a new Swedish thriller with a protagonist deeply depressed about the human condition because of the swine he runs into in his profession as a detective. *Even more depressed than me,* Erica thought. Claire nestled at the edge of the bed.

"Am I interrupting?"

"Claire, never. It's a relief to get away from the angst of the land of the midnight sun."

"I know I must be irritating you," Claire said abruptly.

Erica put the book down. She stroked Dim, who was lying across her legs. "No, you're not irritating. I am."

"You're just so worn out, I think more than you realize."

"I could use a vacation."

"I really hope you'll get some help in. You heard Dr. Kingsley."

"He's been pushing a nursing home for a while; he must have stock in them." *But John hates hospitals.* "I do have some help. A cleaning lady."

"Erica . . . it's going to get worse and worse."

"And so, when it does, I'll get help. An aide."

"But if you got one now, you could get out a little bit, see friends, do things."

"But I don't want to, Claire!" Dim leaped off the bed, offended by her tone. "I mean, I've loved having you here. My friends come over; I watch television, read. But I have to be *here.*"

Claire, so pretty with her cap of skillfully gilded hair, her soft, brown eyes and high cheekbones, began to cry. Ever so softly. Erica dug her nails into her palms. *She* was not going to cry.

"Mona's petrified of what happened when she had to call the ambulance. She told me at breakfast; we had a long talk. And she's terrified of what's happening to you."

"To *me*? She said that? Oh, that's beyond the pale. Do you know the panic she puts me through? Stoned on I-don't-know-what, it changes from week to week. My only goal is to get her to graduate high school. Then, I'm done."

Erica looked at her hands. *Liar.* They were shaking, with red marks on the palms.

Claire stared at Erica through streaming eyes. "Oh my God, Erica, you don't know how crazy and angry you sound!"

"Please don't…say that." Erica fell on her stomach across the bed and buried her face in the blankets, closing everything out. Like it was snow she was sinking into. She could move her arms and legs and make a snow angel, as she and Claire had done during childhood winters, as little Mona had, too, plump and golden in her snowsuit. "I am not crazy!" Angry? Yes, but she'd long gotten over the taboo against female anger, courtesy of the women in AA. But crazy was different. The fear of it had tap-danced around in her head for years when she'd been a drunk and druggie and done crazy-ass things, and that same fear had bled into her early recovery from addiction, with the familiar harpies of anxiety and depression, shame and guilt—all the things that chased addicts, secrets that had eventually been told and released. Yet, even so, even after years, decades, of increasing emotional balance—an absence of proof of craziness—she knew it hadn't gone away. That fear never went away completely.

She lay there and dozed, dreaming about making snow angels with her little sister. Fallen angels. She felt hot fur on her head and her legs and heard John's labored, croaking voice below, then Claire's soothing voice. Erica didn't move yet, she clasped the memory of the snow angels, how they would run into the house, their mother saying, "Take all that stuff off by the door! Don't drip snow everywhere!" She would make them cocoa with tiny marshmallows, stirring the hot milk at the stove.

Erica turned face down on her bed, mourning the mother who was so good with small children, with their scrapes and fights and measles, but who had changed when Erica and then Claire morphed into teenagers. She had backed away and become remote; she was no help. Erica wanted her mother badly at this moment. But what help could she be now?

She got up and washed her face and brushed her teeth. It was only a little after nine. She'd go downstairs and say good-night to John, read a poem to him if he was awake. She would be even-tempered with her sister. But John was asleep, and Claire was browsing through today's newspaper. "You had a good sleep," she said.

"Yes, and I feel better."

"There's this Meryl Streep movie on; it just started. She plays Julia Child. Have you seen it? I could nuke some popcorn."

"And would you make some cocoa?"

At some point, Mona appeared from her room, made more popcorn, and plunked down beside Erica on the couch. It had started to snow outside; they watched it drift down through the gap in the curtains. They were just like normal people, watching television, snacking. Well, except for John, nearby. *The maddening thing*, Erica thought during a commercial, *is that Claire is right. I can't go on like this. I can't, John can't, Mona can't.*

"Want some?" Mona asked, passing her the bowl of popcorn, larded with extra butter and salt.

"Sure," Erica said. "Why not?"

THE LAST MARTINI

Erica sits on a rug, surrounded by her little classmates, listening to Mrs. Hanson read to them from a large picture book. She loves kindergarten. It makes her feel cozy and safe. Mrs. Hanson says, "I have something to show you, class." She turns the book around, holding it so the children gathered at her feet can see. In large, block letters are words they can't read yet. The teacher points to each one and reads aloud, "Grief is not a curable disease."

Erica stands up in protest. She shouts, "This is supposed to be kindergarten!" But the letters have been imprinted in her brain.

"So, just try to keep him comfortable now," Doctor Katzabiyan had concluded back in April when John was moving toward death. Erica had switched from Dr. Kingsley after one too many mentions of a nursing home; the new oncologist was a man in his forties. Erica had learned from their encounters that Dr. Katzabiyan battled a sweet tooth, like her; loved to travel, like her; and that the origin of his unusual name was a blend of his and his wife's, Jewish and Hindu. The doctor knew a good deal about her as well. They talked increasingly less about John, she realized.

"We'll keep managing the pain aggressively, of course. But it is palliative at this point. I am very sorry, Mrs. Mason-Grey."

Erica let the doctor call her that, her blended name, though no one else did so. She would have let the doctor do anything if he could help John. She understood, though, that all he could do was keep John as stoned as possible. The day before, John had fallen to the floor again, her fault for thinking she could let him maneuver to the bathroom with the walker, which was about twenty steps from his bed. She'd had to call the ambulance again, and he ended up back in the same room as the last time he was in the hospital. Waiting, she sat beside him, reading aloud from a new biography about Thelonious Monk and, then, just stroking his arm. John had the ecstatic, whirling-dervish expression that sometimes came over him when they IV'd ever-stronger pain meds.

"The daffodils are out now," she told him suddenly. How she had longed for spring! "And the forsythia, not that I like that metallic yellow much, but it's something."

His jaw was clenched, but she thought he said, "Yes."

She got a paper cup of filtered water and a straw, and he tried to drink. John's drink of choice had always been a cocktail. He was a connoisseur of wine and the proper martini. With the clarity of hindsight, she realized that it was his last martini, the summer before, which had marked the change from a man with a bad back to a man dying. Though they had never discussed it directly. Elliptically, yes.

They had been at their old friend Lee Wanamaker's, retired art critic, expert cook and maker of martinis (according to John), eating little savory samosas while Lee stirred her signature silver pitcher of martinis to the peak of perfection. She carried John's glass to him, brimming with best-quality vodka and vermouth, along with proper olives. He'd thanked her and taken a healthy sip. At once, the color drained from his face, and he was suffused with sweat. He stumbled to the bathroom, retching.

"Oh, poor baby!" Lee had exclaimed. "Was it the samosas?" She appeared to be nearly as stricken as John, white-faced with concern.

"But we all ate them," Erica pointed out. "I'm fine, you're fine."

"It must be a sudden flu. Alka-Seltzer?" Lee offered. "Aspirin?"

John flopped in a chair and shook his head. Beads of sweat dripped onto his shirt.

"Home and to bed," said Lee. "And call the doctor in the morning, won't you? And let me know?"

Erica, whose night vision was uncertain, had taken the wheel of the Subaru, leaning forward owlishly.

"How are you?" Her scalp prickled. Stupid question.

"Like crap." John groaned. "Can you stop the car?"

She did, and he hung out the door, vomiting.

"I *must* be allergic to something I ate there," he rasped, slamming his door.

She drove on. "But we've established it can't be the appetizers. You didn't eat anything else!"

"It can happen. Oh, Jesus," he groaned. "I think it was the martini."

She turned her attention for a moment from the road and stared at him, crouched in the new position he'd taken since his back had started plaguing him. She swerved.

"Watch the road!"

"Sorry." But was it, she pondered, the vodka that made him so sick? Probably a twenty-four-hour virus. Because John was a legendary bon vivant, the perfect kind of drinker, like a polished European. Erica admired him for this. It was a talent, a social skill, like playing tennis well or sailing or something—something that she could not aspire to but didn't begrudge. Well, just a little. This drinking-like-a-gentleman habit had stood him in good stead. The art director who seldom overdid it, who became well-watered and blooming from his judiciously paced wines, liqueurs, and beloved vodka martinis.

Erica couldn't help it; she stole another glance at him. He was pearl-white, shaky, and rubbing his back awkwardly with one hand. "*I* know!" she said. "It's those pain pills for your back. Combined with alcohol." Percocet, wasn't it? He hated taking them, because of the fuzziness they induced, yet she'd noticed he'd been getting into a bit of a routine there, never missing a dose. "You're probably not supposed to drink with them."

"Yeah, that's probably it. Shit, not that they're helping much." At home, John had gone straight to bed. He'd not had a drop of wine or spirits since.

Funny how his consumption of drugs might outdo Mona's. Since the Percocet, there'd been a steady rain of ever-stronger painkillers: Vicodin, then oxycodone, then morphine, fentanyl patches, plus an ever-lengthening and changing list of other drugs. Medical marijuana wasn't legal yet, but several friends had offered to get him some weed. Not to mention, and how could she forget, the chemo combos. Erica's prayers veered wildly: for Mona to get off drugs, for John to be as high as he could be. She forgot to pray for herself; the list was crowded enough.

Two months after John's death, on an August day too humid to sustain Erica's mania-driven discarding activities, she realized while she was brushing her teeth that she needed to get a haircut. Denise at Lovelocks said she was in luck today; tomorrow they were closing for the annual two-week vacation. She and Denise had come to a truce, established over many visits: Denise could wrestle Erica's moody hair into her version of acceptability, but with a minimum of blow-drying fuss. Today, Erica made a slicing motion. "Cut it short, please."

"You're sure about that?"

"Yes." Now Erica would never be one of those old babes with a long, silver braid. Oh well. "Not a trim. A serious cut," she clarified. "And no blow-drying at all today, all right, Denise? I'm just not up for it." Of course, Denise knew nearly as much about Erica's problems as her closest friends did, as hairdressers have, from time immemorial, served as confidantes, often as effectively as therapists.

"OK, Denise, you *can* style it," Erica gave in. She should be presentable for that trip into the city tomorrow to meet John's financial guy. She had never met this man; John had taken care of all that. Well, it was his money.

Early the next morning, head sleeker, Erica found a not-very-old, tan, linen skirt and a blue blouse for the meeting in Manhattan. No comfy old khaki shorts and paint-stained T-shirt, her uniform at home, for this: she was about to meet her financial fate. As the economic sky was currently falling again, Wall Street hyperventilating, she spent most of her time on the train imagining the job she'd have to get to supplement John's pension, since being an artist didn't count, money-wise. Maybe she could sell plants or something at Home Depot? Books at Barnes & Noble? Or scarves at a counter in the maul? Or maybe some art-teaching thing, but those jobs were hard to come by, and she'd been out of that loop for a while. Staring out at the suburban landscape flashing by her on the train, she drifted back to the argument she'd had with John, years ago, when she told him she wanted to quit teaching art and just do art. She'd come to resent the work that had kept her afloat in her single, Manhattan days, mainly because of a coveted, rent-controlled, tenement apartment. But with John's salary, hers barely made a difference.

Funny, she thought, *how that heated discussion happened only a year before Mona was conceived.* She'd come close to screaming at him that night.

"But you always say you like being around the kids and their energy; you like meeting the faculty and the free perks you get there at the college, that health club, the concerts, and lectures." Like most men, John was deeply defined by his work. He didn't like everything about it, of course not, but even the negative stuff seemed to energize him. He would have liked a shorter commute, but he'd adjusted: home by seven, discard the bespoke suit for jeans, work in the vegetable garden in the warm months, play the piano in the winter, have a cocktail, then dinner. Then, when Mona came along, he was often the one to bathe her, read to her, tuck her in. John was all about work and leisure as a package; he needed both and, in his mind, everyone should.

Erica worked up to her main point. "Actually, I'm tired of young people, their fuck-you attitudes and pretensions. It's a struggle to get most of them just to show up for class." She paused, took a sip of her seltzer with lime. John was drinking wine that night. She heard herself veer from the reasoned script she'd planned and become querulous, one of her faults. "I do a lot around here, you know, with the house and the shopping and the cooking. I can cut back on personal stuff, if necessary. I can clip coupons." He was about to respond, probably to say not to be dramatic. She hurried on. "I need to get back to my real work, and it takes serious time to do it. All this classroom stuff is stealing my energy. I'm too tired when I get home."

She knew John could not understand this. John only stopped producing when he was sick. "Well, make a schedule. Get up an hour early." He was bound to say something like that, and she was both resentful and humbled. But she wasn't like John; she had a more finite amount of energy or drive. And she was more of a drifter. She thrived on what others called dead time.

"Not everybody's a workaholic, you know!" she said loudly and childishly, another mark in her faults column.

"That's supposed to mean what?"

"You know what it means. Oh!" And she had cravenly, help-lessly, given way to tears. "I'm really just a painter." *Add preten-tiousness to the faults list?* she thought, grimly.

"Oh, well then." He stood up.

"Right. Just walk away. But it's true."

She heard his home office door shut, a hair below a slam. An hour or so later, when she'd made rigatoni with sauce, eggplant, and sausage and a green salad, he reappeared. "I'm sorry," he said.

"I'm sorry too," she said. "I shouldn't have called you that. You're an incredible person."

"You are too. Of course you have to do what you want; I just worry you'll get too isolated."

And so it proved to be; that year before Mona's arrival changed everything once again. Once the last term was taught, the final proj-ects discussed, and, because they were required to be, graded, Erica cleared out her cubbyhole office, had a farewell coffee with a few other teachers, and soon found she had too much time to herself. She tended to fiddle, "fritter away time," as her mother used to say, make coffee, and read the *Times* thoroughly, even the business sec-tion. The old house made demands she hadn't noticed. Should she strip and refinish those scruffy old floors? She'd walk Bilco, their dog before Paco, make a meatloaf, then scones, and think about going to her studio.

Finally one morning, she carried her coffee to the bright lit-tle room, pulled out the easel, and began again, as tentative and self-conscious as she had been in the tumult of her post-drink-ing days in her twenties; her brain felt fried for a while. She had almost always drawn, or colored or penned or painted, portraits. Gradually, doodling, she found herself calling up characters she'd met in the AA meetings she now went to, haphazardly, in the burbs. It was absolutely not the thing to sketch them at meetings, so she had to rely on her memory, and the translation via memory led to a process where she could embellish and distort with impunity—could be kind or savage—and she did. A year later, newly pregnant, she had her first local show at a co-op gallery in a large, wealthier town. Charcoal and pen-and-ink portraits of AA people. She called it *Anonymous*, of course. She turned then to a project she'd begun in early sobriety, but had never completed. The only job she could get at first after she stopped drinking had been cleaning apartments. She'd already done a series (while drinking) called *Cleaners in the Dark*, sparked by encounters she'd had while working late as a typist at a law firm with immigrant workers who arrived when everybody went home for the day (except for Erica, who was working on a special project for the overtime pay). The lights were dimmed as vacuum cleaners roared and windows were dusted and wastebaskets were emptied, and the people who did this work became, to her, beautiful. That had been a modestly successful show for her.

And now *Cleaners in the Dark II*. She had begun with a self-portrait (thank God, she had gotten another office gig soon after, as she was a terrible cleaner). Years later, she added the curly-haired, always-smiling Guatemalan woman she saw coming and going from the old church where in the basement the AA meetings were held. Next was the janitor she glimpsed at her bank when she went to the ATM after hours—a whippet-thin, prophet-jawed West Indian. Her sense of isolation began to fade. She started going to local art events and met people: a round, old woman who had lived in Greenwich Village in the fifties and still painted wonderful dancing couples; another woman her age who did warm-toned abstracts; a guy who painted stadiums of sports fans, each fan exactingly depicted. There was another show at a small community art center of *Cleaners II*, with wine and cheese and a modest, well-disposed crowd, and John there and proud of her swollen, six-months-pregnant belly. Some sales, now a modest savings account. Never enough to live on, but that had not been the intention.

Having taken on the job of bill payer from John once she'd quit teaching, Erica was humbled at the scope and extent of what it took to live decently. Neither she nor John was much of a spender—he had the used Beemer and the used piano, and she drove a sensible Subaru. They ate out, but not high-end, went to local concerts and movies. Yet it simply cost a lot to live.

She jolted awake in the train as it pulled into Grand Central and thought, *Oh yes, he's gone, two months now, I'm a widow,* and walked down an essentially treeless Park Avenue under a merciless, white-hot sky, though luckily it was only a few blocks to the green-glass tower where John's financial man met her on the seventeenth floor. He actually wore striped suspenders and a bow tie and, in a little conference room, was very soon assuring her that he was "plain vanilla," whatever that meant. She was given coffee, and he showed her a raft of papers. "The key thing," he said, tapping columns of figures, "is this." She was going to be comfortable for the rest of her life. Because it turned out John had a hobby, a talent, maybe a vocation, of salting away bits and pieces of unusually fruitful deals, investments she knew nothing about.

Financially illiterate, she listened, taking in little, with a smudged sense of elation, relief, and guilt. Also resentment: why hadn't John told her about this sizable socking-away of money? "So," said the financial man, "take a nice long vacation, Italy, or someplace like that. You deserve it. Decisions will need to be made, but not at this moment, no. Take this home and read it. Ask me any questions; there's plenty of time." Erica descended in the elevator of the green-glass building in a daze, gripping the heavy envelope, walking slowly into the surge of office workers heading for the train station. Clipped and buffeted by the hurrying crowd, she turned off into a side street that was calm by comparison. Maybe she should celebrate. High tea at the Plaza? But she just wanted to go home. And think. She was modestly, but undeniably, rich, a condition she had never expected to encounter. *Thank you, Plain Vanilla Man.*

Now knowing that she was safely cushioned, Erica was perplexed that she felt compelled to work harder than she had in years. The cleaners' portraits had taken her in a new direction. She began to scout out more Guatemalans: easy pickings in her town, which was overflowing with them in its rundown old houses in the old village, much to the local rednecks' discomfiture. She was pulled in another direction, too; she needed somehow to educate herself about the great unknown that had been in her marriage. Money. She lugged boxes full of old tax forms from the attic, to page through them. She found that, just as she couldn't stop looking at the financial past, she needed to know if there were more secrets in their twenty-five years together; more boxes were brought down, several filled with photo albums of John's stiffly posed and unknown ancestors. Others were just filled with crap: a mildewed sleeping bag and blankets, rusted window screens, a broken, fake Tiffany lamp. Out it went, all of it, in compactor bags.

During one semester of her sophomore year in college, Erica had discovered acid, mescaline, and then Black Beauties, which everybody used at exam time. Speed. Dexedrine. The crash was so pitiful that she stopped taking them, but now she was reminded of that feeling of endless soaring power as she zoomed through boxes, hurled out piles, maybe collections, of nails and screws and old cans of paint. Dragged trash bags, again and again, to the curb.

Back up in the fiercely hot attic, reaching for yet another box, she wondered if John had been a borderline hoarder. Erica found one that was full of cards, the ghosts of birthdays, anniversaries, and Christmases past. One addressed to her flapped open, and she read, "And most of all, I am glad there is you. All my love, John." She sank to the floor, flooded by the heady, hormonal, early years together. All that good sex! And how did they get from that to the end? Oh, she knew it's what happens. Of course, the excitement wears off and, if you're lucky, there's peaceful sex, the contentment of being together, but sometimes, along the way, you hide a yawn after making love, and you stop thinking about it much. And the last year together didn't count. She'd become a nurse and he her patient. But she'd been cold at times; she'd snapped at him. "Please stop thanking me. It's my job; I have to do this." His gray, gaunt face and felled, suddenly ancient body would overwhelm her, and she had had to fight the revulsion that would come over her. She swore she wouldn't patronize him but acquired a nursey briskness all the same. With the person dearest to her.

Hadn't she gone to see him every day in the hospital, those many times, and, after that, to the hospice? Yes, but she'd always wanted to leave soon after she got there. The worse it got, the more quickly she wanted to leave. The hospice center was full of the expected, disturbing odors, despite being clean; it was noisy from the televisions blaring at the wheelchairs. Yet, on his last day on earth, she'd arrived to find the nursing home quiet, hushed almost. He was strapped into the wheelchair so he wouldn't fall out. The staff no longer changed him into his old corduroys and plaid shirt and sweater, but he was in fresh pajamas and his thick robe. The aide, Nilda, was patting his face with a washcloth.

"Here, I'll do that," Erica said. Perhaps Nilda, a Dominican, would do if she expanded the Guatemala series?

"He don' want his lemon ice today," Nilda told her. "I give him water."

"All right. Anything else I should know?"

"The Father, he come in the morning." This would be Father Locke, the priest of their little Episcopal church. "To pray on him."

"Good. Good." Erica wheeled him from the room to the corridor with the long, tinted window that let in an underwater kind of light. John began making scrabbling movements with his hands—little, crablike motions—and she realized he was trying to tell her something. She bent to hear his gossamer rasp.

"Do you want more morphine?"

But perhaps not. John inched his hand toward her hand and, with infinite patience, moved them together toward his bent head. This shape-shifter, this body snatcher! How could it have been only a year ago that he'd had his wonderful, thick hair, his well-cut suits, his busy life with his lunches with old friends—he had a gift for friendship, much more than she did. They'd gotten the adorable creamy puppy, Casho, and John had been training him, patiently most of the time..

They were alone in the hallway, which was not often the case, as John's friends had been coming in a steady stream to say goodbye. Even Mona had come. They had all left gifts, books and magazines, flowers and fruit, even—God knows why—a bunch of balloons.

"John, we're going to be all right, Mona and I," she said, kneeling beside what was left of him. "I promise. I swear it to you with all my heart."

He pressed his parchment lips to her hand, a light kiss. It penetrated like a bee sting on her skin, and she gasped.

A sound like a whistling kettle pierced the nice, dense fog of Erica's nightly Ambien-induced sleep, pierced the dream in which she had moved into an apartment with unexpected rules—you couldn't go into the room next to your bedroom; you were living in a dangerous area; actually, no, you weren't living here, it was up three flights of stairs, on the other side of the enormous complex; and so on, a variant of a dream that she had been having for years. She really, really wanted to settle this living arrangement once and for all but was pulled away by the whistling kettle noise. It was the phone, relentless in the dark. What time was it? Three fifteen. Erica didn't want to answer; she wanted to go back to sleep.

She picked up the phone. "Yes. Yes, it is. No! No! Yes." She didn't get up, not for a while. Shouldn't there have been cracks in the walls, lightning flashing, a voice from the clouds? All the things she hadn't done for him rushed in with a silent sucking noise, especially not sleeping on a pallet next to him, so he wouldn't be alone when it came. How could she have left him alone with it? But she had been bled of all but the most basic emotions. She must get up now and survive. As she did so, Erica stumbled over the heap of Casho, the sentinel who had taken up a new position beside the bed for the last week or so. He got up with a grunt, familiar with her panic, and was immediately on guard. He had known only confusion for many months, but this time, Erica did not comfort him. She threw on jeans and a shirt, opened Mona's door, and remembered Mona was at Misty's again; she practically lived there these days.

She let the dog sit in the front passenger seat, a first for them, as she drove up to the nursing home. Casho was very pleased, of course, and stared intently at the still-dark, empty roads as Erica sped through the night, this cautious driver who had never gotten a speeding ticket. She was half-hoping she'd see the flashing, red light of a police car, half-imagined how she'd throw herself on his or her mercy and get a ride from the sympathetic lawperson while she wept quietly on the way; Casho in the back behind the grille.

"Wait here and don't bark," she told Casho in the parking lot of the darkened nursing home.

Casho gave her a long dog look, stretched out somehow on both front seats and sighed. Nobody does sighing better than a dog. The place was locked up, of course: all those drugs floating around a nursing home were an addict's heaven. But she was buzzed right in.

"Mrs. Grey?" said the heavy woman at the desk in an awful, flowered shirt and shapeless pants. "The night supervisor is waiting just down the hall."

In his room, she forced herself to sit and then to touch him; it had to be done, but she feared it, as if he'd jump up laughing and say "surprise!" And she was surprised at the warmth she felt. She should have been here. She was a selfish, terrible person, sleeping in her own bed with all the comforts of home, abandoning him to this. They'd closed his eyes. And everything had been discussed, but she was breathless at this new development. This was him, but it was not him. What travesty had been committed that the substance and the light of him had been stolen and in their place, this?

She heard a dog barking, no, keening. Their dog. No, her dog.

It was not as dark when she emerged to the parking lot. A pale-violet light was blooming. No, she thought professionally, the sky held pink, gray, and yellow besides the light, purplish tinge of this dawn. Seeing her, Casho threw himself against the car window. She let him out and he ran into a thicket and peed, an improbably long stream, then ran around in loops.

"Casho! Come!"

He gave her a feral glance and skipped into the interesting weeds.

"Oh God!" The true prayer, the one that spews from the gut. Erica slid to the ground, and the dog was immediately there, heaving himself on her. He smelled of intimate encounters with something rank. Dogs love to roll around in decay. "No!" she prayed, seeing John again, Olympian, waiting to decay. "God, no!"

She had to go to Misty's house now and tell Mona that her father had died.

HOLIDAY GRIEF WORKSHOP

Erica senses a man watching her as she is trying to scrub out large crimson stains from a rug. She abandons her efforts and begins sweeping piles of dirt heaped in the corners of the room, still feeling his presence. As hard and fast as she sweeps, she can't keep up with the dirt. And the man is getting closer. She shouts, "Help me!" and wakes up.

That first December after John's summertime death, Erica gets lost while driving in Connecticut, trying to find a Holiday Grief Workshop she'd signed up for during some brief and dubiously hopeful moment. She's late when she finally tracks down the address on an obscure country road. Erica hates being late to anything, even a holiday grief workshop. The leader, or no doubt "facilitator," looks up and stops talking as she sidles into a room dominated by a large, oblong table covered by a tablecloth festooned with reindeer. Everyone watches as she pulls out a chair.

"Sorry," she says.

Sorry for being here, she immediately wants to add. For starters, the facilitator is an elderly man in a gray cardigan. Not what she'd expected. And all the other attendees are just plain old,

too. Mostly old, white people, but with a sprinkling of other ethnicities, including a tiny, balding Chinese woman. Only two are
men, the facilitator and a deflated-looking man who, on second
glance, is really not that advanced in age, though white-haired.

"Welcome, indeed," says Gray Cardigan Man.

She ponders that. *Indeed? What indeed?* But he's moved on.

"Comments? We're talking about changes we might make
for Christmas or Hanukah," he explains courteously to Erica.

Or Kwanzaa, Erica adds silently.

"Yes, I have to say something." A pink-haired old lady, with
too much makeup. "All these years, I've made the turkey and all
the trimmings at Thanksgiving, then the ham or roast beef, et
cetera, plus, of course, pies again at Christmas. Well, I don't want
to do it anymore. But they expect it, you see, so I have to." She
dabs swiftly at her eyes.

"For me, it's cookies," a large, black-haired woman weighs
in. "My grandkids would never eat store-bought."

"And for me, latkes, brisket, and *sufganist*," says another
elderly woman, also with intensely black hair.

Why do elderly women do this to themselves? Erica wonders
idly. The vivid hair and bright makeup. Would she end up the same?

"What's Sufa-ganic?" The not-so-old guy leans forward
across the table.

"Hanukah food," the Intensely Black-Haired Lady explains.
"Well, I'm not doing it this year. Enough! Let the younger ones do
something already."

"Is this something we should think about?" queries the facilitator. The others seem variously sour, crushed, or, in the case of
the tiny bald Chinese woman, bewildered. And then there's Erica,
who's planning to get takeout this Christmas; and who would rush
out the door this second, except she can't move.

"OK, fine, don't make the whatsit for the Hanukah, I respect that. *I* draw the line at getting a tree," a husky voice booms. "That's where I draw the line. By the way, do you have trees for the Hanukah?" she asks the black-haired woman.

She shrugs. "Some do."

"Would *you* like to add something?"

Erica realizes the facilitator is speaking to her. "Oh," she says. "What I want to know"—she realizes she feels a little peculiar, feverish—"is how many holidays will it be until I'm not in a bad movie? Nothing matters anymore, certainly not things like trees, cookies. Oh, never mind." She pushes back her chair. "I have to go, sorry."

The facilitator follows her into the hallway. "Is it the first one?" he asks softly. She sees that he is kind.

"Yes."

"Well . . . this one you just get through." He clears his throat, produces a pamphlet. "I think you would find *this* group to be more of a help, more age-appropriate." He taps a color photo on the front page of a pamphlet. The circle of women is of varying middle-ages, her age. "The Modern Widows Club," she reads.

"They meet here twice a month."

A functioning group of the MWC! "Oh my," she says. "OK. Thanks."

"You're most welcome."

But she suspects that she's done with grief workshops. For good.

It is definitely going to be an Ativan evening after that senior holiday experience. Her doctor, dear Ronnie, who knows her best of anyone in the world, as well as Ginger and a couple of other people know that Erica now takes an antidepressant and half an Ativan, too, but only ever later in the day—well, almost only ever—and then an Ambien to sleep; Erica, who for all these years "in the program" has faced life free of chemicals. Well, but when she had gotten sober, they hadn't invented these things. Prozac came out and was supposed to be a miracle drug, but she wouldn't know. Erica had learned to wear her anxiety and depression like a reversible sweater. But not now. Even though all these mood and pain pills are dispensed like candy throughout the land, she's careful. The thing is, she must function, she has to, for Mona.

The next day, as she is drinking her second coffee, on a whim, she perversely decides to celebrate the holidays after all. Mona will soon be home from college for Christmas break. Their first Christmas without John. She digs Christmas stuff out of the attic, the star- and reindeer-shaped cookie cutters, and the jolly, red table linens. She buys a tree from the fire department sale, the smallest one she can find, and easily slips it into the stand. It is so small she starts to cry, remembering the seven-foot trees she and John used to wrestle with; the thing always had to be perfectly straight (John), which could take some time and had sparked more than one spat. The ornaments can wait for Mona. Then she locates the CD of Bing Crosby in the Santa hat. Except for some gifts for Mona—certificates this year, cash, some pricey choco-lates—Christmas is set. She's already sent Tom a check and a card.

The phone rings. In the background, Bing warbles about chestnuts.

"Mom!" Followed by sobbing and a dial tone.

Erica instantly begins to hyperventilate as she dials Mona's cell. Busy. She paces, breathes in and out, tries the phone again and again. Finally, Mona calls back. "I need to come home now. *Right now, Mom.*" Her imperious tone is undermined by more sobs.

"Why? What's wrong? Are you OK?" Questions that she's asked her daughter too many times to count. Pointlessly, she adds, "The holidays are coming up and you'll have a long break then."

"Mom, don't hate me, but I haven't been going to classes for a while. And I have to get out of Brooklyn. Now. It's urgent, Mom!"

And so it is that Erica finds herself, fearful and angry, on clogged, mean-spirited highways and, at last, inching her way along the streets of the borough of Brooklyn in the full darkness of a five o'clock December afternoon. Where everyone drives aggressively. Panel trucks and buses are the most fearsome, all seemingly driven by crack addicts or anger-management candidates. She gets repeatedly cut off. To be fair, they all do it to every other vehicle on the road, too. She's shaking by the time she gets to the row house in Greenpoint where Mona rents a room. Erica's been inside it just once, when she helped Mona move in on a sunny September day. A hopeful day. They had walked around the old Polish neighborhood, had a pierogi lunch. Now she stays in the car as instructed while Mona brings out trash bags filled with her stuff and bits and pieces of furniture.

"What about the futon, the dresser?"

"I'll get them another time." Mona sinks into the passenger seat and implants her headphones. Dry-eyed, she doesn't seem particularly upset now.

Erica starts shaking again, now from anger only.

"Mom! Let's get out of here already!"

"I'm just getting myself together." But does Mona hear her through the noise of her iPad?

Erica does her breathing and decides to wait until she is out of the traffic insanity and back on the smooth familiar highway in suburbia before she attempts a conversation.

"Tell me what the hell's going on!"

Mona yanks out the earpiece. "What?"

"Tell me! What happened? And . . . where is your car?"

"Oh, the car." Long silence. "I sold it," she says through clenched teeth.

Erica swerves on the highway. "You what?"

Mona speaks rapidly, almost shouting. "You're driving erratically! Chill, Mom! I sold it because I needed to; I would never have done it, but it was a real emergency, and then yesterday I . . . I got caught doing something by one of my roommates."

The car veers again. "Got caught doing what?"

"I don't want to talk about it, OK?"

"Well, tough, talk about it."

Now Mona does start crying. "I needed some money, OK?" She collapses, but Erica has to keep driving. How many times in these past couple of years of Mona's chaos has she felt like her heart is being run over by a truck?

Remember: Mona is a drug addict. Mona is a drug addict, she reminds herself. Each time it brings fresh panic. *Well, you were a drug addict too!* she reminds herself. It was just different stuff then, not this malignant heroin. And, with her hands numb from clenching the wheel, Erica remembers a night when she was about Mona's age. She'd ingested some street drug she and her girlfriends had bought from the local dealer, a guy they knew only as Crazy Dave. She was walking around with her stoned friends, all of them in bellbottoms and floppy hats and love beads, and then everything went white in Erica's head, like a snowstorm. When she came to, she was lying on the pavement. Alone. Her "friends" had split. And all these years later Erica has the sudden, absolute conviction that, if she were Mona's age now, it wouldn't be street acid and Panama Red and cheap wine for her. No, it would be heroin. She too would have crossed the Rubicon on a ship of pain pills cadged from Mom and Dad (John's cancer meds!) and landed on some desert island, a junkie. Thousands and thousands and thousands of children are addicted to opiates; they steal, lie, overdose, end up in jail, then rehab, then back to jail. Or die. Thousands are dying. Schools ignore or get rid of them. The government puts them in jail. She would have been one of them for sure.

No comfort in knowing that, though. Or that Mona is just another casualty. Nineteen, skin and bones, bad complexion, awful hair, spinning down. Fleeing Brooklyn, breaking her mother's heart, this adored addict child now sobs out something that astounds her mother. "Everybody has a boyfriend but me. I have nobody."

"You have other things to think about!" Erica screams. "Like your life!"

In silence, they continue home, where Casho leaps ecstatically on Mona; Dim and Dimmer circle, sniffing change. "I got a tree," Erica says for no reason.

"Cool." Mona is already sliding back into her remote hipster guise, raising an eyebrow at the painted wooden Santa by the fireplace that Erica has placed there every Christmas of her life. "That Santa's cheesy, Mom." She drifts upstairs, her bags left by the door. Erica opens one cautiously. The funk hits her of clothes long unwashed, salted with cigarette smoke. She resolves to leave the bags there for Mona to deal with, a resolve she knows she will break. Then she smells something else, an acrid burning. She pounds up the stairs and throws open Mona's door. Mona is in bed, with a hash pipe to her lips.

"What the fuck?" Mona complains.

"Give me that pipe! You have half an hour. To come downstairs. Dressed. Or else you are out of here tonight. That's the fuck what." Erica wrenches the pipe from her and slams the door.

She crams some dirty dishes into the dishwasher, left over from the night before. She paces. *Breathe.* Gets the folder with the plan that Ronnie and Claire and even Ginger have urged her to create, each in their own way, over the past few months. And for the first time in many years she could really use a drink.

Mona clumps down the stairs in a Hole T-shirt and red, velvet pants torn at the knees, in a child's size. No hips, waist, or butt left.

Erica is waiting with the folder at the kitchen table, her whole body vibrating. Even her teeth feel ready to fly away. She has made coffee and offers some to Mona, along with a slice of bread and butter, slathered with strawberry jam.

"Thanks, Mom." She sits at the extreme edge of her chair, but at least she's there. Devouring bread and jam. She probably never eats.

"Here's the deal," Erica says in a voice she doesn't recognize. *Breathe.* "Our insurance covers some inpatient, but not all. You're lucky, because we can pay the rest, thanks to your father. Look it over and make up your mind. The choice is yours."

"What if I don't want to go? Which I don't." Mona is so thin her chubby cheeks are now the sucked-in planes of fashion ads; she's a skinny mess, but Erica is fairly inured to this, after John. Cancer was the holy war; heroin is the thief of life. Mona has an abscess on her foot, so she hobbles. She has contracted an STD. She steals. She sold her car—correction, the car that her father had bought for her—to a drug dealer. She lasted less than a semester in college. But, damn it, that's not what a mother sees. A mother sees the home movie with the cute, melting moments of her baby, then her little girl. Flickering images of a three-year-old in a pink princess dress and a tall pink hat covered in stars on Halloween, a cold night when Mona insisted on not wearing her parka so she could show off her princess self. The awkward, not-lovely preteen, still willing to wear a dress of blue-green velvet with long sleeves and a tartan belt, standing with a gap-toothed smile in front of the applauding auditorium as she was announced the winner of the first prize in the whole state for her piano composition. And, a year or so later, Erica watching her sail around the ice arena, skating with natural grace, laughing with her friends—all those little friends who are gone now, in college, not on drugs, as far as Erica knows.

It dawns on Erica that Mona is not putting up much of a fight about going to rehab.

"Fuck it!" Mona says. She has not looked at the folder. "Where is it?"

"Just the next town over."

"It's *Wings*? Mom, Wings of Hopelessness?"

"Of Hope," Erica says automatically. She stands up, wobbling, feeling as if she might pass out. Her brain is on a loop: *Please God, please God.* But she knows she can still multitask: insist, press, make this happen, call Wings, throw together some kind of a meal. Oh, yes, and feed the animals. Mona, the cats, and the dog all stare at her remorselessly, because she is the one who must hold it all together.

AA-APPROVED LITERATURE

Mona's in a booth in a coffee shop. A stranger across the aisle is loudly slurping a milkshake through a straw out of one of those tall, silvery, old-fashioned glasses. Mona leans over and tells him her heart has been broken. "Of course it has!" says the stranger. No, not a stranger: it's Kyle from the animal shelter. "Because you're a junkie."

Erica shakes the hand of a heavyset man sporting a red plaid holiday vest in a cubicle at Wings of Hope, the large rehabilitation center ten miles from home. Wings had begun life as the bucolic weekend estate of a wealthy, alcoholic industrialist who was restored to health by Alcoholics Anonymous way back in the fifties or sixties; in gratitude, he donated the property for this rehab center. The festively dressed, portly man in the cubicle is here to begin the process of restoring Mona to health, although he himself appears, Erica thinks, like a heart attack about to happen. But that's not her problem, hers is down the hall, getting drug-tested.

"Jack Bunch. Intake counselor," he explains and launches into a discussion of Mona's options, which he's able to do because Mona has waived her confidentiality rights after a long argument with Erica which had ended with both of them sobbing.

"I recommend inpatient for at least sixty days, longer if you can."

"I don't know . . . The insurance covers four weeks." Yes, she can pay for more. But shouldn't a month, OK, 28 days, of group counseling, institutional meals, and enforced AA meetings be enough?

He shrugs, the universal what-can-you-do body language. "Well, we find with this younger population that the more time we can have them, the better the outcome. But here's another option. Let's assume the test is dirty now. So, she does the twenty-eight, then group outpatient." He hoists a stack of papers. "I'll let you know when we have the results."

Erica goes back to the waiting room, a clone of all the doctors' and hospital waiting rooms she's spent so much time in with or for John. A television yapping—some talk show, very restful—the old tattered magazines and the other drooping people waiting like her. Only here at Wings, there's a different atmosphere in the room, because they're all parents or lovers or relatives of someone who has crashed and burned and sent shrapnel flying at them. Addiction.

After a fidgety ten minutes, she can't stand it. She goes outside and calls Ronnie.

"I'm waiting at the rehab center," she says, "I don't know if I can go through with this."

"No, *you* can't," Ronnie agrees.

This is startling. "Ronnie . . . you think I'm going to cave? Come on, I need support."

"You always have my support, Erica. But this is not something you can do. This is Mona's problem, remember? All you need to do is support her right now."

"She looked like a kicked dog when we got here."

"That's exactly what I mean. She's in the right place."

"I know, I know. Why can't I accept it, though? I feel like I'm abandoning her."

"Remember when you had to get her out of Brooklyn because she claimed her life was in danger? Remember she sold the car for drugs? I can go on."

"Right, right. But this place . . . it's so institutional; it's depressing."

"Does the atmosphere of this place, Wings of Happiness . . ."

"Wings of Hope."

"Yeah. Does the ambience there matter? It's a step up, Erica, because where do you think Mona's going from here if she's not stopped?"

"OK, yes, right."

Ronnie's voice softens. "You've done everything for her, Erica Mason, now you've got to let her deal with her addiction. She's in a safe place where she can get well."

Yes, yes, yes, yes, and yes. But Erica can muster no optimism, no sense of happy endings right now. "Casho keeps peeing in the living room," she says.

"Maybe he's trying to tell you something."

"What, he hates me?"

"Maybe Casho wants the chaos to stop, too."

They say goodbye; Erica goes back to the waiting room. It's another half hour before she's summoned to another cubicle, where she meets Steve, just Steve, the counselor, a shaggy, small guy in his forties wearing chinos, a blue shirt, and a dark-blue tie, an outfit that says "psychologist." Mona is there also, white-faced.

"Mom, I want to come back tomorrow; I need to pack, get organized."

Steve shakes his head. "Mona, you tested positive. This might be your one chance to get clean."

"Please, Mom." Mona does pathetic expertly.

Erica feels about an inch high as she says, "She'll be here tomorrow morning, I promise."

Driving home, Mona curls into a ball, sniffling. "Thanks, Mom."

"For what? I should have insisted."

"For giving me time to . . . adjust to the idea of the horrible Wings."

"It's not horrible. You have to promise you won't go anywhere. We can have a nice dinner, maybe watch a movie."

"Yeah, OK, whatever."

At home, Erica hears Mona moving around her room, packing. She's been given a list of forbidden stuff, quite a lot of things actually, including cell phone, iPad, iPod, laptop, DVDs. Mona shuffles downstairs and goes in the living room. Suddenly, she erupts into the kitchen, where Erica is contemplating what to cook for their last supper.

"Mom! Where are the car keys?"

"I put them away. You're not going anywhere, remember?"

When Erica is in the bathroom a few minutes later, she hears her car start. Shit! But Mona can almost always find her hiding places. Erica is too familiar with being played to dwell on it.

Long after the supper that Erica eats alone on a tray in front of the television, Mona returns, and Erica's anger dissolves into relief that she's come back. High, of course. The next morning is like the years and years of school mornings when she had to fight to get Mona up. She simply refuses. Erica calls Steve to plead with him to save the bed. "You have until four thirty," he says. It's after five when they pull into Wings of Hope again, but they've saved the bed in the detox unit.

A silent Latino aide goes through Mona's stuff slowly and thoroughly, putting aside nail clippers, hair spray and a couple of paperbacks. Erica crams them in her bag. "The nurse'll do a body search," he says, finally. Erica watches Mona droop away down the detox hall. Again, she waits in an awful room. Another suburban mother in a molded plastic chair clutches a plastic bag, presumably her child's rejects. They don't look at each other. This room tries, but fails, to be homey. There is a fake Christmas tree with multi-colored lights and some cheerily wrapped boxes underneath, no doubt empty. Patients, who she will learn are called *clients,* mill around. The aide comes back with more forbidden stuff Mona had secreted in her clothes: cell phone, pack of Salem Lights, lighter, and a paperback called *Smashed.*

Erica pages through the book. "But this is about a girl who gets sober," she objects.

"Only AA-conference-approved literature here."

"Oh, for Chrissake," Erica snaps. She breathes in, says "Sorry," and asks when she can talk to Mona. She doesn't want to alienate anyone who may have to deal with her daughter.

"Call the unit in a couple days, when she'll start feeling better," the man says. Erica can't wait that long. When she calls Mona the next afternoon, Mona says only, "Everything sucks here. I hate this place."

Going through the motions of her days, Erica wonders if life will ever be anything but gray again. She can function, she doesn't want to get drunk or stoned (the big AA victory), she knows Mona's in a safe place; but invisible, tight bands constrict her heart and her head. Signs of life impact her, but faintly.

After Mona is moved from detox to the rehab unit, Steve the counselor calls her in for a family meeting. As she sits again in his cubicle, other counselors, including one also called Steve, stick their heads in and ask her Steve to step out. Like her, they are always dealing with crises.

Mona's Steve finally shuts his door and begins. He's a nice guy, Erica can tell that, but his speech is laced with AA-speak. "*Mokus*"—supposed to be ancient gypsy slang for being unable to think straight, a condition common to people new to sobriety that somehow found its way into the lingo—"surrender to win," "one day at a time," "fake it 'til you make it." For some reason, she doesn't want to tell him that she's also in recovery. Also, she doesn't want to hear his opinions of Mona. It occurs to her that she's afraid he'll tell her Mona's one of those hopeless cases. She points at a photo tacked to his wall of a little boy and an older girl, not yet in their teens. He has that to look forward to. The girl has a big gap in her smile, which makes Erica's heart squeeze.

"Your kids? They're really cute."

Steve smiles quickly. "And they can be a pain in the you-know-what. Now, Mrs. Grey."

"Oh, call me Erica."

"So, about *your* child, Erica. Mona's been evaluated by psych—it's routine," he adds, at seeing Erica's expression. "The evaluation"—he glances down at a paper—"says depression plus oppositional thinking."

"Oppositional thinking? As in, I tell you the sky is blue, you tell me it's green?"

"Something like that."

"But aren't they all like that as teenagers? I was. It seems like part of the deal, almost."

"You know, it's a question of degrees." Steve leans back. "How are you feeling, by the way?"

"Me? Oh, let's see. Numb, but also pick any negative emotion. Anxious. Frightened. Guilty. Ashamed," she adds thoughtfully. "As in, how could I let this happen to her, how could she do this to me? And angry. As in, after everything I've had to go through?"

"Mona's mentioned her father's death. I am so sorry. Losing her father at this critical age . . . I'm sure it's played a role in her progression." Steve presses on. "But Mona's addiction is about Mona. Not about you. Or even her father."

Erica says, "Oh, it is about me—to *me!* I've gone through endless pain because of it. It's like the sun's been blotted out."

"I know it's awful for you as a parent, Ms. . . . Erica." He pauses. "You know there's a program that can help you? Al-Anon. Have you tried it? There's a meeting here I think every Wednesday night."

"I know about Al-Anon, and I've been in the real program forever, well, almost."

Steve looks quizzical. "OK. So you know where to get help. That's great. Look, Mona will be here any minute. She really needs your support, Erica. She's desperate for it."

Erica says, astonished, "But I've always given her my support, always."

"I'm talking about *not* rescuing her. She's already told me about several times you've, ah, done that. She's quite self-aware in many ways. She admits she has to learn to grow up without being enabled every time she gets into trouble."

"Oh God," Erica says. *Here we go again.* In AA parlance, she needs to "let go." Ronnie, her sister Claire, now this Steve, everyone, in fact, who knows anything about addiction, has told her to let go. But there's a steady drumbeat in Erica's head: *Mona's all I have, Mona's all I have.*

Mona, pale and blotchy, her hair not brushed and sticking out strangely, appears at the door and slides into a chair. Detox doesn't seem to have done much for her.

"Hi Mona."

"Hey Mom."

Erica reaches toward her, eager to inhale her scent, feel her body. Her poor frail baby.

To her surprise, Steve suggests that Mona and Erica go get a coffee or something in the cafeteria and come back in half an hour.

They sit at a table near a picture window that looks out upon a dull winter day. It hasn't snowed yet, but it will. Towering pines form a protective, claustrophobic ring around the Wings of Hope "campus," as they call it. There are bunches of other patients in the cafeteria, many of them African American women in this white, suburban place.

Mona points at Erica's coffee. "Guess what? It's decaf, Mom. Everything here is the equivalent of decaf." She starts to chatter. "They've put me on the patch, because they don't allow smoking, and it's making me have crazy-ass dreams at night. Lurid, Mom. Please, please, can you bring me a pack of Salem Lights and some matches next time? Like later today maybe? Just put it in your purse, they won't search you. Mom, *please*."

Erica doesn't know what to say. She supposes it must be too hard to come off heroin and nicotine at the same time. She knows she'll end up smuggling in cigarettes for Mona. "We'll see."

"Everyone's crazy here, Mom, including the staff."

"Even Steve?" Erica asks bleakly.

"No, he's OK," Mona admits. "He gets me, sort of. He said he would have had a hard time, too, if his dad got cancer and died when he was my age."

"Oh." Erica turns her head away so Mona won't see her sudden tears. It was not what Mona had just said; it was the matter-of-fact way she said it. And the fact that Mona seems like a beat-up, little doll. "I'm so sorry about all this," she whispers.

Mona leaps up and grabs her in a tight hug, gulping down a sob. They go back to Steve's office. On the way, Mona again begs her to bring cigarettes. "Also a few tops, a sweatshirt, some books. They let you read some regular stuff once you're out of detox."

Erica nods. "Non-AA-approved?" And then she remembers suddenly, "I need your Christmas lists."

Since she was a baby, Mona has made a Christmas wish list, one for herself, one for those she called "the poor people." And in less than a week it will be Christmas.

That Saturday night, Erica forces herself to go to the annual holiday party she and John had attended for years at Ned and Tony's perfectly restored, Revolutionary War–era manor house, complete with barns, fields, and manicured grounds, which are now dusted with snow to make everything look perfect.

She feels like a cardboard cutout of herself in her black velvet skirt, white sweater, and the red heels recycled each year at this time, as she air-kisses her hosts. Ned guides her over to meet a whippet of a woman in a real-live red diva gown and heavy makeup, Teresa something. "Erica's an artist," he supplies, eyebrows quirked.

"And what kind of artist is she?" Teresa asks, with her own arch expression.

"She's a portrait painter," Ned contributes—inaccurately, Erica feels—but she is uninterested in correcting him. He adds, "And Teresa is one of the world's great hostesses," then wheels off to the next arrival.

There seems little to be said after what, to Erica at least, is a non-sequitur. But she tries. "I guess there's an art to throwing a party, too," she manages, and could throw her arms around dear Ginger who approaches at just this moment. Ginger is locally famed for her conversational skills and is reliably amusing. "I could talk to a wall," she once said and perhaps she was only half-joking.

Ginger gives Teresa a forced smile while extracting Erica. "*That* woman," she murmurs. "You don't need to be around those claws right now. If ever." This will be as close as Ginger comes to acknowledging Erica's low emotional state, but Erica knows she does care. Ginger is the only woman Erica knows who doesn't dwell on personal weaknesses of any kind except as a kind of throwaway joke. Throughout the ordeal of Mona's addiction, Erica's unwillingness and Ginger's ready acceptance of her not talking much about it has been a boon. Hasn't it? There is so much shame, a heavy weight dragging at her legs, like Mona as a temper-thwarted toddler. Behind Ginger's affection for her is a simple slogan: *fix it*. Yet, this attitude has acted, surprisingly, like a tonic. Erica simply has to focus on other things than her problems while she's with Ginger.

"Having a good time? Well, an all-right time?"

"All-right time." Erica's missing John terribly, in fact. "It's kind of like being an amputee without him." She forces a smile.

"He always had such a good time here!"

"Even last year." When he was sick but still game to do things. Barely.

"Shall we get a drink?" Vodka for Ginger, sparkling water for Erica . . . same old.

It's barely nine thirty when Erica leaves. The buffet is being picked over, and the booze is flowing fast. People are voluble and opinionated (Ginger certainly), though some, like Ginger's husband, are sitting with eyes half-mast and a few, like Teresa, are dancing in the roomy hallway in that ill-advised way in which too many adults attempt to relive their youth at weddings and parties. Walking to the car in the clear, biting December air, Erica remembers that she and John had left early last year, too. He tired so easily, but he hadn't had a drop of spirits. He'd declaimed a little of the Bard as they picked their way down the long driveway to the car parked on the road:

> But let your love even with my life decay,
> > Lest the wise world should look into your moan
> > And mock you with me after I am gone.

It would probably be better for her to go spend Christmas with Ronnie and Steve in Connecticut, but Erica doesn't want to be far from Mona. On Christmas Eve day, she finally does the mall, where plummy Christmas carols alternate with histrionic pop versions at every store. Her list is short: man soap for Steve the counselor, large box of chocolates for Mona's fellow clients at Wings of Hope, and, for Mona, a black cashmere sweater (on sale), two graphic novels, makeup, and socks decorated with elves.

Shopping bag in hand, including a tin of homemade Christmas cookies, and a pack of Salem Lights and book of matches stuffed down her bra, Erica arrives at the rehab center, already in darkest night in late afternoon. She's not the only visitor, of course. There are knots of them in the lobby by the fake tree and in the cafeteria that has been done up with tinsel and blinking lights.

Mona's waiting by the tree, leafing through a magazine. She jumps up as soon as she sees her mother. "You came! I was worried you weren't going to!" She clutches Erica fiercely.

"Of course I came." Erica holds up her shopping bag. "I had to fight the traffic from the mall, that's all."

They go to the cafeteria since Erica is craving coffee and Mona decides to have a piece of apple pie. Watching her, Erica decides she looks better, not good, but better. Her hair is losing the blue; she's already filled out a little; her complexion seems less blotchy.

They choose a seat by the window in the half-filled room. The smell of that night's dinner (only an hour away) reminds Erica of elementary school, those steam trays of overcooked stuff she'd always preferred to the bag lunches her mother made her bring. She sits up straight in the plastic chair, holding back tears. "Do you want to open your presents now or later? Whenever you want."

"Now, of course! I wish I had something for you, Mama. Besides this stupid card."

This is not the worst day of your life, Erica reminds herself. *You're used to disaster now, to those you love crumbling like . . . what? . . . Like old Christmas cookies.* She refrains from telling

Mona that getting clean is the best Christmas present she could ever give her.

"How do they celebrate Christmas here?"

"Some dudes did hip-hop carols last night, and this fat counselor everybody hates played the piano and tried to get people to sing along. Tomorrow is the 'Holiday dinner,'"—Mona crooks her index fingers—"which I predict will be cardboard turkey, watery mashed potatoes, gray beans, and more Sara Lee pie. Yummy."

"This should cheer you up a little." Erica hands her the box of cookies and reaches under her sweater for the cigarettes and matches. Because she knew Hank, the sub at the door from "the program," she had whizzed past security with her trio of banned goods: chocolates, cookies, and the totally outlawed cigarettes. She could have brought a carton in.

"Sugar cookies! Oh, wow! They don't allow any food from the outside, it could have, you know, hash or something in it. Did you bring me cigs?" she adds in a low voice.

Erica, whose heart aches at her daughter's casual mention of "the outside," as if this were a prison, slides them to her under the table.

"You're the best. And I'm gonna hide the sugar cookies—screw sharing them. Now, let's see what Santa brought." Unceremoniously, Mona rips open her gifts like the fierce little girl she still could be. Besides a few other parents sitting with their kids, there are a lot of unvisited women of various ages and ethnicities sitting alone or in little groups, with blank or defiant or just plain doleful expressions. They stare as Mona unwraps her little mound of gifts. *Your own suffering is probably nothing compared to what these people are going through*, Erica tells herself. She reaches over and strokes Mona's thin arm with its elaborate tattoo under the Harley T-shirt. *Remember those chubby little arms in the clothes you used to score at that upscale kids' thrift shop?*

"Ooh! J.Crew? Cashmere?" a woman in felt slippers, who has crept forward, comments. "You the queen today, Mona."

"It was on sale," Erica says, hearing the guilt in her voice. Should she risk handing out the illicit chocolates now?

The big hit with the women, now openly watching Mona's gift-getting, is the makeup. All the younger women and girls are heavily made up, while the older women mostly don't bother, but they're all pulled in like moths to the flame of Sephora beauty products. Mona's little fox face glistens.

"And there's something for Steve and, well, the ladies," Erica murmurs. "Nothing fancy."

Mona slides the box of chocolates onto her lap, and Erica has the feeling the ladies will be deprived of these too. They drift off to the hall, where Mona starts to cry exhausted addict tears. "I want to be home with you and the cats and Casho and make a fire and play Scrabble and eat steak."

If you were home, that would last about five minutes before you'd be out scoring. "You will. You just need to get well." *And I need to endure this.*

"I hate this place."

"Mona . . ." What can she say?

At home, Erica makes coffee and opens Mona's handmade card. She has kept all the years of cards, sweet and clumsy, tacky with glue and glitter. Love, Mona, it says, beneath a careful and good drawing of Erica and the animals. Erica sits, staring at "Law and Order" reruns on the tube, Mona's card on her lap. She comes to hours later with a stiff neck, Casho snuffling lightly nearly. She remembers feeling terror in her dream, shivers and wraps herself in the blanket that had fallen off. These endless bad dreams.

PICTURE ME RAW

Erica cranes her neck, peering up at a tall building, where she can see a blindfolded figure standing on the roof edge. Suddenly Erica feels herself being lifted to the roof, but she can't reach the woman tottering on the rim. Traffic noises rise up; the wind whips their hair. Erica freezes as she realizes it is Mona, trying to keep her balance.

The twenty-eight days at Wings of Hope are almost over. Erica and Mona and Steve the counselor are meeting again in his cubicle, where Erica tries to ignore the creeping claustrophobia that windowless rooms produce in the marrow of her bones. Steve is slouching a little, yet she senses he's ready for battle. Because all day, every day, he battles the loathsome symptoms of addiction. He is a good guy, a *really* good guy, so why does Erica bristle? They're on the same side, for God's sake; he wants her daughter to be healthy, yet Erica is wary. She wonders if she's being paranoid, one of Mona's favorite summations of her.

"You're saying all the right things. You're doing the right stuff, Mona, but you know you don't mean it." Erica shifts in her chair, feeling her legs twitch, knowing she is likely to respond to him with something that is not very pleasant. She clenches her hands to the sides of her chair. *Don't say anything.* Because she is afraid he's right about Mona, who has skyrocketed to the top of the class here at Wings in a few short weeks.

Mona, of course, has no scruples about speaking her mind. "*What the?* You're on at me for doing the right thing? Like you're some kind of all-knowing mind reader?"

"No," Steve responds. *He's so calm, so in charge.* Is this what is making her angry? This air of certitude, which drives her crazy about a lot of people in AA. Zealots, she secretly calls them. Like Bill Wilson was Moses, and God handed him the tablet of the Twelve Steps. More to the point, for all Steve's training, force of conviction, and—she grants him—empathy, Mona is just another case for him. For all of his bonding chats with Erica about his and Erica's mutual histories of addiction (meth: Steve, alcohol and street drugs: Erica) and their "time in the program," this is his job. It is not his life, his heart. Of course, it isn't!

"Mona, we're recommending another thirty days here—"

"No way!"

"Then six months in a sober house. There are several excellent places around the county." Steve pauses. "You could start college again or get a part-time job while having a strong home base for your recovery."

"I absolutely, totally, completely, globally will not do that. And you can't make me," Mona says, turning to glare at Erica. "I'm over eighteen."

"Let me speak," Erica says. Steve and Mona stare at her. She puts her head in her hands. They wait. She looks up, feeling defeated—again. "I don't know what to say," she confesses.

"That's OK," Steve tells her. "It's a big decision. We can revisit it. There are still a few days left." Erica has been to every family group meetings and she's sure she has the same wooden expression that is usual for parents here. Living with an addicted child is a form of warfare leading almost inevitably to some form of PTSD. Add to that her own hard-fought battles with the wine bottle at the end of her drinking, memories she thought she'd long ago come to terms with, but here they are again. As for Mona, she is doing her teenage thing. The loud sighs, fidgets, eye-rolling, bluster. Steve doesn't seem to mind at all that she's pissed off. He probably has to prod these kids over and over with sharp verbal forks to get them to start thinking things through. He says, "I have to be honest with you guys. Not trying to scare you—not that I *can* scare you, right, Mona? We've established that. But here's the truth: adolescents, young adults, don't usually get clean their first try. Some of them go out with their bodies all nice and detoxed and, wham! Overdose. Their bodies can't handle the load."

Erica twists in her chair, incapable of holding back an outburst of rage and fear. "Well, that's just so convenient for you people here, isn't it? You get paid. Just bring on the next junkie teenager, like it's a factory. It's not your fault if it doesn't work! Wings of Hope! Really? Really? Wings of Hope?" She's marinating in fear.

"Three young people have died in the last two weeks in this county," he says, apparently unaffected. "Two of them had just come out of rehab. Smack. We had recommended long-term treatment."

"It's *H*," Mona mumbles and rolls her eyes. Smack? That's so *Panic in Needle Park,* that old movie. A bad end will never happen to her, of course: she's choosy about her dealers.

But he has gotten to Erica. She is knitting her hands, squeezing them. Shoulders up to her ears.

"I *get* it," Mona says loudly. "I know what I have to do. I've been hearing it all day, all night. If I didn't get it by now, I'd have to be brain-dead. I'm an addict, and I'm powerless after the first use. And I have to go to meetings for the rest of my life so I don't—"

"But just for today," Erica inserts, at the same moment that Steve says, "One day at a time." They look at each other with the ghost of a smile, more like a grimace.

"Yeah, well, I also need to be around people who aren't constantly talking about their drug exploits and their dealer boyfriends waiting for them to get out." Mona says, her voice rising.

Erica shifts again. She has mixed feelings about Wings, she admits it. It's a big, no-frills place. Her liberal side applauds the chance for all kinds of people to be together here, but that adrenaline-crazed mother protector in her wants to keep her child away from every temptation: if Mona could get sober in a vacuum, Erica would go for it. And Mona always makes friends, but to her knowledge hasn't made any here in rehab; everybody, Mona complains, is either "ghetto" or a "dumbass." Although Erica fears that she may have made potential new connections.

Steve stands up. "Let's talk about this again."

Mona trails out, back to her unit. She spends her free time drawing self-portraits with staring eyes, trying to sneak a smoke and fantasizing about moving to a beach town and working on her tan.

Erica plans to go sit in the cafeteria and page through a magazine, waiting for the weekly family meeting, which will start soon. But Steve walks with her. "Can we talk a minute?" He directs her to the far side of the large room with all the chairs lined up, ready to go. Presumably, it's bad news about Mona. Erica feels that familiar sense of dread slipping over her like heavy fog.

"Mona *is* on track," he says, surprising her. The blanket lifts a little. "But," he goes on, and it settles back down, "*you* know how easily they can be derailed, especially at this age."

"Yes, I do. I was a runner at her age." Catapulting over guilt, anger, loneliness: the fodder of addiction.

"See the woman in the blue top sitting over there? Her son

will probably go to prison next week. Grand larceny. Eighteen. And the, uh, heavyset fellow a few seats down from her? He's already lost one son to heroin."

"That poor man," she says. She feels her shoulders hunched around her ears.

"As you know, I'm not supposed to break my anonymity here, Ms. Mason. Erica but you and I established that we're both in the program. I have to tell you, as I see it, Mona still needs a lot of help with acceptance. She's so young."

Erica begins to tremble. "I know how diabolical it is. I do, Steve, I do. But, tell me, how can I force her to accept it? How can I make her stay here in rehab? She's eighteen."

"Erica, you *can* insist on more treatment. They need longer treatment at this age. Their brains are still forming. They're impulsive. It's a perfect storm for addiction."

"Again, how do I make her do this?"

"Make the consequences very clear to her. If somebody hadn't done that with me, I wouldn't be alive today."

This silences her. What would these consequences be? Kicking her out to couch-surf or live on the streets? Where she'd turn into a prostitute, a professional thief? Get a rap sheet instead of a college degree? *Ah, no,* she thinks, *I don't have the strength. I can't do that to her.* The truth is that Mona's addiction has become something she's agreed to live with, because she's her child and she has to.

On a glum afternoon in January, confronting the last great pile of John's accumulations, Erica takes on his study. It is a superbly cluttered room, which he knew how to negotiate with ease and where certain of his possessions have inevitably taken on his essence. Yes, that fiercely ugly orange and black poncho he'd acquired when he bummed around Mexico after college, the wonderful black felt Borsalino hat he bought at a flea market in San Francisco, his collection of lurid-covered James Cain paperbacks. She cleans out his desk methodically, drawer by stuffed drawer, and finds, amid the old bills, postcards, foreign stamps, coins, and magazine articles he'd clipped and saved, two interesting things: an envelope addressed to Mona and a small, leather-bound notebook at the bottom of the bottom drawer. She puts the envelope aside unopened: it's Mona's. Then she opens John's diary. Death erases boundaries, heaves up secrets. Still, it feels like trespassing, a serious kind of trespassing at that: voyeurism.

> *Erica has the most beautiful body I've ever seen; she drives me crazy in bed. She is fierce, she is luminous, she is my heart's desire. But, goddamn it, she can be a pain in the ass.*
>
> *With Jane, I always felt that I had ended up with her. Nothing was ever decided, and the weeks and then the years piled up. I remember Jane's set face that last day, a bright October, sitting in her kitchen. And Jane wasn't a woman who manipulated. "Marry me." She said that. "Or else go. Just leave." I didn't feel good about leaving. I drove back from Jersey to West Ninety-Fourth, and I remember I went running in the park, picked up Chinese, watched part of a Fassbinder film on television, then fell asleep on the couch. Stuff I'd done forever, stuff I enjoyed. But I felt guilty that I enjoyed it that day. I felt like a shit about Jane. And then along came Erica.*

Erica flips to the last page:

> *I must believe that it is better for people to be hurt suddenly, with passion and love, than to have the situation become*

false. I must put myself out on a limb of feeling and be willing to be crushed when I fall. Thinking of myself this way will give me strength and make me feel. Picture me raw, the positive guts of a man who doesn't want to be rejected, but would rather have this than to reject being rejected in favor of the trivial head and genital relationship, without the heat. I think I must choose Erica.

Erica checks the front of the diary, confirming. It was from the year they had met, circling, arguing, getting each other, diving deep. Erica clutches the book as she roams around the house, feeling light and brittle. A love letter from the other side, yes. He is dead. She has been confirming this in jerks and stalls, but now she feels strongly that there is another death contained within John's. The extinction of a third party: the marriage. This casts its own shadow, she now recognizes. The shadow over his chair in the living room, over the space beneath the old maple outside where he dozed on summer afternoons, over the tables where they had eaten and talked. And of course over the bed. But in other places, too, like the shoe rack that's still filled on "his" side of the closet, the tool rack in the garage.

Holding the diary, moving in and out of the house, she has a sudden impulse to throw the thing into the woods. As if that might free her. Instead, she does the sane thing, placing it in the box in the closet of his study with the magazines he'd art-directed, the articles he'd written, the letters.

She's sitting in a room again, with strangers again, Al-Anon this time. And she goes to every weekly session, despite the inner resistance—or is it revulsion?—to yet another self-help group. Where sitting in a room with people talking about their pain is somehow supposed to help her with her pain. But she listens and she hears. She gets that some of them have far worse problems with their addict children than she does. Is that supposed to make her feel better? In these meetings of parents, grandparents, siblings, friends, and spouses, Erica does not feel better at first. Each time, she wants to bolt from these semicircles of women—they're mostly women.

This room is a preschool during the day; the walls are decorated with finger paintings, big block letters in animal shapes, bins of toys at the edges. It has the effect (she could almost laugh out loud) of making Erica feel that she's regressed. She shifts restlessly on her little chair, scratches herself; she's like a kid with ADD. But after the third or fourth meeting has ended and she's back at home, Erica feels a little better, as if a low-grade fever she's had for a long time is subsiding. Which must mean progress.

One night, she calls Ronnie when she gets home from Al-Anon.

"I just wanted to let you know you're probably right. About going to Al-Anon. Despite, well, everything, I think you're right. I don't want to be there, I don't want to be one of them. And I am."

"Hard to give up the pain when you're used to carrying it all," Ronnie says.

"Also, the terminal uniqueness thing."

She can feel Ronnie's complicit smile over the phone. "Now that you mention it. We alcoholics."

"But I do want my life back. I mean,"—Erica corrects herself—"I know that can't happen. But a life." She is breathing hard.

"And you deserve a wonderful life, Erica Mason, and you will have one."

Erica starts to feel something stir, a kind of hunger, then it becomes a craving, for color, shapes, lines. All those times she'd come back to the white of the canvas, in fear, in longing, excitement, dread. She regards this blank canvas for a long time, begins to fill it with paint—the pure iciness of a winter blue sky, the sexual heat of the orange and gold of a mango, the warning of the unknown in matte black. Paint, its feel and smell, the hospital aroma of turpentine. To disappear into a project! A call from the community center in town is a gift, reminding her about the group show coming up she's supposed to exhibit with. She had decided she would dig into the Guatemala project again when, waiting in the hallway of the church where Al-Anon meets in the playroom, some day laborers had filed by in their best pressed khakis, even a few suits; the women in frilly, full dresses; the boys with their hair combed flat to their heads; barrettes for the girls. More people who tended the lawns and cleaned the houses of white people, many of whose own ancestors, they tended to forget, had also been poor and hardworking—farm laborers, iron miners, workers at the Borden dairy. The dressed-up Guatemalans, she had learned, were part of a congregation of Pentecostals who rented the sanctuary of the church on this night every week. They were everywhere in the village, yet almost invisible to the people who employed them. And, that night, she'd seen them in their best clothes and heard their out-of-tune, lusty singing rise up during the Al-Anon meeting. The next week, she had brought her sketchbook. Now began the painting.

Erica knew who she would paint last: the silver-haired man who prepared her garden in the spring, immaculately, constantly drinking Cokes. When he smiled, at least half his teeth were missing, but he was handsome nonetheless. Her work at the easel went well enough. It was when she was done for the day and turned the easel to the wall that her mood sank in a way that become familiar. Yes, at last she had something to paint. But for the first time in many years there was no one to talk to about it. John had always been interested, a good listener, probing and prodding. She had relished their discussions, which were often heated. What would he say to her now about this project of the Guatemalans? Well, he would tell her she must resist sentimentality. She must avoid a polemic, although she identified with people like them, had lived among people like them in Mexico as a college graduate with no aim or ambition except to paint, a budding alcoholic who smoked a lot of weed. She had learned from living on the cheap in Mexico that the one constant for very poor people is that life is a constant emergency. Now, all these years later, she is the one with the house and the garden and the money in the bank, the overseer of her estate, and here they are, these landless and probably illegal immigrants. They could be picked up and thrown out of the country at any time. She at least can paint them.

Drained and flat in the dark of an early evening, Erica took out John's diary again from where she had put it in the box in his closet. The box, she now noticed, had come from a wine store. John had liked to shop for wine, to try new varieties when they entertained. Liked to talk about wine, savor it, relax under its glow. This had never bothered Erica the sober alcoholic – well, hardly ever. But now she thought about how smooth and warm the wine would be, blooming in her body in a way "civilians," with their better-regulated dopamine receptivity, didn't experience. She thought about it for quite a while, and then she went and found some chocolate in the pantry.

She went back to his study. She wanted to read about their nascent romance again, which had given way to something better, maybe deeper, maybe not.

A piece of paper fluttered out from somewhere in the pages, something she hadn't noticed the first time she read it. She picked it up.

"Nina Never Knew." "Girls were meant to kiss, but Nina never knew." I love that old song, its unfulfilled longing . . .

and without trying much, I formed a picture of Nina, sassy and confoundingly sweet. For years, I sought her, but women never quite measured up to her. They were fine: smart, good-looking, sexy, sometimes sweet, but they would get one of two telltale expressions, eventually. Either that flatness, which said, "Yes, yes, I know, this is soon going to be over; it's goodbye to all this." Or else that glint, calculating like a bookkeeper, toting up the hoped-for mortgage, the vacations to Italy, Bermuda, the kids' colleges. In short, they weren't . . . Nina. They knew. They made their moves. God help me and I made mine. And then, suddenly, Erica with her cloud of pale-brown hair and that Mexican blouse and white jeans at that gallery opening, sandals, toenails unpainted, a little lipstick only and some light perfume. The kind Nina would wear, if she were real. But this girl was real! "Would you like a drink?" "Oh, club soda with lime, please." Her eyes were like an animal's in the forest—questing, unafraid, but ready to run. She was so clean, this Erica, natural, unaware of her power or maybe just careless of it. Erica. The times she says she's too tired for me. Her restlessness, her shutting herself away in her room to paint, her stubbornness. And then she'll take my hand and put it on her body, trusting me with her life. She is the one I needed all these years. To turn away from her would be as much of a sin as I can imagine.

Erica had to move away, from his diary and his desk. She crumpled to the floor. The carpet was redolent of Casho, who had spent puppy time here with John, chewing at the nubs, flinging chew toys, and probably peeing. There were dust balls in the corners. Lying there, she felt she could not stand it: knowing that John had loved her and now she could never again mold the clay of his body with hers. She thought of a strange artifact she'd found once, lying in the grass, apparently blown from a tree, a huge helmet-shaped nest, as thick as insulated walls. "What is this thing?" she'd asked John, when he came home from his art-directing.

"Oh, that's a wasps' nest," he said; he'd been a Boy Scout. He'd thrown it far behind some bushes. Then, she'd come upon the thing a year later, shabbier, but still intact. How long would it take for the carapace to disintegrate?

Erica wept on the musty carpet as she hadn't since John had been taken from her. Wept and began to feel frightened by the demands of emotional pain, as if it were standing over her with a steel-tipped whip. As if she were a child again, always under the command of arbitrary, powerful rules. And, even so, she had a sense, too, of something else moving over her with other, new, and less onerous demands, the scooped-out tentative energy of the newly convalescent. And Casho came in, sniffing and pawing at her, inserting his snout and his limbs on her invitingly submissive posture. The wet nose, the tongue, the happy panting, the faith in her for his next fulfilled need. A memory forced its way through the crashing cymbals of loss: John home from his art-director commute, wrenching off his tie and pouring a glass of wine. "Smells good!" In those first years together, Erica had taken pleasure in making meals that combined his favorites and, not only that, in eating them, too. Food that she wouldn't cook on her own, food that enmeshed them. This particular evening —it must have been warm weather because it was still light out at seven—she had composed a lentil-pork-mustard-thyme pie. Steaming on the counter. But they had looked at each other and ended up half-on and half-off the living room couch, where he bent over her, smelling of sweat and his long day, and they had gripped each other as if to ward off any future parting. The pork pie ended up getting nuked later in the microwave, its flaky crust mushing with the contents.

THE MONA PROJECT

Mona sits talking with her dad in the living room. Without warning, he falls to the floor and is transformed into a large package tied with string. Mona wakes up streaming with sweat.

Erica assumes Mona is just wasting her time while she's in her room, which is most of the time when she is not at her part-time job at the deli that just took her on, or at the group therapy sessions at Jefferson Adolescent Center three nights a week. She doesn't care what Mona does or doesn't do in her room because at least she is safe. Erica has worked out new "boundaries" with Steve the counselor's help, reading them aloud to Mona from a piece of paper. Curfew, chores, monitoring of her computer.

"You've got to be kidding, Mom," Mona told her. "Spying on me twenty four–seven is supposed to help my self-esteem?"

"I don't really care about your self-esteem."

"What? You're my mom!"

"OK, I do. Of course. Once you get clean."

"What? I am clean. See, you just undermine me!" And she'd stomped off to her lair. *Someday, that door is going to come flying off its hinges from being slammed so much.*

Mona knows that her mother routinely scours her room when she's not home (although she neglects to do so in the car, a mistake a CSI would never make). But she doesn't go near Mona's room when Mona is there, so she has no idea about Mona's new graphic novel called "The Mona Project". Mona always brings it with her to the deli, the Jefferson Center, and her furtive meetings with twenty-something local dealers and hides it between her old yearbooks when sleeping.

Mona considers herself to be at once talented and talentless, teeming with ideas but with a vivid fear of being witless. She accepts that she is a fuckup, and, in fact, feels she was destined to become one. She recalls the pact she'd made at fifteen with her then-best friend Maggie to take stuff from the lockers of girls they both hated, which they then stashed in their own lockers. This was an incredibly stupid thing to do, resulting in expensive attorney fees, her mother's embarrassingly downcast appearance in town court, and then probation, which Mona had ignored. Steve had explained the stealing was a "cry for help." Duh! But for what kind of help Mona herself isn't clear. She is still amazed at how powerful it made her feel to take those snots' stuff, just because she could. But, at the same time, it had guaranteed a bad reputation, which she didn't always crave; it meant being shunned.

But Mona has this talent; she draws very well, her teachers and (few) friends tell her, and the "Project" often makes her laugh out loud. Take the scene she's just finished. It's at Bob's Diner, where she'd actually watched this crabby, spidery old man shake an empty maple syrup container's drops on Nora, that Latina girl on meth who works nights. "No syrup left for m'pancakes!" he'd angrily croaked. Like right out of one of Mona's favorite old-time underground comics by that crusty freak R. Crumb. The diner has provided her with several pages of geeks and freaks. But tonight she's edgy. She is going to do a section now on Dad. Face her fears, the way the good old therapists keep telling her. Draw Dad when he collapsed and she found him on the floor in his boxers with the tube and the bag of piss . . . which was possibly the worst thing she has gone through. *So far*, she thinks gloomily. And then she'll do that horrible dream where he turns into a package.

She has to snort some H now, to get ready for this. She had found heroin two days and fourteen hours after she left rehab, in the parking lot of a Dunkin' Donuts. Of course, she prefers heroin—it's much cheaper and rocks even better than Oxys. She has shot it twice, the ultimate magic carpet ride, but she still thinks she'll basically snort it, maybe smoke it . . . Conserve her supply until tomorrow after work or, yes, after Mom is asleep tonight. Not being allowed wheels anymore, except to and from the deli and the Jefferson Center, is so draconian, a word that has stuck with her since she heard Dad say it once about something the government was doing. Draconian, dragons, a magic castle . . . Mona is good and off now. She falls back against the pillows; Dim and Dimmer immediately move from the end of the bed to lie on her. She'll work on the "Project" later. Oh, and get Mom to let her have the car, then head straight to Misty's or Saul's (either or both of whom she may be in love with at the moment).

She intends "The Mona Project" to be a completely honest account, but she's not sure where she's going with it. Still, she will hold nothing back: the stupid, the hilarious, the degrading, the weird, and the dangerous as well as the euphoric. Of the fix. Maybe the "Project" will make her famous online, so she can move out and get a place of her own. True, the "Project" is unfolding in fits and starts, but if she can just stay with it . . .

Mona accepts that more and more of her time is spent in a cloudy, half-assed daze, that her room is a pit, a dump of empty cans, bottles, cereal bowls, chip bags, clothes in need of a wash, and anything else she's through with, including, somewhere, a used syringe or two. She nests in a not very clean bed. All this Mona can accept. The exception is the curtain of self-loathing that comes down upon her when the high is fading. When she feels like a little junkie with a fucked-up life going nowhere. Not so long ago, singing in the shower could lighten her mood. She has a clear, light voice. Once, taking walks or going to movies would help. Now, nothing helps except heroin and doing the "Project."

When she's not in her room at home, Mona hangs out in the kitchen. Erica is on alert for these occasions, when she can try to talk to her. Like tonight, when she hears Mona clomping down the stairs about eight thirty.

"I made that spicy turkey spaghetti sauce you like. Want some? With salad?"

"I'm fine, Mom," Mona says forbiddingly. She gets out the usual, sugary kids' cereal. That and fruity yogurt. At least she's eating it at the kitchen table this time.

"How's the job going?"

"Fine, Mom."

"I thought maybe you could look into the community college for next semester, take a couple of classes—"

"Mom! I'm not your eternal project!" The sound of Mona's cawing voice feels like a hammer inches from Erica's head.

Mona stomps upstairs with her cereal.

A couple of days later, when Mona is supposed to be at her job, Misty calls. "Mrs. Grey? Is Mon there? She's not picking up her cell. We were supposed to meet, like, an hour ago, and it's really important. It's really important, but she's not picking up her cell," she repeats.

"She's at work," Erica says, through slightly gritted teeth. Misty habitually repeats herself in that whine. She has OCD which causes her also to touch every surface around her constantly. Another smart, lost, middle-class white girl.

"Oh, she got a new job? Where?"

"Christo's Deli."

"Oh, she didn't tell me. Oh, shit, uh, yeah, the deli job. She didn't tell me about the deli job. Well, I'll catch up with her later. Bye, Mrs. Grey."

Instinctively, Erica enters Mona's lair. Erica has been good, following her Al-Anon program's advice, "turning 'it' over, letting 'it' go," which has translated into several days of leaving Mona to deal or not to deal with her room. It doesn't take her long to find evidence that she doesn't want to believe but which is there in the mess. A syringe, used, wedged into the side of the bedframe. She slumps onto the unmade bed. Needles were the end of the line back in her hippie days. People who put needles in their arms were crushed Vietnam vets and minority groups—they had good reason to do so, in her opinion back then—or else used-up Beatniks and the occasional fellow stoner. Oh, and rock stars and old jazz musicians. True, Erica and her friends had bought street acid from Crazy Dave. They had snorted coke, thought of weed as an accessory, and, of course, guzzled beer and wine, occasionally vodka or rum. But needles? They were for when you went to the doctor for a vaccination and looked away, wincing. Heroin was for the undead, a strict taboo. Erica sees a loose cigarette on the floor, matches on the dresser. Without even thinking about it, she picks up and lights the cigarette, she who quit smoking eons ago. She goes downstairs, coughing, and calls not Ronnie but Alice, a woman from Al-Anon.

"Yes," she says, listening. "Yes. I'll try to make the meeting." *Hell and damnation.*

Mona shows up at six, after the deli job would have been over. Erica silently holds up a double baggie with the syringe inside.

"You spied on me! You promised you wouldn't!"

Rage in a cornered addict is volcanic. Erica knows this. She pushes forward. "You lied to me about the job; you're not working. I called Christo's They fired you. Of course! I should have known. How can I ever believe a word out of your mouth? Well, this time there will be consequences."

Mona tries to shoves her way past her mother. "You're always guilt-tripping me. You're completely bipolar. You've got to stop!"

"Mona, *you've* got to stop! I'll do anything to help you stop. Please, look at what you're doing." She shakes the baggie. "I can't lose you, you're my baby. You're all I have now!" she shouts.

"That's not mine. I don't do that shit. You're fucking crazy, Mom. You need to be on medication. You're unbearable!"

Erica grabs Mona by the shoulders. "I'm crazy? I'm unbearable? That's rich. You're the one on drugs. You're the one killing yourself! And killing me in the process!"

Mona's face has become unrecognizable to her, and Erica thinks her own face must be, too; it's slick with tears and swollen, as if the pressure of pain is going to burst through her skin.

Mona jerks out of her grasp, plunging upstairs into the hall bathroom, the one room upstairs with a lock. Erica pounds on the door, all her new Al-Anon insights and reasoned behavior having vanished. Steve the counselor had told her this would happen, on the last day at Wings of Hope. "Erica, try not to be hard on yourself or her. Don't expect not to lose control. But, if you do, get right back on track."

"How?" she'd said. "How can I do that?"

"OK," he said. "I'm going to tell you. What happened to me. I was twenty. I weighed about a hundred pounds. I was tweaking, in my dad's garage. I had been thrown out of the house for a while and was basically homeless. Probably dying. And I was beating with a hammer on the '56 Pontiac that, for some reason, he had decided to love back to life. I was going to destroy it. It was the middle of the night, so he heard the noise and came out there."

"Holy shit!" Erica said. "What did he do?"

"It's what he said. Of all the things he could have said. He didn't yell. He didn't seem angry even. He . . . fell to his knees and called out to me. Told me to beat *him* with the hammer, because seeing me like that was killing him. 'Beat *me*, Steven. I can't stand it anymore, seeing my boy destroy himself. I'm done. I can't hurt you and I can't help you.'"

"But you didn't . . . do anything . . . I mean, with the hammer, to your father?"

"No! It stopped me cold, what he said. And I felt cold. For the first time, I heard the truth. See, he'd always criticized me and threatened me and run me down. But this time he didn't. It was as close to a miracle as I've seen. That he ripped himself open . . . and I heard him. The next day I went into rehab and got clean. That was eighteen years ago."

"So, I should tell her to put me out of my misery if she picks up?"

Steve handed her a tissue, and she swiped at the wetness on her face.

"No! See, it's the acceptance. It's letting go. It's 'I can't do this for you.'"

She's pounding on the bathroom door. She's going to lose it. But then she just stops. "You can't stay here anymore! I can't stop you using drugs, but I won't accept it in my house. I love you too much to do that." Silence. Or is that sniffling she hears? Suddenly, there are powerful paws scrabbling on her back, and Casho is saying it too, in high barks. Erica slides to the floor and hugs him, buries her head in his funk-spicy fur, not allowing him to squirm away. In the bathroom, Mona begins to weep.

How much worse can life get? she thinks, pulling away from the frantic dog. And she pounds the floor. Because she is sure it will. Get worse.

MRS. MADONNA

Erica is running a race. She must win it. She sees the finish line ahead and leans in as she flies into a panic and can barely breathe. She drags herself, spent and wheezing, over the finish line and turns around. There is no one else behind her.

In early April, a stupendous late snowstorm is followed by driving rain, and the cellar of her old house floods. All at once, Erica realizes how neglected and shabby it has become. When did this happen? When did the driveway crumble? How long have the cobwebs been festooning the ceilings, the windowsills been cracking and peeling? When she peers in a mirror, she sees more decay: puckers have sprouted on her upper lip, rings around her neck, a general bodily droop. Corruption lurks everywhere. Mildew behind the toilet, dust bunnies the size of baseballs, the old, groaning furnace.

Yet she also welcomes these things, because they are challenges that can be fixed, cleaned up, checked off the list. Get putty, paint, handymen. Miracle face creams, more exercise. She knows that such things are diversions. Anything not to think about

Mona since the failed experiment at Wings of Hope. She makes lists, goes on Home Depot runs, buys cosmetics, and takes longer walks with the dog. Mona should be studying, dating, working, having fun. Instead, Erica sees her only when she needs to do her laundry or get something. Occasionally, she will consent to eat a meal, but hurriedly, head bent to her plate, avoiding conversation. She is camped out at Misty's most of the time and says she has yet another part-time job, caring for twin first graders after school during the week. How she gets there, Erica has no idea.

A welcome diversion will be Ronnie's visit soon from the wilds of northern Connecticut. So Erica attacks the neglected house, cleans the spare room, and, on the day of Ronnie's arrival, roasts a chicken, buys a pie, and makes a salad. When Ronnie arrives, she bears hostess gifts of farm-stand jam and scented soap. Dear Ronnie, last in the line of an old, WASP family, also writes thank-you notes and eats on good china even if it's hot dogs.

"But where is Mona?" Ronnie asks, after settling in her accustomed place on the couch with her coffee. She is a childless woman who dotes on other people's children and her dog.

It is one of Mona's at-home days. When she stamped in last night, she said Misty was being a bitch, and she needed a break. "She's still asleep. But she's looking forward to seeing you," Erica says.

Mona loves Ronnie like a favorite aunt. But not even for Ronnie will Mona get up before four or five in the afternoon when she doesn't have to.

"I'll go and see her before I leave."

"Leave? But you're staying the night."

"Erica, I'm so sorry. I was really looking forward to our spending time together. I'd love nothing better. But, the thing is, Joanie's a wreck. She called me this morning and begged me to come to the city. And my sister hardly ever asks me for help, so . . ."

"Right. Of course. Her divorce came through, though, didn't it?"

"Finally." Ronnie sighs. "But she hasn't been sleeping or eating much. At least you and I can have a good talk now."

They know as much about each other as their husbands do. *Did* in her case. Maybe more. They'd met in the late seventies in Manhattan after Erica had joined AA, to her total shock. Desperate at first to stop drinking and then to find some semblance of order in her life, Erica became hooked on AA's endless flow of colorful characters and their stories (like free theater, with coffee and cookies thrown in) as much as the "suggested program of recovery." Erica couldn't get enough of the stories—intimately detailed, dreadful, often hilarious, told by an endless variety of strangers. This never happened in real life, except at every meeting it did! And all of them had a happy ending, no matter how dreadful the first part. She grew to trust and love from afar the motley crew of alcoholics and addicts, to feel at home in a Park Avenue church basement or the then-funky East Village. Soon she was telling her story in her faded jeans and Mexican shirts and then, when her first winter in the program came, an assortment of shawls over her raincoat. She was still seriously broke and did not have a winter coat. She'd fallen down while drunk the previous winter and bled all over her old coat, ruining it; but, more to the point, she was too disorganized to go out and get another one. In January, a well-dressed woman she knew slightly handed her a large shopping bag at a meeting. After this she did have a winter coat, a designer-suede and ermine-trimmed one at that.

It was not long after that she met Ronnie. Although by then Erica had heard many recovery stories, hearing Ronnie was finding her soulmate. True, Ronnie wore a corporate lady suit and a clipped pixie haircut, while Erica would never be mistaken for corporate, but Ronnie had been a hard-drinking barmaid in some of the same hip, little Village clubs Erica drank in. Then she'd graduated to copping heroin on the Lower East Side, a fast slide to the bottom. When Ronnie talked about her early sobriety, toting plastic bags of her belongings around the city to meetings, crashing on friends' couches or floors and being broke, Erica knew she had met her match. Ronnie was not yet thirty but she was sober for five years—an enormous amount of time it seemed then to Erica. Within days, she had asked the older women to be her sponsor. Ronnie had softened the wild, bumpy road of Erica's early sobriety, in her role as cheerleader, occasional critic, and best friend. When Erica, newly sober, complained about her arid life—financial, romantic, and artistic—Ronnie would tell her to write a gratitude list and go help somebody in worse shape than herself. She also believed, bless her, in bubble baths and pie. Erica would have listened to nobody else. And it worked.

When she and John took the plunge and moved from Manhattan to the wilds of exurbia, with its lakes and woods and horse farms and hardscrabble natives, and Erica went through culture shock, Ronnie kept her steady.

"I can't relate to people who go out to shoot their dinner, I'm serious, Ronnie. Some of them do here," she complained to Ronnie, who had remained in the metropolis.

Ronnie told her to find people like herself. "It's northern Westchester!" Erica adjusted. And Ronnie was always there. Often, now, they traded roles, Erica steadying Ronnie when she was fired, and again when her husband developed his unable-to-work tic.

After all these years—decades—Erica thinks she can usually predict what Ronnie will say about anything. Even so, Ronnie can still surprise her. Today, it's her (latest) wild hair, another business scheme. Since the bottom fell out of the corporate niche she'd been in, she'd tried landscaping and selling health insurance. Now, she's enthused about producing handmade notecards, affixed with color photos of flowers she's snapped.

"I've already sold three dozen to a shop in Sharon," Ronnie tells her, "and I'm going to take them around to a bunch of places when I get back and get on the Net."

Go WASPs! Erica thinks, inwardly sighing. *Isn't the world supplied with enough cards?* "I'll take two dozen," she says. No one should be deprived of hope; Erica has certainly learned that lesson. Ronnie hates her current job as a receptionist at a doctor's office or, rather, she hates her boss, who is patronizingly impatient with her middle-aged computer skills. If Ronnie sees making flower cards as a way out, Erica is not going to discourage her.

"And what about that bookstore that supports local artists?"

"Good idea."

This is what they do: they support each other, but never would Erica have predicted their current situations. Earlier in their friendship, Ronnie had climbed to mid-management and had a pretty apartment and a corporate-type husband, while Erica had remained a painter, living in a rent-controlled tenement with just enough art-teaching jobs to get by and a series of romances that went nowhere. Now, Erica has the big house and the plain vanilla man to manage her financial portfolio, while Ronnie is living with her nice husband who scrapes by, when he's up to it, on freelance editing gigs, and Ronnie has the hope of making ends meet selling flower cards.

They talk, drink coffee, eat some of the pie. There have been oceans of coffee and pounds of pie throughout their friendship. Ronnie suddenly puts her mug down. "But I'm so worried about you! You're strong, Erica, but enough is enough. You have to start taking care of *you*. You've done what you can for Mona. You can't get her well. I know you know this, but I just had to say it."

This, at least, is no surprise from Ronnie. "I know," Erica says quickly. They are both aware she will neglect herself to keep Mona afloat for as long as she has to.

Weeks later, in May, the phone rings at three in the morning. Accustomed now to this dreaded sound, Erica transitions once again from her Ambien-swaddled sleep to full awareness and breathlessness, her body stiffening into battle position as she reaches for the receiver. She's fielded middle-of-the-night calls from Misty's parents when the girls failed to return to their house; an irate parent of a boy Erica had never heard of who accused Mona of stealing fifty dollars from him; and, of course, Mona, many times. The capper had been the time she implored Erica to go to an ATM and withdraw four hundred bucks, then ferry it to a McDonald's parking lot because Mona needed to pay a dealer who was threatening her. No, that wasn't the capper. It was the call from jail to come bail her out after she'd been caught shoplifting at Walmart. Curiously, the bail bondsman the police had given her the number for turned out to be a rough, but kindly soul who advised Erica that "Kids just do crazy things at this age. She'll get over it."

So, this middle-of-the-night call doesn't shock her. It amazes her.

Earlier that day, Erica had driven Mona to a reasonably safe part of the Bronx, to the affordable, safe apartment Mona had found on Craigslist, a block from Arthur Avenue, the old Italian neighborhood. It was Mona's latest attempt to start over. A "geographic," as AA people put it.

Mona was unusually chatty in the car. She said she'd already lined up an interview for a job at a bakery, and she would go check out the local community college. Desperate to get Mona away from the teeming drug scene in exurbia and into any kind of productive life, Erica agreed to pay her first month's rent and security deposit plus a hundred dollars to get settled. She would agree to anything Mona came up with at this point that appeared to offer an escape from the drug world. So, she was driving her daughter to the Bronx. Yes, but it was a clean and reasonably well-kept block, where she could make a new start. She helped Mona lug her trash bags of stuff up two steep flights of stairs to a large room with a bath in this weather-beaten, tidy, narrow, brick house which, by the way, had a plaster statue of the Queen of Heaven on its tiny porch. She learned that Mona was actually subletting the apartment from a Fordham girl doing her junior year abroad. There was plenty of evidence of the Fordham girl, proof of an organized, well-adjusted person in the stack of magazines (*The Atlantic*, Erica noticed, was on top), simple furniture, dishes and cookware (not that Mona cooks or, for that matter, eats very often), and so on.

"Mrs. Grey, you wanna cuppa coffee?" Mrs. Madonna called from the floor below. Mona rolled her eyes. "Oh boy," she said. "You're gonna get your ears talked off."

A short woman in a flowered apron greeted her with a jerk of the head. "Mrs. Madonna," she said, pointing to herself. "Come into my kitchen, Mrs. Grey."

"Well, I actually go by Ms. Mason now." Seeing the frown of disapproval on Mrs. Madonna's face, she cravenly added, "My husband died and I'm using my last name now." Erica was confused, too: it was as if she knew this woman from somewhere. She looked like one of the ladies standing behind the steam trays in the dining room at Wings of Hope. She looked like the woman at her favorite local pizzeria. These women—actually, all tough, no-nonsense working-class women, going back to her grandmother and aunts, made Erica apprehensive. They were such a force of nature, of conviction, while she…wobbled. They made her feel superfluous at some deep level. Yup, that was Mrs. Madonna.

Hers was a compact kitchen that had not seen remodeling,

Erica guessed, since the fifties. Mrs. Madonna's apron was from the same era.

"Coffee?" A percolator. Perfect.

"No thank you. A glass of water would be great."

"Your daughter, she's a college student?"

"Yes." Erica lied because she badly wanted Mona to be a college student. And because Mona had said she'd think about taking classes at the community college.

"That's good. Study and work. I have lotsa Fordham girls here, very nice. I keep a safe, clean house, I tell your daughter that. Never no problems."

Now, twelve or so hours later, Erica is listening to Mona's subdued and trembling voice.

"Mrs. Madonna is kicking me out!"

"What? What did you do, Mona?" *Already, Mona?*

"You have to come get me, Mom. She wants me out now."

"I can't believe this." But she can. "It's the middle of the night. You didn't even last a day? What did you do, Mona?"

"She's insane, Mom. All I did . . ." Mona sighs, a long slithering sound. "I just went out to check out the neighborhood and to that bakery to see about a job. Then, I happened to run into this guy I know . . ."

"You would run into a guy you know at the North Pole, Mona. Probably with some pot or something worse, am I right?"

"No! That's not fair! He just had a couple of beers! So I invited him to see my place, and we were drinking a beer. That's all, Mom, and she comes up the stairs like an elephant, yelling about me having a guy in my room."

"Well, it is her house. Does she have a rule about it? No guys in the house?"

"Yeah, but Mom, this is the twenty-first century! We weren't doing anything!"

"And, right now, it's three o'clock in the morning! I'll come soon, eight or nine, OK?"

"No, Mom, please. She made me take my stuff downstairs . . ." Mona is sobbing.

Erica can't do this. She simply can't do this. The name Pete Rondavel floats into her head. Yes, Pete! He can do this. Her neighbor who's newly sober (Vicodin, booze) and therefore very gung ho about "the program," running around sponsoring newcomers, speaking at prisons. "Please God, please God," she whispers, dialing.

"Sure, no problem," Pete says groggily, interrupting her stumbling narrative. "I'll go get her. What's the address? Hey, Erica, don't apologize, I could use a Twelve Step call."

Erica calls Mona. "Mr. Rondavel's coming," she says. "No, not me! In about an hour." She throws herself on the couch, clutching Dim, who stiffens and flails: true to his species, he is not available for comfort unless he asks for it. Casho paces, circling, then furiously scratches out a watchman space on the rug nearby, all but shrieking, *Can we have some peace and quiet here?* Erica sits, stands, sits, tries not to think of what Mona has really done to have caused Mrs. Madonna to cast her out into the darkness of the Bronx in the middle of the night—thank God for Pete—and she drifts into a confused dream of being in water and holding onto a log that is hot and furry. Dimmer, she sees, jerking awake.

It's dawn when she hears a car door slam. Pete brings trash bags into the living room and shoots her a look.

Erica makes coffee. Like Mrs. Madonna. Mona flees upstairs.

"You gotta get her some help," Pete says. "She's gotta go back to rehab. She's using, you know that." He takes a big swig of coffee. "And it doesn't get better; for sure. I know that."

Erica looks down at the floor. "I know that too."

Mona's back, not doing much about looking for a job, and Erica is stunned to realize that the art show where she's booked to show the Guatemala series is just weeks away, with only three finished portraits and a lot of sketches ready. She stays in her studio for hours, neglecting the dog, not bothering about meals. She's painting. All those years before, when she'd entered the strange new land of sobriety, she found she couldn't do art without a drink, a joint, or something. This impotence went on for some time in the new sober land. She thought it was a(nother) cruel irony. First, the booze and drugs had got so bad she couldn't paint anymore. Now the sobriety thing seemed to be sucking out all her vitality. The part of her brain connected to the creative process appeared to have burned out, and it was her own fucking fault, so she had to accept it. She would have gone back to smoking pot, but those AA people kept repeating the sickening phrase, "it gets better," and all these tips to postpone getting high. For some reason, she did it, delayed getting high, learned tiny increments of patience. She'd have to accept that her artistic life was over. Meanwhile, she had to earn a living. She cleaned apartments for a few people she met in AA, then did office work, and began to think about maybe teaching art. She'd be a eunuch in the harem, but at least she'd be back in the world she wanted to belong to.

But she *had* become an artist again. Doors did open, just as those annoying people in AA said they would. They were always harping on about "it" taking time, and, well, it did. She heard at some point about a meeting for sober artists in SoHo, at that time still a fairly scruffy place that painters could afford to squat in. She went, expecting little. The speaker was a Mediterranean-type sculptor—short, with darkly curled hair—who talked about his own early-sobriety creative desert, his impotence in the studio; how, in a fury, he'd smashed a statue he loved. But he didn't pick up a drink. Then he talked some more about how he'd made friends again with his chisels and stone, while hardly noticing the change. His advice to others—Erica felt it was spoken directly to her—was simple. "You gotta get your ass to the workshop every day, just like you go to a meeting. Just show up. Before you know it, you'll be working again."

Erica had gone home and set up her easel, mixed her paints, arranged her pencils, and stared at the indifferent universe of the canvas. She doodled, she smoked, she drank too much coffee, she did no painting. Until she did. She drew furious self-portraits, began work on a new series, *Cleaners in the Dark II*. When a memory bobbed up, vivid and whole, from her "active" days of drinking, of herself bending over a railing near the East River, watching with an Edvard Munch scream as a dead sheep floated by on its bloated back, black hooves splayed towards the sky, she knew she had a painting.

Middle-aged and battle-scarred, she is doing it now, rebooting the computer in her head. She finishes the Pentecostal church people and arrives at the very last of the Guatemala series. She had recently seen a small, dark man climbing up the steep hill from the village below on one of her walks with the dog. She knew where he was headed, up that shin splint–making hill, then down another one, to the pariah houses where migrants lived, in the woods. One broad hand held a plastic bag—the Guatemalan briefcase. His tan work boots weighed heavy on the incline. He leaned into the alien hill, step after tired step, his face turned, she thinks, back to Guatemala.

POP THE BALLOON

They're in a cave. John looms over Erica, grinning. "I have an announcement," he says. "It turns out there's been a mistake: I haven't died." His smile turns into a jack-o'-lantern grimace, shocking her awake.

Erica is ready for the art show opening in three days, which will include work by two artists she doesn't know from neighboring towns. All she knows is one is a watercolorist, the other a collagist. Today, she's sitting at a little table outside a Starbucks, wondering why she isn't more anxious about it. She's always anxious before a show. She drinks her skim-milk latte and swears she'll never get a skim-milk latte again, and when the sun decides to show, after two days of gloom and overcast, she takes off her sweater. She's waiting for Ginny Salomon, who's still in the queue. They're lucky to have nabbed a table for themselves. It's the middle of May, and everyone is outside, released after a chilly start to spring. Erica turns her face to the sun. This is part of her new self-improvement plan, little forays back into the world, coffee and lunch dates with friends—well, women friends—whom she's known for years, some, like Ginny, going back even before their kids started school.

Ginny appears with one of those thousand-calorie concoctions. She eats as if she is tall and thin, but she is a small woman, inclined to be dumpy. "I'm so excited about your show! It's fantastic you're doing your art so soon after . . ." Ginny trails off, then gamely goes on. "Of course, you've always been so disciplined." This is the thing women who meet as mothers always face: do they have anything in common, really, except the kids?

Erica takes a sip from her latte. "It's what I do," she says. *Do I sound defensive? Should I tell her it's this or fall apart? But we won't go into that, will we?* She's determined to keep the conversation on safe ground—like, how are Ginny's kids? If she's lucky, they'll run out of time before her kid comes up.

"So, tell me, how are Christy and James?" And they're off. In twenty minutes or so, Erica calculates, she can politely excuse herself, make up another appointment. Because it was a mistake, this Starbucks meeting; socializing is too much. Like that dream she has where she's somewhere and suddenly realizes she's naked. But Ginny, who's in marketing, has been kind enough to e-mail and Facebook a lot of people she knows about Erica's new show and Erica owes her some civility. So she makes interested faces about Christy's internship at a local newspaper, James's latest concert with his band "Arms and the Moose," and his progress with new ADHD meds. It helps to think about where they'll hang her stuff at the show. She really wants that wall on the west side of the room which doesn't get the glare.

"It's been so great for him, taking up the drums; it really helps him focus," Ginny is saying. Erica drifts again. She is realizing it is only three weeks until the first anniversary—is that the right word?—of John's death. This time a year ago, she'd been spoon-feeding him Italian ice after yelling—yes, at the top of her lungs!—at the nutritionist at the nursing home to stop force-feeding him solid food. Ginny hums in the background.

She's back at the hospice. Early mornings on the steep road up to the top of the ridge, where the recently built low bunch of buildings seemed to hunch, especially when it was windy. And every day, signing in and going down the halls, past that blaring television in the lobby with the parking-lot-worth of wheelchairs, stopping at the nurses' station for pointless updates on John, continuing all the way to the end, the hospice rooms, Erica felt the air being sucked from her, as if this last-stop facility was oxygen-deprived. In a room, with books and magazines that would never be read, a radio CD player that wouldn't be played, a television that remained blank, lay John. There were vases of flowers, some fresh, some wilting, on the windowsill. It was one of Erica's tasks to see to the flowers. She gave them and the fruit baskets to the aides who did the necessary cosmetic work for John; the freshest, biggest arrangements were for the nice male night aide—Pete? No, Perry —who always stopped to chat with her before he went off-duty. That particular morning, a cluster of balloons, brightly colored as for a child's birthday party, had been added. While John slept as usual, heavily stoned, Erica popped the balloons, one by one, with her fingernails. Paul or Pete—no, Perry!—heard the reports and stuck his head in. He stopped, staring at the pile of dead balloons—like festive, giant condoms—at Erica's feet.

"Who gives a dying man balloons?" she asked and began to cry.

"Mr. John's not in pain," Perry said after a small pause.

Erica shook her head. *Oh yeah? How does he* know *that?* "That's all I want for him now," she said. "But, talking about pain, Perry, I happened to meet a hospice nurse last night,"—a woman at an AA meeting she'd never met before and would never see again—"and we got to talking about John. And *she* told me that, when they get this thin, there's no fat to absorb the painkillers except for there's still a little pocket of fat *under the arms* and that's where it should go in. Do you know about this?" It seemed to her that this was the most urgent topic in the world.

"Well, I'm just an aide," Perry said, "I'll ask the nursing director."

"No. *I* want to ask her, and I want her to do it while I'm here."

"I'll go find her for you." Perry left.

Erica dampened a washcloth, smoothed it over John's now almost nonexistent mouth, his face, and his neck, then patted the skin softly with a dry cloth. He made a noise but remained asleep. The sun through the evergreen curtains at the window by his bed had a distorted quality. They could have been underwater. That time they'd snorkeled for hours in Cancún and, even though they wore sunscreen and T-shirts, got really sunburned! She waited for the nurse. It can take all the time in the world for something to happen in a medical place, she knows now. Another aide came in, a heavily built West Indian woman she doesn't know. John began to stir. "Get you up now into the chair. You want yo' nice, thick robe, Mr. Grey?" They had finally let go of the farce of clothing. His old corduroys and thick, blue sweater and flannel shirts were folded in the otherwise empty wardrobe. Erica held the wheelchair and helped with the robe business, though John was such a slip of a man now that the aide could have easily done it by herself.

Erica wheeled him out of the room and down the hall. It was sunny and warm out. She took him outside to the patio with the pink roses, but John was crabby and restless in the brightness outdoors. She wheeled him back in, to the dining room, and asked for the carton of lemon ice she had brought.

The head nurse bustled over. "Mrs. Grey? Only the fruit ice? We have Ensure, you know."

"Just the lemon ice. That's all he wants," she said, feeling tears again. Impatiently, she wiped her eyes.

"You wanted to know about putting the IV under his arms, Perry said? Well, we know about that. We're doing that. You don't have to worry; we're doing everything we can for him, Mrs. Grey."

Erica kept slipping through the cracks these days. That was how she thought of it, when she didn't remember or care what the rules were: the almighty rules of politeness she'd been born and bred to.

Don't be pushy.

Be nice.

Don't be confrontational.

"Really?" Erica raised her voice. "He hasn't been shaved again, for one thing." She knew she was going off (crazy bitch), but she actually relished it.

"He's been restless today, I see from his chart. We don't like to agitate them—shaving does, you know—when they're restless."

"Well, if he's agitated, give him more fucking fentanyl, morphine, whatever!" Part of her enjoyed these battles of the will. *She* was agitated. "And the other day, this aide, I don't know who she was, told me rudely she didn't have time to cut his nails. They were getting like Fu Manchu!" Didn't these people understand he was still, if barely, a human being? Who needed every bit of what little dignity could be preserved? Oh, she'd had plenty of run-ins with the staff. Though this hospice was much better than the hospital, where she'd yelled at two Jehovah's Witnesses who snuck in with their pamphlets, and at a sourpuss nurse for letting a bowl of hot soup be delivered supposedly for him to eat unsupervised. "He already fucking believes!" she'd told the Witnesses. "He can't lift the spoon by himself!" she'd told the nurse.

They were all used to relatives mad with grief, of course, clinging (pathetically) to details. Claire was right! Erica understood she was now a crazy woman who couldn't go on, but, Samuel Beckett-like, did. Street fights for tiny victories, lemon ice to soothe his esophagus as he died, the dignity of a shave and a manicure.

"I assure you, he is getting all the pain medication he can tolerate," the head nurse repeated calmly.

Before she could make her daily escape from this place, Erica wheeled John down to the end of the hall again, where she positioned him by the window. John drooped, but was kept from falling out of the chair by straps around his chest. She opened at random his beloved collection of poems and read:

> In me thou see'st the glowing of such fire
> That on the ashes of his youth doth lie,
> As the death-bed whereon it must expire . . .

Why was there so much death in the poems John had copied and carried with him? She let the book fall to the floor where it made a loud clap. There was a brief lack of noise before life rushed in, before she heard a patient somewhere down the hall calling hoarsely for a nurse, an aide's trilling laugh, the television's ragged rumble. And John began making gasping noises that passed for speech now.

"What is it, love?" She took his hand, so featherlight and ready with the rest of him to fly away, like one of those damned balloons. *If I were truly a devoted wife, wouldn't I make a bed on the floor and sleep beside him in the hospice, keeping vigil around the clock?* She could not, because there was Mona, there were the animals to tend to, but she knew that really it was because she couldn't bear to stay there very long. She bent over to kiss his cheek in farewell. She didn't want to see anymore; she didn't want to bear witness anymore to his suffering.

". . . and Christy's covering your show for the *Gazette*, she's so excited!"

Erica blinks. Snap. "Oh, isn't that great?"

Ginny is smiling over her coffee cream and chocolate concoction. And it's spring.

"And how's Mona?"

Once upon a time, she and Ginny had taken turns driving bands of giggling girls around to playdates, Girl Scouts, choir practice. Mona and Christy sang Pop-Tart hits in the back seat; they were uproarious girls. And then, around eighth grade, they'd grown shy of each other, taken different turns.

"Well, Mona's working right now and thinking about going back to college, once she figures out a major."

Ginny, a nice person, nods and smiles at this cocktail of truth and fabrication. Mostly fabrication.

NANNY IN MIAMI

Asleep. Insanely loud cat meowing jolts me awake. Dim is yowling and running around on the floor. She has no tail, just a bloody stump! I jump out of bed to get her, but she runs away, leaving a trail of blood. Then I realize an insane psychopath has chopped it off, and I'll be next, and I really wake up, hoarsely yelling as Jack and Topanga are pounding on my door, screeching. "Mona, Mona, what's wrong?"

JUNE 12TH

I love this diary. I love the title. I love this whacked-out cartoon paradise place today. Jack and Topanga. Ramon the Tat King (and his coke). The Slam bar. South Beach. And I love, love, love, living rent-free with no expenses, except for gas and cigarettes and bar bills. I'm getting paid to pick up Jack from school and Topanga from preschool and take them to the beach, the park, anywhere I want, really. They're happy as long as they're with me. Two cute little kids.

I don't love Warren, of course, though he's kind of hot in an old-guy way, and, yeah, I think about the father-figure thing and it creeps me out. Warren is barely around, which is why I'm here, but he's nice enough when he is, and he loves the kids. Warren always gets pizzas with everything on, then Topanga picks off everything but the pineapple. And he gets good wine. Now I drink wine with my pizza! Maybe I should just kiss him, give him the thrill he's hoping for. He drinks a fair amount of rum and Coke after dinner, too, but who wouldn't if they were in the middle of a divorce to that wretched Patty with her practically see-through nostrils at this stage of the coke game. I mean, what mother gives up her kids to a nineteen-year-old nanny twenty four–seven? A rich coke fiend, that's who.

What I hate: Of course, Patty. Ramon, when he tries weird shit on me. Most of my dreams. That I can't do opioids, cannot, cannot. NA meetings where the dealers wait outside, bidin' their time. Those stupid slogans they all use, like they're brain-dead, which they probably are. That addicts are big drama queens, constantly talking about their sordid capers. Dude. Who gives a shit? But here's the thing: I have a plan and it's working. Save money from this job and travel. Write *the* graphic novel of my generation.

Oh, and other things I hate: Thinking about Mom. Especially hate that. She acted so defeated when I left, like I stabbed her in the heart. Everything is *not my fault*, and I hate that she makes me feel like it is. She should deal with her own shit, which, in fact, I've told her. I'm dealing with mine. I have a job, I am responsible, I'm not doing drugs. OK—fuck you! Just pot and wine. A little coke, but I don't even like coke; I'm a down girl. Well, have to go, Topy's screaming, I hope Jack didn't hit her again.

Fuck. Just lying here crying nonsensically. No, sensically. OK, a bit of a crash; no more stash until I can get it up to meet Ramon. Which has to be now but can't be. Because I'm not going to take the little guys to his creepy shop and make them wait in the car. Dude. I will get up soon and find some wine or, if all else fails, beer. I mean, who wouldn't be lonely, stuck with a four-year-old and a seven-year-old? I need people my own age; this totally sucks.

There's always baby drama around here! Like, two hours ago, I almost took Topanga to the doctor, but I finally got her calmed down and cleaned up the blood. Heads bleed copiously. I put a whole bunch of cartoon bandages on it and gave her a popsicle—strawberry, of course—and she finally fell asleep after some *James and the Giant Peach* (I bought all the Roald Dahls for them from Warren's cash. I believe that Dad's reading me those books was the best thing of my childhood), and I also told Jack I was sick of him hitting his sister, and I would beat him up if he did it again, which he half-believed. Ha-ha me, all into nonviolence except when dealing with assholes. Jack's been on his iPad since. Of course, he has every gadget in hyperconsumerist America. I took a shower (again) and have been lying around, chilling and smoking. Cigarettes, dude—I'm not that dumb, even if I had any weed left. Warren would smell it—he's probably a secret pothead himself. OK, cigarettes are not allowed either, but this is my room. Warren wouldn't dare come in here. The only reason I'm thinking about him *at all* is that Ramon hasn't called or texted me back. OK, that Cubano is pretty funny, has good stash, and is a talented tat artist, but, on the other hand, he's problematic. That's not why I'm crying; it's the usual reason. Just everything. It's cosmic! Which sounds so pretentious, but I don't care. I can say anything here. I hate everything. I am a fucking loser who can't get my shit together, a teenager who will never have a normal life, let alone an abnormal one that makes any sense to me. Like, why can't I get a decent tan living here in Miami? Why am I such a pathetic-looking person who still has zits and a bony ass? I hate how Mom always tried to sympathize with me, with that laugh, "Oh honey, you're beautiful. Don't worry about your complexion; it will clear up." And trying to "bond" with me with her hippie tales about acid and her colorful fuckups, the whole ancient package. She does *not* know how I feel! She never put a needle in her arm—or foot, for that matter. A fair number of the people I know, used to know, don't have any working veins left, or have Hep C, AIDS, STDs. Or have OD'd. I hate drugs. They worked for, like, a week, then it all turned to shit. I don't know how it happened.

JUNE 14TH

Misty's coming!!! Yeah! My plan worked: my devious, sneaky plan that Warren fell for. I convinced him he needs two nannies, not one—a day nanny and a night nanny—because I didn't sign on for twenty four–seven and he knows he's taking advantage of me. And I had just the girl for him. Yup. Misty. Out of the shitty, cold, pathetic, nothing-to-do burbs of NYC to golden sunshine all the time. Dude, I am planning some good times for us. Plus, Ramon called so I was able to score a modest amount of weed and then blow him off—not the kind of blow he was expecting. Ha-ha-ha.

Meanwhile, I have to tell about my progress on "The Mona Project." It's fairly insane, which makes it extra appealing. So before I came down here, I took pictures on my iPhone of those bat-crazy dreams in Mom's sketchbook. Some of them actually are a little ho-hum, but some are brilliant, especially that double self-portrait where she's shaving off a beard in a mirror. Of course I've been doing my own version of them in my sketchbook, too, with Jack and Topanga's poster paints and colored pencils, starting with Bearded Mon. Mom would probably be monumentally pissed off at me for using her ideas, but at least I didn't write any more bad checks or raid her jewelry box. My, I have been an evil daughter. But the exciting thing which I know she'd really go for and maybe someday I will "show and tell" her is . . . I am drawing my own dreams now; it's like my subconscious is on meth. I just finished the one where Dad's sitting there with me in the living room. He has a pipe in his mouth and a glass of wine (naturally), and I'm next to him; we're probably talking about movies, and, then, in a flash, he turns into a giant package and falls to the floor. Earth to Mom: graphic novel, dude—that's how you do it!

JUNE 24TH

I was thinking I would write in here every day, or at least every other day, but that's really not the way I roll. Especially with Misty here! Bad, bad Misty brought along a bunch of Oxys she scored cheap somehow—don't ask. Yeah, I knew it was a matter of time. They're too delicious. But I have been very conservative because I have to drive Jack and Topanga around so much. Misty is the night nanny, so she has to make dinner for them, baths, etc., but that still gives us time to be our badass selves. So far, just getting high and watching movies late, but all of Saturday and Sunday until five is free time for Warren's slaves. Last weekend, we hit South Beach for an all-nighter and beach sun, met some sketchy and boring guys, but that has to change. Ramon called and was actually whining in a cheesy way about how I'm messin' with his head and similar shit. Latino dude=possessive. "Go cry to yo' mama," I told him.

JUNE 25TH

Everything's fucked. I can't believe it. Like a really bad movie, naturally. When is my life not a bad movie? OK, today started off as usual. I made myself get up and put the granola in the bowls and cut up bananas. Then came the mad rush to get the two monkeys out the door with all their school shit, and I drove them, a bit too fast, but I'm careful. I never text when they're in the car, and they get to their institutions of lower education only a few minutes late.

I went back to the house. Fiorenzia was there, cleaning the kitchen. I went to my room to get some sleep which I desperately needed, but Misty came in, and we started talking and decided to snort an Oxy or two, and then we just chilled on my bed, listening to some band Misty just discovered called Pony Whack, or is it Whack the Pony? Anyway, suddenly there's this loud knocking on my door, I shouted "Go away!" thinking it was Fiorenzia who wanted to clean, but it was *not*. It was Bitch Mom Patty with a key! Who *never* comes to the house, since the divorce is happening, and a bad one at that, according to Warren's hints and moans. And she had the nerve, being Patty, to barge into my room. Like all cokeheads, she couldn't wait a millisecond for anything. So this scrawny, tanning bed-leather brown crackhead with, what she thinks is sexy, long, black hair (but which makes her look like the witch that she is) busts in screaming at us. "What?" I say, a bit slowly, as I'm in my groove.

"Where are the kids? Where are my kids? It's two thirty; where are they?"

"*What?*" I say, and realize, shit, she's right, the time had flown. I had been flying too. The one day that the mother, who sees her kids, like, once a month, shows up, I have the incredibly bad luck to be caught napping by her the first time I ever messed up. And I, who am usually so clever and resourceful (Misty pointed this out later) could think of nothing to say to defend myself. Like, they're in some afterschool program. Just lie to get her off my ass. But I just mumble, my legs were really not in a position to get off the bed right then. Misty croaks something.

"And who are you?" says Bitch Patty.

"I'm the new night nanny." And then Misty starts *laughing*, and I'm laughing too, and we are *fucked*. Patty goes storming off, and we can hear her yelling on the phone to Warren, who's always at his job manufacturing drones or seaplanes or something, and then she comes back. "You're fired! Pack your shit and leave!" And off she went to get the kids in her unsafe-driver, coked-up condition.

So, I called Warren. I explained to him that I was just tired and, for the first time, overslept, and then Patty came "in a very emotional state"—hint, hint—to let him know she was in her usual state of drugged insanity, which he already knew, that's why he's divorcing her. He's actually pretty calm and not angry, but he says he can't help us with this one. He'll mail a check wherever I want but . . . yeah, right, Warren. So now we are packing. Going back to Moms', mine and hers. I already called mine and made up some lame reason, and she's confused, but, of course, she can't wait to have me back in her clutches.

GUATEMALAN BRIEFCASE

Erica is seated at a formal dining table. A large vase of flowers in the center of the table wafts the scent of Madonna lilies. A waiter sets down a gold-rimmed dinner plate before her with a flourish. On it is a mouth or, rather, a pair of full red lips, garlanded by parsley.

Most of the people milling around at the community center's art show are clustered around Millicent Plainsong's watercolors. This is unsurprising to Erica. Millie Plainsong's oeuvre consists entirely of bucolic views of local streams or hills, an occasional old barn or abandoned chapel, Hallmark scenes that have made the red-bereted artist a fixture of the local art scene. Gary Placksin's obtuse collages draw a thinner crowd. Smallest of all is the group before Erica's Guatemalans. Still, there is already a red "sold" dot affixed to the corner of her painting of the men huddled around a fire in snowy woods, which she'd done after reading a story in the local paper about homeless Central American immigrants. A charred body had been found near a campsite, the autopsy reporting that the deceased had been highly intoxicated. He had likely passed out and rolled too close to a fire. It was surmised, though not proved, that this was death by misadventure. Unless someone had rolled him into it.

Erica is discussing the story behind the painting with Ginger, who is indignant. An indefatigable activist in town politics, Ginger is working to increase services for the swelling number of Latinos who keep moving into the village because of its relatively cheap housing. "So I said to the mayor, really? Do we need another gas station, just because it'll have Dunkin' Donuts too? There's a Dunkin' Donuts five minutes away. We could use that space for a drop-in center with a bathroom for the day laborers. And *he* says—"

"Oh, my God," Erica interrupts. She has noticed a large man with piercing, blue eyes scrutinizing the painting she thinks of as *Guatemalan Briefcase*, the man trudging up the hill clutching a plastic bag. "I think that's my college boyfriend."

"Boyfriend? I thought you were quite the wild thing and didn't go in for commitment then," Ginger jokes.

"Yeah, yeah. Gone was special, though." A brief but important part in the wild ride that was the early seventies.

"Gong?"

"Gone. Well, Sargon," Erica says. "Sargon Harbash."

"Somehow, I know you are not making this up," Ginger says with lifted eyebrows. "Well, see you later."

He's spotted her, too—*Oh my God!*—and is coming her way. Four decades later, and counting, he's still wearing the tooled Mexican boots, jeans, and a Mexican peasant shirt which had comprised his community organizer and agitator outfit back in the day. She confirms that it is him, though he is now completely, and fashionably, bald. How has he recognized her, though? She's not at all the same wild-haired girl who'd sewed an American flag to the rear of her blue jeans, before her World War II vet dad had, in a rare show of force, made her take it off. She's got shorter hair.

of land. Yet Tomás's family, except for one son who came north later, remains in that village, dependent on the money he sends them from his gardener wages. No, he told her, he will never go back. His fate is to tend pretty, frivolous gardens like hers. He, of course, doesn't say that, but Erica thinks it.

So, it is hard to give up the painting of Tomás for this reason, and also because she doesn't like the way one of his legs is bent. She should take it home and get it right; then she will sell it. Suddenly, she is remembering an argument she had with John a few years ago, over another defect in another painting . . .

They stood in front of her painting. She was waiting for John's feedback. Not his approval; he didn't give praise. Not because he was mean-spirited or a hard-ass but because it was a given to him that a professional knows her worth. He was the same with plumbers and waiters as with the artists and illustrators who pitched to his magazine: demanding but fair. What John did well was find the errors, the fudged bits and lazy compromises. He found them and he expected them to be fixed. So now she waited. And he didn't disappoint. Forefinger curved over the figure of Mona skating at the local rink, her body lifted, joyful, a graceful young girl, he said, "This leg doesn't look right."

Erica swallowed. He nailed it, of course. Her husband, attuned to and invigorated by technique, immersed in craft. She'd been characteristically more interested in catching, holding the energy, the happy spray of that flung leg. This was a well-worn path of discussion for them: discipline versus freedom.

"I know I don't have the technique down—but I'm not going to take any more classes," she said, tightly. "But I'll work on the leg."

About to say something, he retreated for once. He had suggested more life-drawing classes several times. "Good. It detracts."

She hadn't gotten the leg right in the end, but she'd been able to let that go. But it's as if, now, she is seeing these new paintings, six in all, with John's eyes. The art naïf quality, which some have found charming or moving, which she has accepted as part of her way of making art, is clear now. It looks a bit clumsy, lacks the virtuosic pitch she will probably never attain. John had been right about the skating picture.

This silent flash of fantasy dialogue can't go on. Because where will it lead? Yes, her work has a homemade quality to it. But isn't this who she is? And the ponytailed guy who is handing her a check likes it. The little old couple like the other one, though they dither about buying it. Two out of six sold and one more, possibly. Half! The show is a success.

Erica looks around for Sargon Harbash, but he seems to have disappeared, and she needs to talk to the curator about the next day, when Christy Salomon, Mona's former best friend in elementary school, is going to do a piece for the local paper on the show. Christy lines up internships. Mona gets stoned. She says goodbye to her fellow exhibitors and the people who linger and want to talk, not buy. At last, she heads for the parking lot, and there is Sargon, leaning against a black minivan.

"Ah, there you are at last. Coffee? Food?"

"Sure! There's a little café down the road."

Settled in the Café Umbra with a cappuccino, Erica leans forward. "There's something I should tell you."

"You're seeing somebody?" He laughs. "Just my luck. Of course."

"No. Not that. It's, well, it's that next week is one year since my husband died."

"Right. I saw it on Facebook. Really sorry, Rica."

Erica ploughs on. "But now, running into you like this, such a surprise. A nice surprise." *I'm blushing*, she thinks.

"Yeah. So . . . maybe we can get together for lunch or some-you're sick from a disease you won't admit you have, which, to remind you, is a symptom of the disease. How is that an insult?"

"Mom, *stop*. Using drugs sometimes doesn't make someone an addict. You just go off; you get crazy on me."

"And there's another insult. Because I am not crazy, and you mean it like an insult."

"So, you aren't going to lend me any money?"

"*Lend* you? That's a good one. How much money have I spent on you? I might as well have thrown it out a car window, the good it's done."

But Mona doesn't hear this last crack; she's back up the stairs. And, later, Erica will find that the diamond ring she'd inherited from her great-grandmother, which had been passed down to the oldest girl in each generation and which she was keeping to give to Mona when she turned twenty-one, is missing from its hiding place in her sock drawer. But, by then, Mona is fifty miles away, lying on the sand and promoting skin cancer. Having pawned the ring on the way.

After any confrontation with Mona, Erica feels drained, sick, and the muggy heat that has moved in doesn't help. She sleeps badly. The next day, she can't settle to anything and worries she'll be bitchy when Gone shows up that night. It's too hot to cook; it's too hot to do anything, so she takes her Finnish paperback, iced tea, and cell phone with her to the Adirondack chair in the shade in the backyard where she falls into one of those sleeps that kick up psychic dust and startles you awake. By now, it's after five.

"I'm out of sorts," she tells the dog, "let's go for a walk." She pulls on a clean, aged, Mexican, cotton blouse that has survived the decades, a kind of cloth diary of her younger life, with its pot-seed burns, mended tears, and an old, faded mango stain which no cleaning product has succeeded in eradicating. "Out of sorts" is her mother's expression, she realizes—a typical understatement by a woman who never appeared to get angry, just snapped and faded out.

Neither she nor the dog pretend to enjoy themselves as they plod through the humid afternoon. Back home, she checks the cell phone—which she'd forgot ten to take with her—the landline, the e-mail. Nothing yet.

It's when she's in bed, asleep, sometime around eleven that night, that he calls.

"Hey! I'm on my way! Fifteen minutes or so."

She addresses her scrubbed face, pulls on shorts and a shirt, turns on lights. All the animals are at unaccustomed attention. And there is the black minivan, Sargon alert and jovial. He has always seemed to fill any room he's in. He's full of jokes about his "made" client guy in Brooklyn, playfully apologetic. "It turned into an all-day marathon. I mean, the moron's facing the Feds," he says by way of explanation for his lateness. He wraps her in a bear hug, sighs. "I'm starving, woman." At midnight, Erica is grilling hamburgers on the patio. He polishes off two, piled with cheese, tomatoes, relish, and hot sauce. "But hold the onion," he'd said, "A noble sacrifice for your sake."

It is at that moment that Erica wonders if she is in love.

HOW COULD YOU EAT THE PIE
AND THEN LEAVE ME?

Erica is trying to run down a crowded city sidewalk while
dragging a suitcase. She is late to a vital appointment.
Suddenly, she turns around and sees that her suitcase has
flown open and her things are scattered all over the street.

"**O**h, yeah, I brought my DVD I told you about," Sargon says, as
soon as he's finished the burgers. *DVD?* Oh, the documentary
film he'd made about his family that he'd mentioned in one of his
late-night phone calls.

"Fucker won first prize in a contest in San Francisco. Big on
independent film there. No money though. Just fame."

"Fantastic!" Erica says. She has sluiced her face with cold
water, made extra-strong coffee, but it's not helping much. She'll
have to pinch herself to stay awake. Because it's clear they are
going to watch the thing now. Twenty-five years ago, she'd be up
for it, but it's almost one in the morning, and she's usually sound
asleep by now, unless, of course, the phone rings with whatever

trouble Mona's gotten herself into this time. And, speaking of Mona, here she is, shuffling into the room.

"Hey," she says, trying to sound sober and failing. "You guys watching a movie?" Mona, who watches movies obsessively, any kind of movie, slides into a chair.

Sargon is fiddling with the cranky DVD player.

"Fuckin' finally it's working. So, welcome to my movie, *The House of Harbash*.

Erica fights another yawn. She is so tired, but, after their weekend dinners and frequent phone chats, it's clear Sargon is both a day *and* a night person. He might stop for a short nap, but that's it. She's got to not just stay awake, but alert: this is his award-winning movie. She takes a deep slug of coffee as it begins with a musical nod to "their" generation, Crosby, Stills, Nash, and Young's "A Very, Very, Very Fine House," which Mona may or may not get. She glances at her daughter, who is stern and smoking, staring at the screen. A camera pans to a large, decrepit house, and the voiceover—his voice—startles her: "This is the house I grew up in." Abruptly, the scene shifts to a machine with a wrecking ball and the house not so much blowing up as caving in, a mighty rain of dust and rubble. Cut again to blown-up shots of a dark-haired woman in shadow, slumped in a chair, refusing to make eye contact with the camera though cajoled in the voiceover. "My mother," Sargon's voice explains. He continues his commentary as the camera closes in on the hunched woman. "My mother was a recluse all my life. The things I remember her doing were having arguments with my father and sitting around, depressed. Yeah, she would do stuff for us, like make food for us, shitty food actually, and then we three kids just grabbed it and went to watch television. I don't know what my dad did; he wasn't around much because of the store. No, the Harbashes didn't sit together at a table to eat. Where she was while we grabbed the food, I don't know. Probably sitting in the dark somewhere. On holidays, we might all sit at the table."

Cut to a bald man in a thick sweater, cap, and Pancho Villa mustache who is spreading out his hands behind tables heaped with stuff, like in *Hoarders*. "Kadeer Harbash, father and packrat extraordinaire. Syrian immigrant who started over in America. Trading rugs, what else? Then it was on to cheap almost-antiques and then just junk. It was everywhere—in the garage, the house, the yard." Cut to the stand-alone garage and another wrecking ball explosion. "Everything else was basically neglected. Like, you might say, a drunk might do, except Kadeer didn't do booze or drugs—he did hoarding." The camera moves, noticeably wobbling, to a close-up of a bathroom, a shabby, early sixties–style arrangement featuring lurid aqua tiles everywhere. Including the floor, or what remained of it. "This hole in the floor in the upstairs bathroom? Raccoons would climb up through it and run around. I swear to God. My sister was afraid to go in there. She used to scream at the raccoons while she was taking a bath, and I would have to go chase them out. Whack at them with a broom. The floor, as you see, never got fixed." In the voiceover, a ghoulish laugh.

Erica is now fully awake. She thinks, *This is pathetically sad*, realizes that her mouth is hanging open, and shuts it. Sargon doesn't notice. He's leaning forward, intensely watching himself in the next scene, pre-wrecking ball, as he heaves a sledgehammer at a wall. "My boyhood bedroom," continues the narrative. The voiceover becomes yells and curses as he destroys an entire wall. Cut to the exterior, the more efficient iron ball destroying walls again. More clouds of pulverized house. "Beautiful!" says the voiceover.

The film shifts to another place, another mood: a dimly lit room in what appears to be a hospital or institution. Gradually, the camera zooms in: Sargon walking toward another man, younger and with a full head of black hair, who jumps out of a chair and throws his arms around Sargon. "Sargie! Sargie! Sargie!" cries a high, little-boy voice.

The voiceover continues, "Andy is my younger brother. Now, Melody, my sister, didn't want to be in the movie, which is typical. But Andy did. Andy's a retard. Sorry: profoundly mentally challenged. He lives in a group home. We're very close, which is unusual for the Harbashes." Cut to a view of the demolished family homestead from across the street. A rubble-strewn quarter acre now. "After the city demolished their condemned house, my parents moved in with my uncle down the block. I myself have not been back to the neighborhood since."

The End

Sargon leans back, puts his cowboy boots on the coffee table, and Erica feels a flare of irritation at that. She doesn't know what to say.

"So," Sargon says, rubbing his hands together.

Mona says in a neutral voice, "This is, uh, for real, dude?"

He swivels. "All of it."

Mona says, "Well . . . your family is insane. Other than that—"

Erica's face is burning. "Mona!"

"What? It's true. And mine is too!" She jumps up. "I'm goin' to Misty's. It's crazy around here!"

They hear the door slam. "God, Gone, I'm sorry. She gets so upset. But that was terrible. Rude." She puts her hands to her eyes and begins to cry, unwillingly, in short, soft gulps, even as she's wondering in a rush: 1) How could *The House of Harbash* have won a film contest? Maybe there was only one entry; and 2) Well, who cares? I want to roll around with you on my wide bed as long as we can. And 3) Oh God, Mona . . .

"Hey, Rica, don't cry on me."

"I'm not, I won't. Oh, come here, you!"

He comes to her, stands behind her chair, and she feels his considerable weight leaning into her, his face moving to hers. For the first time after a marriage of a quarter century, she's going to sleep with a man who isn't John. She leads him up the stairs. How strange to feel him behind her! He stands on the landing, a large, appealing man.

"You know, it's cool if you change your mind."

"Oh no," she says. He follows her into her bedroom. Erica is almost levitating from desire. She wants Sargon to undress her slowly and take her fast the first time. Instead, he removes his boots and goes to the bathroom, emerging with a towel wrapped around his tubby waist. Erica, meantime, has undressed and slid under the sheets.

An hour later, the exact middle of the night, she saw, looking at the red eyes of the clock, she is recalling how taxing sex can be, how razor burns irritate her skin, and there's the chafing. At some point, he had joked that she was "some sort of contortionist" and, soon after, he rolled onto his back with a big sigh.

"Sorry," he said a moment later.

"No, it's OK, we're both tired." Not OK. But the game is on, and she is going to press toward the goal. She reaches over and gives his cheek a slow, melting kiss. Another round, and this one will be better. It has been so long. But he rolls away.

She tries to sleep. In a few hours, she has to get up. Casho is at first imploring, then indignant about his breakfast. She lingers downstairs, makes coffee, brings up a tray. Sargon's awake and, cupping a hand above the sheet over his crotch, says, "Pepe was ready for you, my Viking goddess, but he couldn't hold out any longer."

"Whoa! *Pepe?*" It's one thing—a bad thing—for a man to name his penis, but even worse, it's the name of a former lover, a handsome Peruvian pilot she'd met while backpacking in the Andes with two friends one Pisco sour-fueled summer after college. Pepe it was who had rescued them while stranded in a feudalistic Incan town that had been taken over that very day by Maoist guerrillas who had shut everything down. In fact, that was the beginning of a civil war that would rage throughout Peru for years. Erica, Lydia, and Sally were at the closed-down airport, but the bar, luckily, remained inexplicably open so they sat drinking Pisco sours, clueless about what to do next, when these two guys in pilots' uniforms appeared. Pepe and his copilot bought the next round and somehow managed to corral a cargo plane shortly after dawn. They flew over the majestic Andes down to Lima on the coast, and she and Pepe became inseparable for about a week, until he had to fly. Pepe assured her he'd see her soon, probably in Miami. Ah, those days before the internet and cell phones. She never heard from him again.

The Pepe of today is appended to a man past sixty, as far from being a sexy, Latin, bush pilot as possible. In fairness, she will never see fifty again. She knows that such excitement lies squarely in her past. The past; that means certain hard-won experience. And any woman who hasn't lived in a cave knows how carefully she has to maneuver in this kind of situation, where a man has christened his private parts. Yet really, does she care about the implications? Not much; that's how far gone she is.

They have a good day, notwithstanding the inauspicious night and early morning. She makes food and lazily gardens, while he does lawyer stuff on his cell phone and laptop. Mona comes home, and Sargon takes a nap in the spare room. Then he wants to go out to eat. Erica remembers a good Italian seafood place run by Albanians (a growing trend in the area)—it's not far—in a Victorian manor house that had begun life as a bordello in the 1800s. At this restaurant, Berto's, Sargon plays the Arab card, bonding with the maître d'—who assumes he's a Muslim; Sargon is a Syrian Christian—in the time it takes to order from the heavy, overpriced menu. Subsequently, the busboy, waiter, and nearby diners become fans during the lengthy meal. This is what, she recalls, Sargon used to do back in the day, at spaghetti joints, Chinese joints, bars, anywhere in fact: he always ended up at the center of whatever was going on. But Erica doesn't want to be noticed, in part because her own painterly path as watcher of life is deeply grooved, but also because, hey, what kind of romantic tête-à-tête is this? It isn't. But this is what Sargon likes to do: perform. *Well, out of bed,* she thinks a little peevishly. It makes perfect sense that he became a trial lawyer.

And, while he and the maître d' are swapping Arab man kisses in farewell like brothers, Erica wonders if she really is falling in love. *Grieving for Dummies* had warned about such things during the early stages. Well, it's been a year. And, if it isn't love, she'll take it.

Back home in bed—two nights in a row!—stuffed with sea bass and pasta, they manage a few embraces before falling asleep. As ever, too early the next day, this one full of the gauzy, sick-looking light of a very hot day, Casho barks her awake. Erica throws on her ancient, beloved kimono and trudges downstairs to feed the dog and cats, and there is Mona peering into the refrigerator, her size double zero jeans sliding down over what used to be hips. Her hair is an Amy Winehouse cool-slut beehive.

"You're up?" This is unprecedented.

"Actually, yeah, as you can see. Got home late after a concert, but I couldn't sleep, and now I'm starving."

"Well, how was the beach?" Erica hears the chirpiness in her voice, is powerless to stop it.

"Mmm, OK. Where's the food?"

"There's plenty of food. Eggs. Bread. Fruit."

"I'll make some toast. Is there coffee? Wow, *you* again?" She whips around and stares at Sargon, who has approached noiselessly.

"Yup. I'm an old friend of your mom's."

Mona snorts. "Yeah, I got that. And a filmmaker." She pronounces "filmmaker" like Erica says "drug dealer."

"Nah, I'm a lawyer. That was just me trying to clear up the wreckage of my past. It's an AA thing."

"You too? Wow, like you and Mom can have meetings together and share your *experience, strength, and hope*. Mom! Is there only rye bread? I hate rye bread."

She's about as subtle as Casho's barks, Erica thinks. Might as well have said, "Why the fuck is this guy still in our house?"

"So have some cereal."

Mona fires up a Salem Light, still glaring. "There's no good cereal, Mom."

"So have yogurt, I don't care."

"I'm just saying." She shuffles over to the kitchen table and sits down heavily.

"Hey, I'll have the toast," Sargon says.

"Oh, fuck this," says Mona and goes upstairs. They hear her door slam.

Erica, feeling the heavy, invisible cloak of her codependency nestle upon her, rises to Mona's defense. "She's just so upset about the stuff that's happened in her life. And it makes her impossible right now."

"Hey, I know what kids are like." He has two, a daughter he adores and a son he doesn't talk about. "*You* don't have to apologize."

"I should go talk to her." The codependency cloak, as she well knows, drowns out reason.

Mona is sitting on her bed, smoking. Erica sits, gingerly.

"You OK?"

"Mom, what is he doing here again?"

"He's my friend and . . . we're enjoying each other's company." *Christ, did I just say that?*

Mona snorts, a grinding, nasty sound due to all the drugs she's put up her nose. "*Whatever!*"

Two can play this game.

Erica tugs an arm free from her invisible cloak. "I didn't hear from you once while you were at the beach! You were supposed to call me."

"I just forgot. We were having such a good time."

"Really? Well, you appear to be wasted. Is that your definition of a good time?" They glare at each other for a long second. Wasted. That had been a favorite word in the college crowd she ran with. Sargon and Fishy and Lalo and Annie and Happy Jack. Also trashed, wrecked. Yet they had been innocents compared to Mona's generation, shooting, and overdosing on opiates.

"Thanks for your support, Mom."

"My support? When haven't you had my support? I do everything for you," *which is the problem*, the chorus of sanity hisses in her head. "And what thanks do I ever get? Just a crap attitude." After a tight silence, she veers onto another mutually hated theme. "Anyway, you have to start looking for a new job. That should be your focus right now." Mona is constantly getting, then losing, jobs. Erica doesn't even want to know the reasons.

"What*ever!* You're always on my case." Mona beams a glare of such high malevolence that it would be laughable in a movie— shlock melodrama. *Very Very Very Fine House* material.

But, as usual, Erica can't bear these hateful scenes and, again, switches gears. "I just want to see you healthy and . . . and doing things again. I know it's tough, with Dad gone. Don't, don't be so hostile about Sargon. He's fun. In fact, look, why don't you come with us to dinner next weekend? Sargon is coming back then."

"Oh, like being with that bald psycho is going to help me get over my father, is that what you're thinking? We'll be a new, happy little family? Why would I want to be with you and your filmmaker boyfriend? That's fucking crazy." Mona makes another awful snorting sound, as if she can barely breathe, and hawks into a tissue.

"Mona, you sound terrible!" *What am I thinking? How can I shove a man at her when she's falling apart?*

"It's just allergies. Anyway, I'm tired. I'm going to sleep."

Mona is always "tired." She sleeps through golden days and stays up all night. She doesn't do anything that Erica knows about, except watch movies on her laptop, hang out with Misty, do drugs, and, at some point, get into more trouble.

Erica realizes that Sargon will have heard this latest ugly conversation. How could he have missed it? They were yelling at the top of their voices, as if that was the only chance each had of being heard. But, when she goes downstairs, he says nothing.

They're at a Latin fusion place someone had told Erica about, with trashy, tropical décor and a menu including Mexican tacos, Chilean sea bass, Puerto Rican arroz con pollo. Erica feels her neck and shoulders begin to relax. It has been a difficult day with Mona, nothing unusual about that. She is refusing to even pretend to be looking for a job, but the difficulty isn't that: it's the escalation of their arguments to a point where Erica doesn't recognize Mona or, for that matter, herself. Mona, a howling, door-slamming banshee; Erica collapsing, almost disembodied in her distress. The animals have all found corners to burrow in, away from the ugliness around them. Mercifully, Sargon was not there for the latest, most explosive "conversation." He was at the nearest Apple store to deal with his strange-acting laptop. Though, when he came back, he behaved a little strangely, Erica thought, as if his mind were elsewhere. He hugged her, but stepped back when she wanted to kiss him.

But, now, they both seem in a playful mood, or willing to take a stab at it.

Scooping a large dollop of the guacamole that is almost as good as Erica's renowned secret recipe, Sargon is amiable. He crunches blue corn tortillas. "Look, I just wanna say, about your daughter, I know you're worried about her, probably smoking too much weed and shit like we did, but it's gonna pass. My daughter wouldn't speak to me, literally, until she was practically out of college. Now, we're tight. And remember what we were like? Parents didn't fucking exist."

She nods but can't look at him. He doesn't know the extent of Mona's drug use, because Erica doesn't want him to. Shame rests heavily on her gut, no matter how many books she reads, or Al-Anon and Wings of Hope parents' meetings she goes to.

But Sargon has moved on, plunging into the pool of their shared past, safely sealed. "I never forgot you, you know. One of the two women I never forgot. Even though you blew me off."

"This again? No, I did not! You went and married Nora. And I never really knew you. You were planning protests or buying another round at the bar, always making everybody laugh. We would get together—*hook up* as they say now—then you'd disappear for a while. You were chasing after that Nora Espinosa. Don't bullshit me, I know it."

"That was after you blew me off."

"That's not how I remember it."

"You were my Viking warrior princess. Like the time you told that cop off at that protest for Black Studies on campus: he coulda cracked your head open!"

"He was hurting that African American girl!"

"That's what I mean: a Viking warrior, with that long, curly, light-brown hair and the sweetest ass on campus."

They burst out laughing. She can't believe it: they have had

hours late, practically in the middle of the night *and* wanting to be fed. Was she like the mama he'd never had? She's feeling the elation of the last weeks, the charged, drug-like effect his presence has had on her, start to deflate.

"How's the paella?" he asks presently, his own plate of arroz con pollo disappearing fast.

"It's good, except . . . it tastes like there's Rice Crispies in it."

"Really?" He reaches casually over and forks up a taste. "I'd say more like puffed rice. That's fuckin' weird, man."

And the way he uses *fuck* in every sentence, also *man* and other out-of-date expressions.

Erica excuses herself and goes to the ladies' room. The familiar, dreaded shit storm of anxiety has advanced, marked most noticeably by the sense that she might throw up. In the bathroom, decorated with primitive colorful masks, she dry-heaves in the toilet. Well, this is bringing back memories! *Breathe*, she tells herself, *say the Serenity Prayer*. In early sobriety, she'd had to do this constantly, recite the friggin' Serenity Prayer over and over until the chaos ebbed. She sits down on the toilet seat lid, wishing suddenly for a little Cuban cigar. Maybe it's not anxiety? Maybe it's plain, old anger. That sense of being kicked again by the universe.

"OK?" Sargon asks her as she scrapes back her chair.

"Oh, fine." To prove it, she drinks her coffee with a flourish. She's going to kick this unease's ass.

On the way home on all those winding, country roads that usually provide bucolic comfort—but not tonight—they hardly talk. They listen to music, his music, since it's his car. More precisely, his tank-size minivan. The music, Tom Petty, and the huge car irritate her despite her resolve to be calm. Once they're back in her house, she makes an effort. "*Más café*?"

Which is a mistake, as it just winds them both up. He launches into one of his ambulance-chasing court case tales. "Hispanic dude, dishwasher in a diner, illegal of course, twisted his back severely slipping on grease in the kitchen. Terrified of getting deported. Wins the settlement, over three hundred thousand dollars. Then I see him completely by chance one day, on a ladder painting a friend's house! 'What the fuck, Ronaldo?' I say to him, 'You really wanna get deported?' Fuckin' idiot."

"And how much did you get out of the case?"

"Half," he says. "What? That's how it works. I did all the work; he gets a shitload of money. He's probably still painting houses. These guys never stop working."

"I don't think it's fair. Half!" And he had allowed her to pick up the check at the Latino fusion place. Never mind that she had the money.

"Well, that's the system, Rica." He stirs his coffee. "Anyway, as you may remember me saying," he continues, his tone a step lower, "the divorce cleaned me out."

In bed in the dark later, they lie still, like a long-married couple, Sargon on her side of the bed, which, she admits, disturbs her. Because it means she's on John's side of the bed and, even though she has been there all along with Sargon, she has now that Princess and the Pea sensation that she is lying over the imprint of years and years of her deceased husband's body in the ripped white T-shirts and jockey shorts he always slept in. At last, Erica falls asleep. She dreams she's on a pebbly beach, staring up at an ugly, postmodern house with bars over all the windows. And it is Sargon's house.

Late the next morning, they make love. Technically. *Don't blink*, Erica thinks.

"God, it's hot in here," Sargon says when it's done. He falls against the sheet, slick with sweat.

Erica has always gotten by fine with her arrangement of

fans. "It's the dead of summer." She stares at his broad, big body and swallows hard. *Oh, what is to be done with men? You feed them, listen to them, stroke them. Is it too much to ask for this one thing? To be well and truly fucked? Instead of this hard-won, half-staff finale?* Cravenly, she puts her arms around him.

Almost immediately, there's the sudden blare of hip-hop (that musical nail down the blackboard for her) and the slam of a car door, announcing that Mona has arrived after another night at Misty's. "Mom?" she shouts almost immediately.

So that's that, Erica thinks. Though it is perfectly fine for two grown-ups to make love in the daytime, it feels all wrong to her now.

"Stay here," she says. "Take a snooze? I'll go deal with her." She ties her kimono, hard.

Mona is sitting on her bed. She does not look good or, rather, looks worse than usual. "Mom, can we talk?"

"Of course. Here?"

"Down in the kitchen." Mona adds, "What about that, uh, Sargon?" with a false casualness that makes Erica want to throw her arms around her and beg her forgiveness.

"He's taking a nap," she says evenly.

Mona shrugs. "Cool," she says.

Erica makes coffee, and they sit at the little, round table where she always thinks of little Mona shaping Play-Doh, finger painting, doing her homework. Eating a thousand picky meals.

"I found a job, Mom! There's a job on Craigslist, a nanny job; it pays well, a free room and stuff. They checked my references from babysitting, and it's mine if I want it. It's in the city," she adds, slurping her milky coffee.

References? What references? "But . . . is that a good idea? The city is . . . you know . . ." *Full of drugs. Danger everywhere for a hot mess like you. Don't go. I won't let you go. I can't stop you from going. Oh God, she'll be so far from me.* She won't be able to handle *it, she'll get fired, she'll end up down on the Lower East Side with all the junkies. No, that was my era; the Lower East Side is gentrified now, OK, parts of Brooklyn, the Bronx. She could get attacked. And I can't stop her.*

"Mom, this is a good job. I need to earn my own money, and I love kids, and I need to feel, you know, better about myself. This is the perfect opportunity."

"There are no perfect opportunities," Erica feels compelled to state. "When?"

"Two weeks. The other nanny is leaving, so I'll get a week's training with her. You see? I've thought it all through, Mom. I learned a lot from the Miami job, you know. I can handle kids."

"Yes, but we . . . you need to know about the parents, make sure you have a contract."

"Mom, I'm gonna do this!" Mona pulls out her cell phone and goes outside to the patio. Erica sighs. Everything Mona thinks and does now fills her with fear. Mona in Manhattan, living with some random rich family.

She goes back upstairs where Sargon's backpack is in a corner. The bed is made, sort of. In one of those moments when Mona would call her "psycho," she considers going through the backpack, searching for clues. Clues about what? Instead she picks up little Dimmer, breathing into his clean fur. Why do cats always smell so fresh and dogs so funky?

She finds Sargon downstairs in her studio. He has turned around her easel, which she always keeps facing the wall when she's not working, and is looking at the drawing in progress.

"Hey," he says, turning around.

"Hey you."

"What happened to the dapper dude with the long hair?"

He swivels around and then turns back to the sketch of an

overweight, bald man in three-quarter profile, leaning back in a chair, cowboy boots resting on a table. Him.

"It isn't fair to judge something that's not finished yet." Reality is just the clay for an artist, and, anyway, she sees the figure through the eyes of infatuation, maybe even love. But, to him, it must be kind of a shock. Maybe cruel.

"I guess the young guy is drinking tequila on a beach down in Mexico. Long gone. Gone, get it?"

She moves to put her arms around him. He steps away.

"I'm going to eat this easel if I don't get some food in me," he says.

"Is that a threat?" Erica's laugh sounds false to her ears. But she's irritated. That Mommy-feed-me thing again. Of course, most men do that sometimes. John had. As if he was helpless to do anything about food except eat it. But he had paid for the groceries, and everything else, while Erica had quit her job and had time to paint.

Mona emerges again later, lured by the smell of chicken sautéing with onion and garlic and tomatoes and olives. Erica is scanning the newspaper. Sargon is lying on the couch with his laptop, cell phone, and coffee.

Erica boils fettucine and preps the salad.

Mona grabs a banana and a bag of chips and a bottle of water.

"But there's all this good food, almost ready."

"Maybe later. I'm going to hang with Hawthorne and Molly."

"*Hawthorne*? Is he OK? He was supposed to paint the living room, last I heard."

"He's fine, Mom. He got this job as a mechanic, so he's been super-busy."

"What about Molly?" Hawthorne's lovely girlfriend, another train wreck. "I wish you wouldn't hang out with her."

"She's Hawth's girlfriend! What am I supposed to do, tell

him he can't see his girlfriend? Can't you ever stop trying to control my life?" Mona hoists her old bag to her blade-thin shoulder and leaves. Of course, Erica thinks, they're going to do drugs together. Of course, Mona has to heave her guilt and shame and anger at her mother. Erica hears Hawthorne's old car rattling in the driveway and Mona's utterly different tone of voice.

Sargon finds Erica crying in the kitchen with the food all ready to go.

"I'm just so worried about her." She stirs the pasta, which glistens with oil and grated cheese, colored with the snips of parsley she grows in a pot outside. "Sick with it sometimes," she whispers.

Sargon fiddles with the coffeepot, milk, spoon. "It's just a tough age."

Erica realizes he has said this before, maybe several times. She shouldn't talk about Mona. It's a turnoff and it's not his problem. But, slumped at the table, she continues. "She's probably doing drugs this minute. Oh, well, screw it. I'm being a drama queen again. Anyway, she's got a job in the city. And that's all I'm going to say about her tonight, I promise."

"Don't apologize," he says.

They eat out on the patio, and it's delicious.

"And there's banana cream pie for dessert," Erica says. She made it herself the day before, the first one since John got really sick. John had loved fruit pies, tarts, apple cake.

"This is really fuckin' good."

"Want another piece?"

"Why not? It's great pie. You outdid yourself."

"Hardly." But she's smiling as she gets another, smaller piece, thinking he really should cut back a little on the caloric intake.

He eats it fast and sets down his fork. And, at the very moment when it is reasonable for her to expect a sigh of contentment or a little compliment again or maybe even a hug, he pushes the plate away and says heavily, "Look, I'm sorry. But I have to go. I can't fuckin' do this anymore."

The world around her changes instantly, like when she is dreaming. For that matter, as she has learned, it can happen when you are awake, too, though rarely. In, say, an accident. You are driving along, minding your own business, not texting or indulging in other distracted-driver behavior, then there's black ice on the road, and you hit it, and the brakes don't work, so you hit a tree; this has happened to her. Or some doctor, the tenth or twelfth specialist you've seen, tells you your husband's back pain is not back pain; it's terminal cancer. Or *now*. You meet a man you once knew after decades and, all at once, you feel young and frisky again together. But, really, you're on black ice, and—here it comes—you're going to hit another tree. There are many, many steps that lead to this transition, of course, but they're too complex and rapid for her brain to follow, especially now.

"Can't do what?" she says shrilly. His face has changed. It's closed over, like one of those metal grates that gets pulled down over a storefront. His eyes are oddly vacant, like one of those people who became pods in *Invasion of the Body Snatchers*, which was one of her favorite movies as a kid. "What?" she repeats, more loudly.

"This. This is the last time. I can't do this." Despite herself, Erica is intrigued in a ghastly sort of way by what is happening. Cushioned by good old adrenalin, she considers his remark. There seems to be an echo.

"*Last time for what? Pie?*" God, she is shrieking at him.

"You have . . . well, a lotta stuff to deal with, I get it. So, me? I'm gonna go back to the monastery."

"*What* monastery?" That word again. "Why do you keep using that word? What do you mean, *monastery*?" Shock makes you stupid, she knows this.

"My house. Where I live in solitary splendor—OK, more like squalor. So, I have to go now, Rica."

"This isn't happening," she tells him.

Sargon stands up like a sleepwalker.

Her neurotransmitters are firing away, trying to interpret this completely unforeseen eventuality, but there's a lag: Erica hears and understands only at a basic level what he has said, and repeated several times now. Swimming through the natural chemical soup, her brain seems to be shooting out flares. Maybe they're clues. "So it's Mona?"

"Well, your daughter does need you. Obviously it's a, uh, bad time for her. But, uh, it's not that. I can't do this. I have to go."

This time Erica does hear clearly. She follows him up the stairs, where he is scooping up a T-shirt in the bedroom, some socks, stuffing them into the backpack she had wanted to snoop in.

From the doorway of her room she says softly, almost whispering, "What is wrong with you? We go out, we laugh, we sleep together, we make plans. You just ate two pieces of my banana cream pie!" The blood seems to be draining from her head and racing toward her heart. She turns, goes back downstairs, out to the patio, and picks up the empty plates. She lets them fall with a crash on the flagstones, where they scatter into jigsaw puzzle pieces never to be solved.

Sargon says stonily from just inside the house, "Oh, the DVD."

She races in. "Oh, your fucked-up family? Please, do take that, too." She is clumsy and her throat is constricted. Though she wants to shout at him, hurl herself at him, she is icy now. Casho, scenting the fragrance of strife, looms, serious, at the edge of the room. "I am too healthy for this!" Erica says, gasping.

Silent, he heads for the door to the driveway. Erica and Casho follow him. It's about ten o'clock now, a blurry sky and still hot out. Sargon gets in his minivan. Erica approaches. She says, very quickly, "My husband and I were very, very close; we were best friends. My daughter is heartbroken and lost. When you and I met at the art show, I was so glad. I didn't have any expectations; those are gone for me now, and I didn't ask anything of you! Did I? *You* came *here*—you came!" Her arm whirls to smack him. He steps away.

"I'm going now."

"But . . . I might love you!" She is shocked by this, and it will keep her up for many nights. She doesn't know what she means by it. Does it matter? But, after some time, she'll realize she was speaking to someone from the past, the Sargon who had maybe existed when she was twenty-one. Someone else long gone.

"I might love you too," he says in a strangled voice and begins backing his van out of her driveway. Erica waits to feel something big, crushing, horrible. But she feels nothing as she watches the black car vanish over the hill. Casho approaches with his favorite, ancient squeaky toy in his jaws, on happy feet.

In the house, standing at the sink, she pours suds over the dishes she hasn't broken. Suddenly, she's dizzy. This morning, she had felt incandescent with desire for this man, despite her, well, misgivings. Hadn't she? Yes, she had. After she washes the dishes the old-fashioned way, eschewing the dishwasher in order to be doing something, she sends Sargon an e-mail. He'll find it when he arrives at his house—no, monastery—on the Cape at first light. And then he'll delete it.

She types, *Why did you eat the pie and then say you had to go?*

Because now it is his timing that plagues her as much as, maybe more than, the rejection itself. In novels and movies, and in her head, things usually move to some kind of resolution. It might be unsatisfactory—it is often conflicted or unclear—but people are owed an explanation, and they get something. Most of the time. And what kind of a person eats the food you have prepared for him, has a second helping of the pie you've baked, and then, just like that, dumps you? Aces you out. OK, he had said Mona "needed" her. No shit! But why such extreme withdrawal and *why then*? Erica feels weighed down by this unfathomable act, like she, too, has eaten too much pie, a whole pie. Lying in bed, she recognizes the heaviness: grief. Ah, it has been there all along, after all, just biding its time. Her Big, Fat, Funeral Heart.

THE BAD DREAM NOTEBOOK

Erica must perform surgery on a man with her heavy kitchen scissors, removing a lumpy growth on his side. She cuts into the mass, and a worm emerges. She is deeply disgusted.

Erica comes awake in the middle of the night, panting and sweating, almost sick with the afterlife from another bad dream. In the morning, she decides at last to make an appointment with a therapist. Anna Potsche has been recommended—several times—by a woman she knows in AA. Potsche sees her two days later at her office, a shoebox of a place located in a strip mall between a dollar store and a supermarket.

The dubious location of the therapist's office adds to the press of unease frosting Erica's anxiety. This is not the first time anxiety has driven a reluctant Erica into therapy. In her early sobriety, a profound disquiet, sizzling and hissing, had motivated her to fork over a good chunk of her paltry paycheck to another therapist, also called Anna—though she's forgotten her last name. Anna One, although she had a Park Avenue office, had given her a reduced fee. She was, in fact, a kind-hearted, Eastern European émigré, and it was this kindness that kept Erica going for a year and a half, despite Anna One's bookish, probably Freudian training (though Erica never asked about this, assuming it was off-limits.) What Erica remembers clearly from those sessions is the black couch upon which she always sat, never reclined, and Anna One's unusually small, dark eyes. Also, a remark, atypical for the carefully neutral Anna One. It was that Erica's mother had been "particularly unimaginative in her childrearing skills." This had caused Erica to feel fiercely protective of her mother and angry at the therapist. Later, she came to apprehend that she was swathed in guilt about her mother, who was never cruel but always withdrew at the first sign of upheaval. And there were many upheavals. Weeks or months after Anna One's critical remark, Erica noticed that her anxiety level had lowered to a simmer. Soon after, she quit therapy. Prozac had not yet been invented, and the current pharmacopoeia was still a gleam in Big Pharma's eye.

Anna Potsche's little office does not have a couch, which would take up too much room. Instead, there is a cozy arrangement of two comfortable chairs and a little table away from the desk, and that is where they meet, like friends having a chat, almost. Potsche is masculine-looking, energetic, full of personality, and immediately establishes that she, too, has been "in the program" for many years, which is reassuring, because it's a safe bet then that she's allergic to the bullshit drama that alcoholics and other addicts seem drawn to, perhaps inexorably, due to a propensity among people recovering from substance abuse for too much self-regard coupled with a strong critical sense. Also, long-term sobriety in a shrink is good, Erica thinks, as it's usually accompanied by a highly-tuned sense of the absurd. And, Erica learns, Anna is a clinician at Wings of Hope, so she'll probably know about Mona.

All these things turn out to be true.

After the get-acquainted questions, which take up most of the session—John and then Mona and a quick sketch of the Sargon fling—Erica confesses that she's been putting "this" off for some time and has had to drag herself to come. Anna cuts to the chase. "So what's your biggest concern right now?"

Without hesitation, Erica says, "Dealing with what a fuckup I am. No, seriously, I know my assets. But all I can think of is how I've failed my daughter, Mona. As a mother. Well, that's redundant. Also, sometimes, I seriously question my . . . well, stability. Being unstable was a big concern when I was drinking and for a while afterwards."

"We'll get to the mother thing, but first I want to know more about this stability concern. Are you afraid you'll pick up?"

"No. Not that." Erica shifts. Sighs. "It's hard to put into words . . . I have these terrible dreams, for one thing."

"Well, why wouldn't you? You just told me you lost your husband to a difficult, lingering death. At the same time, you've had to deal with a daughter whose drug use has gotten really serious. Don't you think you'd be unstable if you *didn't* feel unstable?"

"I suppose you're right."

"OK. Look, these old overworked sayings . . . like 'feelings are not facts,' well, you and I both know that they're true. You and I are both alcoholics with a great track record, but crises *always* stir things up, no matter how much time you have."

Erica squeezes her eyes shut. "Crises," she mutters. "That hardly describes the hell I've been in. But here's the thing," she goes on more loudly. "I mentioned I had a brief . . . what? I don't even know what to call it. Affair? Series of trysts? I don't know what it was. With my old college boyfriend. Who is, by the way, also an alcoholic, and let's throw in cocaine. OK, he's not a newbie, he's been in recovery a while. So he planned for us to meet again after decades at this art show I was in, and I became like this . . . puppy, whining and yapping for affection. One year after John died! Only one year! If I had gone on some internet dating site and posted, 'Recent crazed widow wants highly unstable and fucked-up older man,' that's one thing. On the other hand, he was magnetic. And he made me laugh. And I actually thought about the future without being totally depressed . . . And then, with absolutely no warning whatsoever, he says he can't do this anymore. *This*? Immediately after he had polished off two pieces of the pie I baked for him with my own hands."

To her embarrassment, Erica begins to cry. Anna Potsche hands her a tissue. "Maybe you needed a distraction," she says gently.

Erica sits up, wiping her nose, on high alert. "A distraction?"

"Yeah, you know, a man in your life. Someone to have fun with."

"But he just flipped out on me! I absolutely did not see that one coming. And I haven't heard anything from him since!"

"That might be a good reason to be grateful he left when he did."

"Well, I'm not grateful. Fuck grateful. Sorry." Erica rolls her soggy tissue into a tight ball. "*And* I betrayed my husband and neglected my daughter."

"How? Because you have needs too? That makes you a bad person? Erica, you're a woman who has gone through and is still going through the highest level of stress. You responded to this guy. He ran away. What did you do wrong?"

"Then . . . you're the therapist—why do I feel that I betrayed them?"

"I'm not a therapist, remember? I told you on the phone, I'm a social worker and alcohol and addiction counselor. Does that matter to you? We need to clear this up right away."

"No, it doesn't matter to me. It's all the same pot."

Anna Potsche laughs briefly. "OK. Now, back to you. You understand, Erica, that letting go is a messy business. And grief? It takes hold of people in all kinds of ways. Be gentle with yourself."

"That's what my friend—sponsor—Ronnie always says."

"Great minds . . ."

They decide they'll see each other once a week, for starters.

Fall, leaves turning, crisp apples, and shorter hours of daylight always say *school* to Erica and so, this late September, she finds it easy to think of her sessions with Anna Potsche as a class. Like a senior seminar. And she finds it easy to talk to her, although Anna, doing her job, of course, has a way of steering her toward topics she would like to postpone or skip. As when Anna says, in their third or fourth session, "Tell me about you and your husband."

Erica realizes she hasn't talked about John or their marriage for months. It's not that she's avoided doing so; the subject just doesn't come up unless she brings it up, and people, even close friends and family, don't go near it anymore. Maybe they've been waiting for her to do so, while she doesn't want to be a bore. Anyway, yes, she does want to talk about him. But where to start?

"Everything was pitched high between us from the start to the finish," she plunges in. "Sex, of course. For a while. But we also . . . well, drew off each other's energy, mentally, artistically. He pushed me in ways that were good for me. With my work, with people. And, especially at first but even after years together, we'd have these long, heated conversations on the phone, on the street, in bed. And we could really piss each other off. He could be impossible, and I behaved badly at times. I knew I was testing him.

"Once, I got so frustrated I threw a container of Chinese takeout at him in his kitchen. This goopy stuff was running down the wall, into the burners on the stove. He stormed out of the apartment, and I cleaned it up, and I remember thinking, *Just go, this is not for you.* Because I would feel so conflicted. It wasn't this mad, wild love affair for me. I'd had those, and I didn't want them. OK, I wanted them, but I didn't want to pay the price again. John was this great, edgy man plunked down before me, and I had to accept him. Does this make sense? John was the best thing that ever happened to me, man-wise, but I wasn't used to someone like him. What? Oh, solid, trustworthy, stable. Intense and completely sane. I knew I could survive on my own; I was painting again by then and had been sober for a while, seven years—eight? I'd been in some minor shows around the city, nothing too important, but still. And I was teaching studio classes at a community college, which paid the rent.

"John had been with a girlfriend for years, but that had ended before we met. He was really a confirmed bachelor, I mean, he had lovers but he always kept his own place and when we met, he fell for me, hard. And the strange thing was, after a year or so, I was the one who decided either we get married or split up. John, I think, would have let things go on, the two apartments . . . But I was sick of that kind of life. I wasn't really thinking about having children, I have to say. But I was sick of some guy moving his stuff into my place, then moving it out or me schlepping it to his . . . I think, I *think* we were both surprised that we got married. And then we became each other's best friend.

"We were married a few years when I got pregnant. And, of course, then everything changed. I remember we had this huge, like, seminal fight when she was about four or five. And I remember how it started. I was complaining about how badly I had drawn something—hands, that was it. I used to complain about my technical inadequacies as an artist sometimes, but I was just venting. Well, this time he jumped on it: why didn't I do something about it, take a life-drawing class or two, for example? See,

John was extremely knowledgeable about art, which was how we'd originally met. He was an art director at this magazine, and he loved art, of course, but he wasn't an artist. For him, it was about the technique. Me, well, it's never been about that. I remember I just started weeping with frustration. Here I was taking care of a young child and a house, working as an adjunct at the college, which means not just teaching but evaluating projects and having office hours and lesson plans. And then trying to get an hour or two in in the studio. And John was going off to the city every day, being with interesting, stimulating people and getting home about the time Mona was ready to go to bed. I was full of resentment. Because motherhood did swamp me; it could be crushingly boring and it sucked up all my available energy. I felt like I couldn't do anything well."

"Ah," says Anna.

"I completely overreacted. I said . . . things. Mona came down from her room in her little pajamas while I was yelling and, God, was I ashamed. Then John said I was being impossible and went into his office, slamming the door. Leaving me to deal with Mona.

"What did I do? Well, I made us some cocoa, and I explained to her how sometimes she and her then best friend Emily would get mad at each other, but then they would make up and be best friends again, and that grown-ups could do that, too. It wasn't very nice, but Daddy and I were best friends and loved her more than anything, and I took her upstairs and started reading a story. And John came in and finished the story."

"And how is that not doing motherhood well?"

"I didn't want to. I wanted to go to my studio."

"But you stayed with her. God, Erica, you are hard on yourself."

"I thought it was a rule that therapists remain detached and not judge their patients."

"First of all, I'm a social worker with lots of training in family counseling and addiction. My style is practical. Nor am I into judging you. *You* are. Now don't get mad. We all do this to some extent. Let's get back to you and John."

"We didn't make up right away. But, on the weekend, we went on a long walk, and then he helped make dinner. It wasn't . . . it wasn't perfect between us, you know? And sometimes he bored me or I bored him. But that was the last big fight we had. We just didn't do it at that pitch anymore, like we both agreed where the line was and didn't cross it. And we made it through, somehow. We made it through."

Anna hands her the box of tissues.

The never-to-be-completed drawing of Sargon is parked in a drawer with the detritus of years of other half-finished, half-hearted, or half-baked projects. While buying the usual household supplies at a box store, Erica ends up in the aisle that sells art stuff for kids. With no plan in mind, she feels the urge to buy fat boxes of crayons, markers, and colored pencils and a sketchbook. In the studio, she turns the pages slowly, as if their crackling purity will give her inspiration. How many times has she sat with a blank canvas or sketchbook, waiting for ideas to uncurl, flower—or wither? The excitement and dread of the chase. It is time for something new.

The Guatemalans had been a turning point in more ways than one. Some of the new art supplies are for the children of those immigrants from that beautiful, ravaged country. She'd been approached about teaching an art class for these kids at the community center—a volunteer job—and immediately agreed. She's still somewhat fluent in Spanish, thanks to her hippie wanderings in Mexico (when she was not much older than Mona). Ever since the plain vanilla man had proclaimed her financial freedom, Erica's felt a gnawing need to give something back.

She strokes a sleek, blank page of the sketchbook. After all this time, Erica has learned to be more patient, to wait for the synapses to move, the signs to come. When she was younger, it could be torment to sit before a blank canvas, and it is still uncomfortable, like an itch; but now she knows that something will eventually materialize. And, at this point in her life, it's less about seeing, more about feeling. Because her sight is smudged by grief and trauma, it's worked on her like the myopia she was diagnosed with as a kid. She'd thought, until she got glasses, that the world was blurry by nature, and it had been shocking, almost unwelcome, to view sharp corners and defined expressions. There is now a similar kind of frail, myopic insubstantiality on the screen of her inner sight, her artist's eye.

Then it comes, like a faint rumbling, the inchoate sense and the flicker of an idea, shuttling between the place where dreamscapes are bred and the new territory of light and color and shape. In the trance that seduces the embryonic idea, Erica gathers her bits—literally, scraps. Fabric scraps, clippings from old newspapers and magazines, bits of glitter and ribbon, stalwart instruments, paint and brushes and pens and markers. All for the bubbling muck of her mad, mad dream world, which she's been keeping a casual log of in that sketchbook: *The Bad Dream Notebook*.

Leafing through it, she stops at the dream she described to Sargon on their last night together: the dinner table, the gold-rimmed plate with its pair of scarlet lips garnished with parsley. The translation to canvas comes so easily that Erica feels like she's cheating. In oils, of course, the heavy folds and thick light of a four hundred-year-old Dutch still life spiked with the hallucinogenic content of, say, a Salvador Dalí. For a few hours, she is sealed from her unhappiness, from Mona, rejection, and the incomparably indigestible subject of death. It can't last—of course, she knows that—but seize this high she does.

Every day, she creates her dreamscapes, often cheating in the process: certain memories are cast for her like dreams, so she uses them (although she draws the line at using other people's material). She sketches a remembered semicircle of little children, sitting at the feet of a fat teacher in a fifties print dress who is holding a large picture book on her lap: *Storytime*, it's called. But it isn't a placid, pleasant childhood scene: the five-year-olds are at exact eye level with the spread of Teacher's thick-stockinged legs in black, sensible shoes.

Working on *Storytime,* the bright edges of the classroom surrounding the dark view up Teacher's skirt, Erica decides to put some music on her little CD player. She wants something mellow but with a tough heart. Miles Davis and his quintet are perfect for doing battle with this collage of innocence stripped away.

"What's that noise?" Mona announces herself in the studio. "It's like a sick elephant trumpeting." The nanny job in Manhattan had lasted for about a month. According to Mona, it turned out to be pretty close to around-the-clock, just like the other nanny job—a clear violation of her contract—and one day Mona just packed her bags and took the train home to Mom. But she seems to be doing better. She is taking a couple of art classes and doesn't disappear for days on end. It's something.

"Mona! You know you're supposed to knock first!" This is the first and most important of Erica's few rules—to maintain an inviolate space.

"But that shrieking woke me up. I thought there was a herd of elephants in here."

"That's Miles Davis!"

Erica turns her back.

Storytime hasn't liked this interruption, but she flirts with it, teases it, cajoles it. In the following weeks, months, the project pulls her in, the feel of a washed or layered page, the coaxed images, the rise and fall of tension in her neck and shoulders. *The Bad Dream Notebook* satisfies some unmet need that uncoils and sighs within her as Erica inhales the wax of a crayon, snips images and words, rolls them into place, pats them carefully down, swirls oils. She becomes aware that she is not locked into time, is not trapped like the characters in these bad dreams. She is moving again; she is bringing the night terrors to heel.

Most of the time she's in the studio; Casho lies nearby until the smells and maybe the oddness of what she's doing push him outside to reassuring markers: grass, sky, scent of creatures. At night, he climbs the stairs to accompany her as she sleeps (sometimes adding to the material for *The Bad Dream Notebook*). She knows she talks in her sleep and yells—John had complained about it—and drools and snores. Once, she wakes up from some upsetting dream that vanishes instantly to find Casho staring at her rather sternly. Is it possible, Erica wonders, that the dog thinks she's crazy?

"Believe it or not, I seem to be quite productive these days."

"Oh, *I* believe it. What's important is that you believe it," says Anna Potsche.

Erica shakes her head. "Sometimes, I'm excited with this project. But then I'll think it's childish. Insignificant. But, yes, I am working. Right now, it's a painting of a dream I just had. I'm in a foreign country with, of all people, my friend Ginger's sister, who died recently. Brain cancer."

"Want to talk about it?"

"Yeah. The thing is, Kate, the sister who died, was one of us—a drunk. But a high-functioning drunk, plus she smoked a lot. Had a glam job and a glam, fucked-up husband. My friend Ginger blocks all of it out, of course. At least, she never talks about it."

"Too bad."

"Yes. It is. So, the dream. Kate suddenly announces she's leaving this gloomy resort. She grabs *my* suitcase and starts running down the street. And I go into a panic. That's the second dream about a suitcase I've had since John died. Well, the symbolism is so obvious; sometimes, I think my subconscious is a little stunted. And Kate had cancer; John had cancer. But, anyway, I chase after her. And I almost reach her. But, of course, then I wake up."

"How are you painting this dream?" Anna never asks stuff like, *What do you think it means?* But she is interested in how artists work.

"Charcoal and colored pencils. A noir street at night, some sickly, yellow streetlights. Nobody's around. Grays and purples, yellow-greens, and I'm really fixated on getting the streetlights right—lurid-fluorescent, but not bright. Kate—in profile, of course—very tall and pointed, with my suitcase dangling from her long arm. I'm a bundled-up figure. I haven't figured out anything else, really, except I'm wearing lime-green Adidas."

Anna smiles, pauses. "The fact that you keep working . . . it's wonderful."

"I suppose so," Erica says, dubiously.

But, at their next session, when Erica starts talking about *The Bad Dream Notebook*, Anna stops her. "It's wonderful you're painting. Vital, really. But we probably need to talk about the other stuff in your life recently. For instance, how's Mona doing?"

Mona . . . "Oh, right, stop babbling about your silly art projects, Erica. Let's throw some cold water on your face. You can't expect to feel good, can you, when your whole life is a bad dream." Is this really what she's saying? Yes. Hear the buzz saw of self-pity whining away? That's her, Erica. But screw reason and manners. "Mona Grey, drug addict! That's my girl. Mona Grey, thief, liar, unemployed—unemployable—dropout, skin-and-bones nightmare of a daughter. Who I produced. My fault. My misery. My little girl. 'How's Mona doing?' Do I ever know? I think she's shooting up again, with horrible people. Should I say it? *Other* horrible people. And *nothing helps*. She gets jobs, loses them or quits, starts classes, drops out, seems healthier, gets back on drugs again. It feels like I'm walking over hot coals barefoot, and you know what? All the Twelve Step programs in the world don't really help. The last time I went to AA, this woman I know was freaking out because her old dog had died. I used to like this woman. But she said he was a member of the family, and I hated her. I wanted to slap her. Hard. Because *how dare she*? She doesn't know what pain is—*losing a dog*? And I love dogs. She doesn't know." Now the shame and relief of tears.

"I am so sorry you're in such pain. You know I have to ask this again: are you thinking of picking up?"

"What? No! I might as well slash my wrists as go back to booze. But my life is a nightmare. And please, Anna, don't remind me about gratitude! It's incredible to me that I can brush my teeth right now, let alone do art. Reasonably good art! But, basically, I'm on maintenance anxiety attack mode all the time. Will she get stabbed or shot in some drug den? Or overdose. She could OD anytime. Over a hundred people do every day in this country. I can't believe anything she tells me anymore. She could be OK; she could not be. Like last weekend, this guy on a loud motorcycle showed up in the driveway Saturday night. I was in my robe and slippers. I heard the bike, looked out my bedroom window, and there's Mona, handing him some cash as he gives her this little package! A drug deal! At my house! Then I'm running outside, screaming that I'll call the cops on him, and he roars away. Meanwhile, Mona's screaming that he's her friend, he just needed to borrow some money. While she's standing there, stuffing this baggie down her pants, and I'm lunging at her trying to get it. Even then she lies!"

Erica gulps. "The next day, I decide I have to find somewhere where I can just sit and be safe. You know? Shreds of sanity are still there. So, I decide to go to church, and I want to look presentable, like something other than my Raggedy Ann self. I open my jewelry box to get some earrings, and I notice John's wedding ring is not where I keep it. I turn the box inside out; I look everywhere. It's not there and I *know*: she stole it. But it's my fault because I didn't lock it up. And she'll never admit it. I have to lock everything up. I never, ever thought I'd have to live like this. But she'll do anything for drugs. Lie, steal, commit felonies."

Anna says slowly and emphatically, "But you know, Erica, that this is what addiction does to people. It takes everything from us, sooner or later. You know this. You know it's her addiction doing this. It's not her. And although I am so sorry you have to go through this, I am glad you're talking about it. It's such a burden for you. Let people help you."

Patient Anna, wise Anna, prepping her for some new jump off the cliff. When she will tell Mona, "No more!" and, this time, mean it? Erica knows this.

She says, "I don't know what to do anymore. But I can't kick her out. I just can't."

"OK," Anna says. "Then don't. Not yet," she adds.

A SEVERED HEART

Erica's in her red and white swim team suit, pulling and kicking as hard as she can in the hundred-meter freestyle race. But she keeps slowing down until she can barely move. Suddenly, she realizes she's not in the water but on land. She is hauling herself over bare earth. Yet she has to keep swimming.

Erica calls the manager of her bank in a panic as soon as she gets her current statement. It takes five transferred calls, the usual torture of being trapped by tinny, holding music, and an exact and extracted repetition of her pieces of identity and concerns for each new bank employee, until it's agreed that a hacker has made the ATM withdrawals that have drained her account. She'll need to destroy her card and wait for a new one.

Except that she knows it wasn't a hacker. Well, technically it is. Her own child. She tells herself she should be used to this. She tells herself it could be worse. She won't be wiped out because of a loss of hundreds of dollars, as some people most definitely are. She still has nice things—things that are hard to pawn—and, glancing out the window, a garden currently showing off. Which makes her remember the Al-Anon meeting where a woman had choked out the most amazing story of waking up one morning and not having a rose garden anymore. At first, she had thought, deer? But deer don't dig holes and remove plants by their roots. It turned out that her addict son had dug up her beloved roses in the dark, with the help of an illegal immigrant, for a client's landscaping plan. "The most enterprising thing he'd done in years," commented the Al-Anon woman, clearly having worked it through. Well, was there anything they wouldn't do to get drugs? No. Erica cuts up her bank card, picturing her house naked of its furniture. Erica is always freshly surprised by how bad it feels to get ripped off again.

She calls Ronnie, who quit her job at the doctor's office to work on her greeting card business, so fortunately she can now talk during the day.

"What's wrong?" Ronnie says immediately.

"What else? Mona. I just found out she's been stealing from my checking account. I was down to five dollars. Thank God for the plain vanilla man at the bank."

Ronnie doesn't say anything. Erica begins to sweat. "OK, OK, I know what you're thinking. I should kick her out or turn her in." She pauses, and Ronnie remains silent. "I'm falling apart. I'm a mess. I think about her every moment. What if she's been assaulted or is lying dead somewhere from some bad shit? How did I get here? What did I do? I know it's not my fault; I know it's the drugs that do this to her. I can't turn her in. So what can I do?"

"Well, you already know what I think. That girl . . . Look, why don't you go somewhere, get away from this constant turmoil? Go to a beach and read paperbacks for a week. When you come back, you can decide what your next step is with her."

"Well, if I do that, she might sell the furniture while I'm gone; she might give away the friggin' house to some dealer and leave me homeless."

"Oh, then take her with you!" Even Ronnie's legendary patience has to have an end. "Yeah, it might be a good thing for the two of you. Being on neutral ground, away from the chaos. But Erica, I strongly suggest you first make her accountable for stealing the money!"

"I don't know," Erica says, "how you can stand listening to this crap from me over and over."

"Me either. But you're my best friend and I love you."

The deal they work out, she and Mona, would probably not get a stamp of approval from Al or Nar-Anon, but Erica has only so much fight left in her, while Mona is not yet twenty and is filled with the addict's demonic talent to oppose, block, thwart, and otherwise refuse to accept responsibility. So Erica gets the short end of the stick, but reasons it is something: Mona, in exchange for a trip to Cancún, would make reparations by thoroughly cleaning her room. Erica thinks that probably only another addict's mom would understand the significance of this. And the fact that Mona actually does it.

The cheap, off-season Cancún package she has bought includes a slightly seedy, pink-washed concrete high-rise. But their suite is large, with separate bedrooms, a television and a mini-fridge in each, and a balcony with an angled view of powder-blue ocean and several pools, from which kids' shrieks rise, though muted by the ocean. Even though it's October—hurricane season—they've lucked out, and no storms are predicted for the next week.

Mona lights up a Salem Light. "Awesome view."

"And reasonable," Erica adds. They're sitting on the sliver of deck, drinking Cokes, resting after the incredibly long wait to get through Mexican customs in the dank, un-air-conditioned airport. It was not the Mexico that Erica had lived in once she'd finished college. The rent for one week at this two- or three-star hotel would have paid for maybe three months of her expenses back in the day. Cancún then was just marshland on a beautiful coast. What hasn't changed—she's sure of this—is how easy it is to score just about any drug. She had certainly availed herself of that convenience, easily getting Quaaludes (long since banned for being ridiculously addictive) as well as pot, coke, uppers, and opiated hash. So, how long will it take Mona to score?

She feels compelled to give a probably useless mom lecture. "Mona . . . Mexico is not like the States about drugs. I mean, Americans caught with drugs here go to jail. The thing is, you do *not* want to be in a Mexican jail. They are filthy, for one thing."

"Mom." Mona sighs, hugely.

"Please just listen for once. When I lived in the Yucatan, there were a bunch of American kids your age—my age, then— locked up in the local *cárcel* for years. The ones who didn't have money to bribe the *Federales*. They didn't get enough food, any medical care—one guy supposedly had TB—nothing. Please, *please*, remember this."

Mona stands up and goes to the rail, where she stares down at the ocean, smoking. "But you used drugs when you lived here."

Erica joins her. The sight below is of indistinct but mostly unbeautiful bodies sprawled across the beach. "Yes, I did. The difference between us is I had no one to talk to, to give me good advice. And, actually, I almost got busted once. I had copped some weed in a park from a Mexican friend—Friend? What am I saying? A dealer—and it was in my purse. And two cops came. It was just luck that the guy I copped from was some well-connected politician's son, so they didn't hassle me. Mona! It was terrifying. I was very fearful and unhappy then. I thought the drugs helped. I made a big mistake and I paid for it." Suddenly, she wishes they'd gone to a city, somewhere exotic. Istanbul, Rio, Hong Kong. That would be a real diversion, as Anna would say. Although, maybe doing nothing but relax on a beach is better. And Mona? She is never sure anymore what Mona needs.

Erica, who packed haphazardly for this trip, has remembered to bring a sketchbook, drawing pencils, magazines, and a thick, hardcover book that she grabbed on the fly from John's study simply for its title: *A Severed Head*. Tough, grisly mysteries are her meat and drink these days.

Mona leaves the balcony. Soon, Erica hears the blare of the television in her room. She wants to suggest they go down to the beach or the pool together, but, as Mona would say, "like that's going to happen." Instead, Erica keeps staring at the beach below: David Hockney meets Lucien Freud. A surfeit of overweight, reddened, white people in beach chairs attended by small, brown people with their trays of drinks and snacks. Should she do a sketch of this? No! She doesn't want to give a shit about anything this week. Let Mona spend all her time in her room watching TV, then probably venture out, despite her warnings, to find a drug buddy, of whom there are surely many on the beach. Why should she, Erica, always have to care so much? Very bad mom, that's her goal for the week. The white flag is up. The battle will resume after this beach vacation.

Among the items Erica threw in her suitcase is an old bathing suit whose tired fabric puckers around her like a deflated balloon. She puts it on, adds flip-flops, picks up her straw bag stuffed with the book, shades, and sunblock, gets her room key and is ready to descend and become one of the Hockney–Freudians. A last glance at the balcony. There! Isn't that Mona? There, at the very edge of the sea, is a bikinied Mona talking to a skinny, dark-haired guy. But the girl turns, and it's not her daughter. Perhaps this girl has a mother staring at the ocean, too, motionless. Worrying about her daughter.

Erica doesn't leave the room. She flops down on her huge bed in her swimsuit and eats a handy granola bar and some dried apricots she's brought along, and then she falls asleep.

Twelve hours later, she wakes up, ready now to do nothing more than flop into a lounger by the pool after breakfast. Mona's door is locked. With luck, she is asleep in her lair. Erica has a muffin and coffee at the beachside café, then heads for the pool, where she props *A Severed Head* before her like a shield, not that anyone is likely to notice one more middle-aged woman in a saggy one-piece. Later, she wades in the bathtub-warm ocean, remembering that *this was the very week* she had been invited to come to Sargon's house on Cape Cod, an offer he made during their first night together. With Mona! "You and your daughter come up to the monastery. The Cape is crawling with tourists in the summer but it's beautiful in October."

That word again! He'd laughed when he said *the monastery*, and she'd teased him. "What kind of monk are you?" Why hadn't she picked up on this blatant clue? Why had she immediately buried it? He'd snapped their infant affair in two like the stem of a flower. And almost two months have gone by since then. Can it be that she is just a tiny bit relieved he had run off into the night? She draws letters in the sand with a big toe: FUCK YOU. It is immediately washed away to CK and then nothing.

Almost in spite of herself, Erica feels good as she wanders along the beach, this meeting place of primal energies constantly recycled, flushed in and out. She ambles past adorable children, busy with sandcastles, dripping ice cream cones, splashing in the waves. She lets the quotidian world blur and sag, go out of focus, as she remembers baby Mona's fat tubes of legs running along another beach to her dad on his hands and knees, shaping sand stuck with shells, a feather, pebbles. It had really happened, hadn't it? The games with balls, the pony rides, water parks, birthday parties. There are photo albums to attest to it from that predigital age. Erica had inserted the snapshots into those corner brackets and written little explanations: Maine (5), St. John's (7 and 8) Mexico (10). But the memories don't stick now; they melt away like ice cream on this hot beach. Other toddlers are real now. She feels the burn of the sun and heads for the beach umbrella where she'd left *Severed,* certain that no one would swipe a book with that name, which is turning out to be not a murder mystery but just as grisly.

Mona, to her surprise, consents to have dinner together that night in the resort dining room. It is the wrong choice, Erica realizes when they arrive; it is a formal and empty room, an archipelago of white tablecloths. And seemingly no waiters; at least, none in sight. Yup, they should have gone to the noisy, poolside grill. Yet she's hoping that she and Mona can sit across a table from each other and have a real conversation. Just this once. Mona wears a wrinkled but clean loose, long top, ripped jeans, and a photoshoot level of makeup, while Erica is in a cotton tunic and serviceable, white pants, her hair curled by the sea air, a widening splash of silver at her temples now. She's pulled it back into a clip.

Eventually, they are handed menus, the thick parchment scrolls that mean high prices, and are served iced tea by a solemn, Mayan-featured waiter who then disappears again. Erica sips, biding her time. Maybe Mona will actually tell her what's going on. Maybe it's too much to ask. But Erica waits for the smallest sign.

They order the fish tacos, which come with their sides of sour cream and radish swirls and guacamole. Mona remains a closed book to her, wan and sullen, but at least she's here.

Erica finishes her tacos, which are quite delicious, and leans her elbows on the table. "So, Mona—"

Mona easily parries the fraught, impending speech. "Mom! I heard about this mall in town. Can we go shopping there tomorrow?"

"But we're in Mexico. The Mayan Riviera. What about the pyramids? Tulum is just up the coast."

"This girl I met on the beach says they have good stuff supercheap at the mall. And I really need some decent clothes."

That part is true. "Well," Erica says, "If we do that tomorrow, let's go to the ruins the next day. Deal?"

Mona orders ice cream and, for a moment, Erica is back in the toddler past again, when ice cream could end tears and a sandcastle could absorb an afternoon. She turns away, blinking.

"Mom."

"What, Mona?" Erica looks at her with hopeless longing. Not for the first time, she wonders how she and John produced this Mediterranean beauty. Who does have her mother's addiction-prone genes, however.

"Did you ever hear from that Sargon again?"

"Whatever made you think of that? Him? No. I haven't. And I don't think I want to."

"What a weird name: Sargon."

"I told you, it's Arabic for king."

"*Right*. King of bullshit. Umm . . . those *cowboy* boots he wore? And that weird movie he made smashing up his house? *And* he rolled his eyes around a lot when he talked. Very weird, Mom."

Erica sips her coffee. "I suppose so," she says. Ronnie's theory was that Sargon is gay: on the down low, as she had put it. Oh, *whatever!*

And, then, Erica bends over the table, tears leaking. "I'm terrified, Mona."

"Mom! Mom! Don't, Mom! The waiter's coming with the check. You're so embarrassing." She throws out her arms in exasperation, and her loose sleeves balloon away.

"It isn't always about you," Erica says. She wipes her eyes with the side of her hand.

"It's embarrassing to be with your mother who's crying in public."

"Well, then, why don't you stop breaking my heart?" This is irrational: addicts don't have a choice about using. Until they do. And that's all she wants. Erica pushes back her chair. "I'm going to the room. Just give the waiter the number for the bill."

"Mom!"

But Erica is in full weeping mode now; she has seen the cluster of ugly track marks inside her daughter's arms, when her sleeves fell back. Erica flees the dead space of the restaurant and stumbles, like the drunk she once was. What would Mona do if I went and got good and truly wasted at the Tulum Bar? On rum, I think. She had liked her Cuban rum, back in the day. And they would have some here. Or perhaps brandy. And maybe a joint. She won't, of course; it's insane. She's an addictive type, too. Pain gurgles through her joints at the thought of Mona's little fox face at the table, her thin chest, her pock-marked arms.

Once and only once in her entire life, several years ago when Mona had been invisibly morphing into a sullen, defiant teen-ager, Erica had slapped her. A brisk clap on the cheek, of medium sharpness. It had stopped the snarling. Then Erica's millisecond of pleasure at shutting her up had plunged into self-loathing. Her own mother had never laid a hand on her. In that era, it was, "Wait 'til your father gets home." (The anticipation of punishment over an endless afternoon was far worse than the few, fumbling attempts her father made to exert discipline.) Erica had never allowed herself to get to that state again with Mona.

But seeing the track marks that Mona kept hidden from her so well with long sleeves or makeup, Erica has come very close to slapping Mona again, right there in the restaurant. To make her see what she is doing to herself. Nothing else has worked. Shuffling toward her suite, she doubles over for a moment—people going laughingly past her must think she's had too much to drink, what an irony—remembering Sargon, how joyfully she had shut the door of her bedroom to be with him. But was that the reason she'd been so happy, so light? Or was it because Mona—but not John, not yet—ceased to exist in those moments? She'd pushed her worries about her daughter away. She'd actually told him Mona was fine, just pulling the teenager bit. Was it because Erica didn't want to deflect any attention from herself?

In the suite with the king-size bed that mocks her aloneness, Erica can find nothing with which to distract herself. Nothing except CNN and Spanish soaps on television. She picks up her book and listlessly leafs through it, tired of the endless number of betrayals and affairs in *Severed;* they only serve to remind her of Sargon. But he's already a grey ghost. It's John she misses.

She drops the book and falls back on the bed and lets the pain of loss wash through her. She realizes that she's lying on the left side of the bed. And for twenty-odd years, that was John's side. A silly, widow thing? But it feels wrong to be here. Invasive. As it had felt invasive when Sargon, who of course had no idea, had claimed her side and she'd been forced to take over John's territory, being unable—unwilling?—to ask Sargon to switch sides. John would have disliked Sargon; she'd known this the moment they set eyes on each other in the art center. John had a gift for friendship but also had a terrific, built-in shit-detector. When they went out, Erica always knew when they met someone if he or she was for real by watching John. If he stayed focused, the person was genuine, worthy. If he became distant, he or she was a phony. If he was served a stupid or rude remark, John fearlessly lobbed it back across the net; she'd seen him do this to the president of his company, widely regarded as an ass, at a company picnic. He had a temper. And he would have marked Sargon as a grandstander, a bullshitter, a user. Above all, he would have been furious at the way Erica had been treated.

Erica has a satisfying mental picture of John shoving Sargon hard in the chest.

Mona comes into the suite and gets a cold drink out of the mini-fridge.

"Look, can we talk?" Erica asks, sitting up, remorseful like clockwork.

"Oh God, all you do is lecture me."

"Well, I want to apologize. For leaving the restaurant so abruptly. I know this is a bad time for both of us."

Mona shrugs. "*Mom*," she says. "No biggie. I get that you're lonely. You liked that Arab dude and . . . you had a really tough time with Dad." She adds, "But you're not exactly ready for a relationship."

"Some speech. I'm just so tired of worrying about you, Mona."

Mona's head drops. She puts an arm around her mother and lays her head on her shoulder briefly. "Well, I love you, Mom."

"I know. I love you, too." Getting a glimpse of the old Mona is always a crusher. A reminder there is hope, that cruel, necessary survival tool. Then, the next shock comes, will come—the sick, mean Mona will be back.

The next day, they take a cab to the shopping mall where Mona buys a bikini and a sundress and Erica an embroidered caftan she will probably never wear. Back at the resort, Erica sits by the pool with *Severed*, wherein a dizzying number of affairs that turn betrayers into victims and vice-versa have piled up to the point that she can't keep track of them. Head lolling, heat-drugged, she falls into a doze, the book slipping to the concrete, dampened, as she wonders, half-dreaming, if she is both victim and betrayer like the characters in the novel. *Maybe yes? Well, OK, yes, I am*, she thinks, and dreams that a hurricane is racing toward the beach—toward her—coloring the powder-blue sea pewter.

The sense of danger wakes her—these endless ominous dreams, this breathing in short spurts as if she were in a marathon. Under her straw hat and large sunglasses, Erica is glad to be invisible, hidden in a chaise, or behind goggles doing languid laps in the pool nearby. *A Severed Head* keeps her going again until sunset's requisite flare of strawberry blonde streaked with orange over the lowering ocean. At last, shaky with hunger, Erica goes to the room, takes a shower, and orders in a chicken Caesar salad. She falls asleep immediately after she eats it. The white curtains remain open on the square of sky and from the windows drift the sounds of families, in the pool, at the grill, adults intermittently loud with boozy laughter. If she dreams that night, she remembers nothing.

In the morning, Mona walks into her mother's room. "Can we go down and have breakfast? I'm starving."

At the umbrella-covered table on what is not going to be a beautiful sunny day, Mona wolfs down waffles, and Erica picks at scrambled eggs.

"Mom! Are you still pissed off at me or something? You just sit there."

Erica munches toast, considering. "No. What I'm feeling is fear, Mona. Like I have no idea where you were last night, and so I have to think the worst. That's the way it is now. I'm frightened for you all the time. But you know all this. Plus, I'm missing Dad, I think."

Mona latches onto this safer topic. "Me too." She pours maple syrup on a waffle, gaining the seconds her brain needs to go into its creative state. Lying is like bungee jumping, doing comedy improv, sketching pages of the "Project." It brings its own kind of high, a minor glow (then the crash), but a glow nevertheless, and Mona is ranked by her peers at the top of this particular class, helped by slightly chubby cheeks, slightly snub nose, and liquid, brown eyes. *Don't pile on too much detail: you may need to remember. Don't get sloppy, and do not underestimate your audience. Who could be, was, a guy you'd blown off, a dealer you owed, the cops if you were driving a little carelessly, Misty occasionally, and boy did they fight those times, but usually it was Mom.* And no way would she impart to her what she had been doing yesterday. Not that it was anything special, but there was that Mexican *Federales* twist. Lying in the sand, gazing at the twinkly stars, laughing her ass off, on the shrooms those Mexican guys and girls had laid on her.

"Well, I'll give you my report," Mona said, thinking swiftly. "OK? And yeah, I'm missing Dad, too. Yesterday, what I did was walk the beach for hours and just thought about him, stuff we used to do. And how he used to get so mad. He'd blow up in restaurants when the food wasn't hot enough, remember? Or his martini wasn't the way he liked it, like they forgot the olive or some shit? And that time he yelled at that bus driver at the airport who wasn't helping with the bags, and everybody looked at Dad like he was crazy. I hated it when he yelled."

"Why on earth were you thinking about that stuff? He was usually very even-tempered."

"Because some kids were horsing around, and they knocked over this little kid's sandcastle, and the dad was shouting at them, and the little kid was crying."

"Well, he had very high standards, your dad. But especially for himself. He was hardest on himself."

"I know." Mona huddles over the table. "Remember when I told him he had to stop smoking his pipe or he'd get cancer? And he got really mad."

"Yes. He . . . was frustrated. He wanted to quit, but he couldn't."

"He wouldn't! And then he got cancer."

Oh, middle school, the hush before the storm, when kids get drummed into them the evils of smoking, booze, drugs, careless driving, and sometimes unprotected sex. Then, the next year, they can't wait to do those things. Mona and her Salem Lights!

"But then, coming back here, I started to remember all this stuff we did together. Remember, he taught me how to skate and cross country–ski?"

"And play tennis. And those duets you did on the piano."

"And read Sherlock Holmes when I was little."

"I used to have to tell him to stop reading; it was getting so late."

"Those old movies we watched. *The Postman Always Rings Twice. Rear Window. The Four Feathers.* And he would always fall asleep in the middle."

"He did? I didn't know that."

"Oh! And speaking of Sherlock, remember that cape he bought when we went to San Francisco, and he wore it out to dinner that night, and I pretended I didn't know him?"

"Well, it was chilly, and he hadn't brought along a coat."

"Not *that* chilly. He could be so goofy." Mona sniffs. "I miss him so much. Oh my God. I feel . . . I just really, really wish I could talk to him again."

On their last day at the beach, Ronnie calls while Erica is poolside, still wading through *Severed.* This is a very thick novel.

"I should have called *you*," Erica says, guiltily. "I've just been slothful. Yeah, a real vacation! Well, she's . . . We have had some conversations, yeah, but I don't know if I'll ever get the letting-go thing. I can't trust her, but at least we're talking. Oh, and we went shopping together. But also, I keep thinking about Sargon. Path–et–ic."

"It's not pathetic!" Ronnie says in the staunchly supportive way that makes her, at times, sound angry or highly indignant. "You

cared about him! And he walked away when you were very vulner-
able. A man that fearful of commitment . . . imagine how hard it
would be if you had kept on seeing him and then he did that."

"That's what Potsche says, too. She actually called him a
diversion. Ha! But Ronnie . . ." Erica lowers her voice to a con-
spiratorial whisper. "What I can't wrap my mind around is how he
could sit there, eating all that pie, then immediately announce he
had to leave. Forever!" she booms. "I keep deconstructing him, us,
but it's no good."

Suddenly, they are laughing. Every time one stops, the other
starts again.

"You couldn't make this shit up!" Erica pounds her fleshy
knees, gasping. Suddenly, Mona appears, in micro-shorts and a
bikini top. Fresh from a trip to the resort's hair salon, she now
sports highlights of platinum blonde. "Mom?" she says.

"Ronnie, just a minute. What?" Erica looks at Mona's head
and bursts into laughter again.

"Mom, what's *wrong* with you? You score some shrooms or
something?"

Erica doubles over helplessly, holding her stomach. "Shrooms!
I can't stop," she gasps. "Ronnie, can I call you back?"

Mona flops down in a beach chair with a copy of *People*,
available in the resort gift shop at twice the US price (Erica had
checked). "Mom," she says, though without the usual harshness,
"you need to stop acting like a teenager."

"Oh, and why is that? You think anybody here cares what I
act like?" She can't remember the last time she had a good laugh.
"Hey, want some ice cream?"

"It's like eleven o'clock in the morning," Mona says.

"So? Screw what time it is." Erica scrutinizes Mona's pouty
face topped by white hedgehog hair and starts laughing again.
Maybe she'll run down to the ocean and peel out of her suit, let

the water run over her body. She glances down at her old L. L. Bean suit. "Oh my God! I can't stop!" she wheezes.

"Mom! It's not *that* funny, whatever it is. Mom, you're drooling!"

And when was the last time she'd felt like she was the irresponsible kid and Mona the adult? Never, actually.

THE MODERN WIDOWS CLUB

Erica is onstage, ready to perform before a live audience. She's rigid with anxiety, and the crowd presses in from all sides. Her idea is to improvise like a jazz singer but she starts off-key and freezes. The crowd begins to boo. The scene shifts. She's outside the club, and the audience is gathered inside at picture windows, watching her. This time, Erica chooses an old-time, Bessie Smith blues number. The restive crowd at the windows grows quiet as she nails it, soaring and rumbling. At the rousing finale, Erica opens her arms wide, taking in the applause.

"You're in a mood." Anna Potsche looks a question at Erica, who is not saying much.

"I don't really want to be here today. No offense."

Anna, of course, is unruffled. "Why is that?"

Erica frowns at the display of tchotchkes ranged over her counselor's desk, these little, cheesy tokens of clients' gratitude. She feels distinctly ungrateful and doesn't want to talk about it. Even though it's her dime. *Oh, what the hell?*

"I'm sick of support groups," she begins.

Anna waits. She is so good at waiting.

"I was doing some cleaning the other day, because, no matter how much stuff I get rid of, there's always more stuff, and that's the thing about this country—do you know we throw out almost half the food we buy? Anyway, I was going through my desk, and I found this pamphlet I got somewhere, from this grief support group. The Modern Widows Club—MWC. Of course, everything's an acronym. I'm looking through it, and there's this little section on intimacy, as they call it. And, then, I just fall apart, yet again, because I know I'll never find a man like John again. *Don't be greedy, Erica*, I tell myself, but really—Sargon? What was I thinking? I wasn't thinking; that's the problem. I was lonely. I wanted to be held. I wanted to feel someone else's skin.

"I'm not making a lot of sense, I know. These days, I'm all over the place. I'm scared of life being a bore again, you know? Well, OK, of being alone. I'm almost done with *The Bad Dream* and working is the only thing . . . I mean, when I'm working, I'm OK with my life; I forget everything else. But then when it's coming to an end, a good run at the canvas, it starts again. Like I wake up and *Oh, right, here I am. By myself.* And then I can't imagine a new idea, a new piece of work, nothing; the future's just a blank, which I'm going to have to fill, somehow."

"Can you put a name to that particular fear? I think it would help."

"Why? Why would it help? We've been talking for a year, almost a year, and I'm just afraid. Terrified, sometimes."

"You've talked about it. You've also been understandably concerned about Mona. And that connects to everything else, the fear you've expressed."

"Well, because Mona is . . . Mona is most of the bad dream."

"Mona's illness," Anna says softly.

"Yes. No! It's her. She brings back all the pain of when I was her age, but it's much, much worse when it's your child. I talk about it constantly, and I am doing better with it, but, you see, there is no lasting relief. More than there was, but . . . the fear is so huge."

Anna nods. "Yet a few minutes ago, you began by telling me about this big positive thing in your life—your latest art project."

"All right, yes, I did! But you of all people should get this, that even though I can't wrap my head around these terms—modern widow, addict's mom—that's what I am at the end of most days."

"But not every day, Erica. You just said it, you're doing better. Now, when was the last time you just did something fun, not paint, not go to a support group meeting?"

"I went to Cancún for a week."

"Yeah. Last fall. With your addict. Well?"

"You sound like Ronnie, my sponsor. She's all over me to do good stuff just for myself. Treats, she calls them."

"I want to meet that woman someday. That's your assignment for this week. Treats. Fun."

"I think I can do that," Erica says. The room seems to be pulsing suddenly. She blurts out, "Maybe I am ready to do this— well, live, go on—on my own."

Anna Potsche nods her head. "And stop coming to see me, right? Just like that? You're OK with that?"

"Yeah, I think so." When Erica then manages to quell her sex's self-effacing and placating verbal disclaimers—"I'm sorry," "But only if you think so," "I feel your pain/need to make you feel better," and so on and so on—she thrills with possible empowerment.

"You can always check in, you know."

"Thanks. I will if I need to. And Anna . . . you've been a great help." She puts the final check on the tchotchke-covered desk and they hug goodbye.

Erica goes straight to the mall and buys a great-fitting pair of jeans and expensive face cream. She buys good chocolate at a chocolatier to eat before she goes to sleep. She makes a movie date with Ginger. And she lingers after her weekly AA meeting, instead of going right home, and has a conversation with a guy called Ben Sanders who she's seen around for years, but never paid much attention to, beyond clocking that he's reasonably good-looking, has a nice smile, and always says hello to her.

"Are you coming to the barbecue?" he asks.

"What barbecue?"

"My second annual anniversary blowout next Saturday. At six. I hope you will."

She hears herself say yes, she'd like to.

Ben Sanders has very nice, dark-blue eyes.

He likes to walk in the November woods and try new restaurants and hear live music and take in movies. He always brings her gifts: an orchid, a spice grinder, a T-shirt. A recently retired sound engineer, he loves to fix things unasked. He rewires the stereo system that hasn't worked for years, predating John's illness, and fixes the broken panel of a faux Tiffany lamp which has been sitting on the workbench in the garage even longer. Erica is happy, or mostly relieved, when they have sex: he's affectionate, enthusiastic, and uncomplicated. Their conversation is pleasant. She wishes she was more into him. It's unfair to compare him to John or even Sargon, but she does. She senses that Ben will never be edgy or thought-provoking. Maybe this is just what she needs right now. An uncomplicated, nice relationship. And meanwhile, Mona is simmering on the back burner again. She's a tad more responsible; her moods are less severe. These are the positives.

After dating for a couple of months, they're in a new, fashionably loud restaurant. They've finished their very good fish tacos. Ben pushes his coffee cup, leans across the table and takes her hands. "Let's get married."

"What?" Erica pulls away and grabs her cup for ballast. "I didn't hear you."

"LET'S GET MARRIED! You don't have to say anything now. Just think about it. We're really good together, Erica."

"Ben." She's suddenly aware of the pervasive smell of grease and fish, the blast of noise from all the voices. "We've known each other for like two months." She shakes her head. "I'm not—"

"Hey, no pressure," he says. He looks away. "Let's get out of here."

She starts making excuses when he calls and he's always fine about it, which makes her irritable.

"Sure, later this week then?"

"I'll call you," she says. She starts a new painting, slapping ruby red, aubergine, ebony on the canvas. Wound colors. She's got to end it with Ben and not in a cruel, Sargon way. She invites him for lunch.

"What did I do?" Ben says tightly, throwing down his croque monsieur. They are sitting on the patio under the umbrella and she just told him it isn't working out, it's not him. The dumb clichés that are all she can say. He slumps.

"Nothing!" Erica says. This is like being a teenager again, she thinks.

Ben lurches up, pushing back his chair. "So that's it." His voice drops and takes on an uncharacteristically bitter tone. "I can never catch a break. Women." He stomps off across the lawn. She hears his car start. Did Sargon feel this shitty when he dumped her? Erica kicks the patio table leg.

A few months later at her weekly AA meeting, Erica sees Ben holding some woman's hand and an unreasonable quick spike of jealousy rushes through her.

Fall is fast winding down and with it the uneasy ceasefire around Mona's addiction. Erica again finds drug evidence, a couple of tiny baggies with gray-white powder, stuffed in the back of a drawer in Mona's room. The years of dealing with Mona's troubles and addiction seem endless, although in fact they amount to about four. The frantic, dreadful phone calls to and from teachers, counselors, psychologists, policemen, bail bondsmen, lawyers, other parents. The many thousands of dollars spent on therapy and rehab, the unknown amount of money that Mona's ripped off from her. The places Erica has gone, searching for help: Al-Anon, Nar-Anon, Wings of Hope family group, Anna Potsche. And the long talks with Claire, Ginger, and, above all, Ronnie. Trying to stop the train wreck, trying to stay above water. And—what an American concept—trying to have fun! But it all comes down to this, every time: the drugs win. They have taken her daughter from her, and they are taking Erica down.

By nature, given her own troubled past, Erica feels sympathetic to the tumult and instant gratification of adolescence. Her own bewildered, often-sullen teen years remain forever vivid to her. But all her empathy, understanding, love, prayers, support, threats, warnings, punitive action, demands for change, have changed . . . nothing. She holds the tiny, lethal packages and crashes to her knees.

When she was little, Erica's siblings teased her, because she would bury her face in her hands during scary scenes on TV programs and at movies. "You're peeking!" they would yell, as she watched through her fingers, knowing she could shut out the image before her at any time. She could control it. Not now, not this scary movie. She is out of play, out of cards, out of ideas, and out of excuses.

She calls Ronnie, but this time it's not to rail against the fates. "Every time she's relapsed, I feel crazier." Erica thinks of her sister

Claire when Claire told her she seemed angry and crazy—and her own vehement denial. Well, not anymore. "As you know better than anybody else. Ronnie, I'm sorry I have leaned on you so hard. Yes, I *am*, Ronnie. You don't deserve it. But, you know, she would hit a quiet patch, and I'd think, *Finally, she gets it.* She'd find something or somebody, a job or a new friend. Like that internship at that film institute in her senior year in high school? And the nanny jobs, college. Everything would start out well again. For a week or two or maybe a day. But it's done; nothing comes between her and drugs, and it can't go on anymore, at least not in my house."

"I'm so glad to hear you say this!" Ronnie says. "It's terribly hard for you, I know, but this is what she needs if she has any chance. And you need to get your life back."

"I know. Finally, I get it in my gut. And for some reason I'm not freaking out, Ronnie; I just want to get this over with. She wasn't home, of course, when I found the heroin; I'd never have gotten into her room otherwise. I also found several syringes. I buried them in the backyard, and then I took the dog on a walk and thought of all you had said to me, you and everybody I trust, what you have been saying to me for so long. I don't know how you could stand it! When I got home, strangely enough, Mona was there, making spaghetti sauce of all things—she rarely cooks. And we had this freaky conversation, like everything was normal. We ate the spaghetti. She said she was going to an AA meeting later, that she's got a temporary sponsor."

"Hmm."

"Well, it's probably bullshit, but she wants so badly to seem normal."

"She wants to please you. She thinks the world of you, Erica."

"She has a hell of a way of showing it. Oh I know, I know, we've established ad nauseam that she's an addict. I was pleasant with her. Thinking how she'd freak out when she found out the drugs were gone. Which she did. And then I told her it was over; I'm done."

Erica had sat at her kitchen table where the dinner plates remained and the bowl of hardening bits of spaghetti sat as Mona raged. At last, she said, "We're done here. Done! You and those pills and heroin. Heroin? It sucks the life out of everyone it touches. Whether you're stupid or gifted, you end up wasting your life. And it's sucking the life out of *me*; this addiction is killing both of us, and I can't go through that again! I won't let it happen here. I won't rescue you anymore, understand you anymore, give you one more chance. I'm done. Mona, you have to pack up and leave, and I'll watch you while you do it."

"How did she take it?" Ronnie asks.

"I was prepared for anything. Knives thrown. Whatever. But she just sat there, sobbing. Then I told her either she needed to choose a rehab—I'd looked into several, all a plane ride away—or else leave the house tonight."

The next day, Mona is on a plane to The Grove in Palm Beach, Florida: land of a thousand rehabs.

SCRABBLED

It's her new home, an apartment of long, dark rooms that she has to share with a stranger. She has no furniture, and the front door lock is broken. Mona pleads with the building manager, who is offstage and thus invisible to her. Please can she have that little, sunny apartment at the end of the hall? But it's take it or leave it and Mona knows she has no other options.

"Hi, Mona! My plane just landed. I'm so excited, too! I'll be there in an hour or so, soon as I get my bag. Love you!"

Mona hangs up the phone in the living room. They don't let them use cell phones, although a couple of the women have burners that they keep lightly buried in the garden around the Grove. But Moira is extremely good at figuring out their ploys and eventually finds the phones. Rumor has it she once called in a drug dog and busted half the house. Surprising herself, Mona actually likes her house manager. She gets that Moira's doing her job, keeping the twelve women—her "motley crew," as she calls them with a smile—on the path. For the first time in recent memory, Mona likes having rules. It's been fifty-eight days. First detox, then this little, pastel-pink, converted motel on a nondescript side street. Nearly every hour is accounted for except free time from three to five, when she can read, sketch, hang with the crew. They all swap stories about their addiction, mainly. Everybody likes the Grove, except Madison. She's nineteen and has flunked out of Betty Ford and some place in Cali that she claims cost twelve hundred thousand dollars. "This place is totally sketchy," she says. "A converted motel? With, I mean, a car repair shop two doors away? And you know what they're doing there, right? Probably?" Madison is an heiress. At the other end of the spectrum is Feather, who never speaks. She's from a rez, so this must seem like luxury to her.

They are allowed to smoke at the far end of the backyard, by the chain-link fence covered with bougainvillea. Mona huddles there now with Angie.

"She's on her way," she says.

"Are you nervous?"

"No . . . yeah. I mean, my mom is pretty cool basically. It's just, you know . . ."

"Yeah," says Angie. "Like she might be judgmental or something?"

Mona's fingers are trembling as she takes a drag. "It's not that."

"It's the stuff with your dad?"

They get up at six thirty, make breakfast, shower, clean the kitchen, make their beds. Have the morning house meeting, read the meditation, get the plan for the day. Get on the shuttle at eight thirty that takes them to work or the therapy center: group/psychodrama/yoga/art/sound. Then lunch, individual therapy, shuttle to the Grove, free time, five thirty make dinner, clean up. Six forty-five shuttle to the AA/NA meeting, eight thirty night house meeting, nine thirty lights out. Weekends: shuttle at free time to the beach/mall/park. Angie came in a week after Mona; they have managed somehow to get to know each other deeply already.

"Yeah, well, I don't want to talk about it."

"'Scuse me."

"Don't get your knickers in a twist, Ange."

"Huh?"

"He used to say shit like that. My dad. He used to wear a Sherlock Holmes cape. And bow ties. 'I won't dignify that with a response'—that's another thing he said." She cries, leaning into the fence. "I miss him so much. When he got sick, I wouldn't go see him. I couldn't."

"Yeah, Mon, but remember what Dominique said in group? We're sick people, not bad people. We all did fucked-up stuff."

"I know." Mona wipes her eyes. "It's just, my mom would get this really sad expression, and I couldn't stand it. I'd have to, you know, go cop something."

"Mon, you aren't thinking of . . ."

"I don't mean now. Before!"

"Oh God, Moira's calling you!"

"Your mom's here, Mona."

Mona wipes her face with her hands and threads her way through the palms and flowers to the gate where she tackles Erica in a bear hug that almost knocks her over.

My God! Erica thinks, breathless, *What's happened to you?* The sunken chest and cheeks are gone. Her daughter is now a plump, young woman with round apple cheeks. She holds onto her mother as to life itself, until Moira, a wiry woman, shakes Erica's hand firmly and invites her in. Mona leads Erica on a tour of the Grove. With its Buddhas, lush plantings, and soothing colors and fabrics, its offerings of art and music therapy, psychodrama, acupuncture, yoga and meditation, it appears to be the polar opposite of the institutional Wings of Hope. Yet there is the "plain vanilla" part too, the talk therapy, the mandatory Twelve Step meetings . . . Women, mostly young but also a few older ones, are sitting in the living room reading the Big Book, the AA "bible." Erica is introduced to Angie, Madison, Feather (who's allowed to sit in a corner by herself and barely lifts her head to acknowledge anything), Tabatha, Mary, Soledad, Katy. Erica can't help but wonder how many of them will make it. And Mona?

"I'm in recovery too," Erica tells them. "It's completely possible."

"Mom . . ." says Mona in her warning tone.

"What was your DOC?" Tabatha asks.

"My drug of choice was booze, but, really, anything in a pinch. Except heroin." She adds in an undertone, "so far." She'd just read an article in the *Times* about all these middle-aged women who got addicted to painkillers, got cut off, and ended up like Mona, hooked on heroin.

"Anything but H? But did you do Percs or Oxys?"

"Tabatha," Moira warns, arms folded.

"They hadn't been invented yet."

"What the—you must be like an old-timer!" Angie's eyes are huge. She's the chattiest one of the bunch. "What about meth?"

"We had our speed, trust me. Not my thing. I liked Quaaludes, which made you bounce off the walls and were banned later for being so harmful. But basically, we were into psychedelics, weed, and booze."

There's silence. Erica adds, "And it all gets you to the same place."

Mona has been shuffling around. "Let's go see my room, Mom."

In her shared bedroom—two twin beds, a closet where a few garments forlornly hang—Mona says with quiet fury, "Mom. Why'd you have to say all that stuff about your addiction?"

"What? I'm in recovery, too."

"Ange is my roommate. She's completely bipolar. Now she'll bug me about you nonstop."

"Really? Why don't you just tell her I'm sober awhile, and she can be, too."

Mona sighs gustily. "Yeah, OK. It's not a big deal, I guess. I just get upset easily. And I get that it's part of early recovery—we talk about that stuff all the time here. But you're my mom. This is about *my* recovery, not yours."

And Erica remembers those early days. Actually years, though she's not about to tell Mona this. The extremes, the hyper-sensitivity about yourself. The hard work of trusting a process you know nothing about, for a minute, then a day, a week . . . Mona's a baby bird. Like a hummingbird. *And I'm an old hen.*

"You're right. This is all new to both of us."

"I'm doing fine, Mom. Moira says I can enroll in the community college here and, oh! I didn't tell you. I got a job, at the Gap—there's a big mall close by."

"That's great, Mona."

"Now that I'm sober, Moira says I can do anything when it's time."

They end up on the shaded patio where Mona finds a Scrabble board. Squarely between them they put the much-used letter board with the tiles, ice cubes merry in glasses of iced green tea, oatmeal cookies—"We made them last night, Mom"—and the heat of a South Florida afternoon. And Erica is squarely between this time and the summer afternoons of her childhood with her mother, who came from the last generation that mastered bridge and croquet in the time before television and computers. That closeness. And Mona is in the past, too, thinking of herself before the fall of puberty, those winter afternoons, snowbound, with Dad, sometimes a friend. Mom was there, too, but it's Dad she needs to remember. She has never felt such a force of loss and yet

belonging as now, and she sort of gets that these feelings are inseparable for her, here on the patio of the Grove Recovery Center for
Women. Tabatha and a few others come out and watch them play
Scrabble, but they are really watching a mother and daughter. This
is what they want, what they all want, really. And Mona becomes
casual, flippant with her hoarded joy, fooling no one.

The other women drift off and Erica and Mona finish the
game. Soon, it will be time for Erica to go. She will see Mona for
two hours again the next day. And, after that, she'll have to go
back home, to her obligations.

Mona wins by five points. She is flushed with victory. She
pours more tea. "Mom? While you're here, I want to make my
amends to you. My therapist says it's too soon, but . . . I need to.
OK: I hate that I was a thief. I stole from you. I took your jewelry.
Dad's meds. I'd go to the city and ride the subways and . . ."

Erica knows these things. But she doesn't want details. Yet
Mona wants to be released from her grimy past, so she listens.
Mona's in that first flush of sober life; her nerves are unprotected,
are exposed to the air, when everything can thrill you or hurt you,
when the slightest criticism or the smallest rejection can plunge
you into despair. But when you also want to make up for lost
time. Erica listens. In her lap, she digs her fingernails into her
hands. And keeps listening. How Mona would end up slumped
in a doorway in the Village, too stoned to move. How she became
adept at stealing wallets on subways. And from friends. They are
both crying. And then it's time to leave.

They are allowed to go out and have breakfast together the
next morning at what Mona calls a "real great Cracker place," the
aptly named Dixie's.

Mona picks at her cheese grits. "I had a bad dream about
Dad last night." She won't say more, except she "needs to get to a
meeting."

"I wish I could go with you."

"No, Mom!" Mona sighs. They return to the Grove, and Erica holds Mona. In her addiction, Mona had lost all her curves. Her period had stopped. God knows what else. Now, she's gaining weight. Her complexion is just a little mottled. Her hair has been cut.

Erica hands her a shopping bag with the wrapped gifts she'd tried not to cry over: a black top (the only color—or non-color —Mona will wear), some Sephora, and paperbacks. "Do not open until Christmas," she warns. It is a week away. She's getting to be an old hand at this.

"Ooh," says Mona, surprising her mother with her own wrapped gift, which will turn out to be a colorfully hand-painted-by-Mona sign: NAMASTE.

Erica puts in her study and when she looks at it, she feels a warm glow.

She has the day ahead of her at Palm Beach before the flight back home. She doesn't want to sightsee, which leaves the beach. But she really just wants to sleep and sleep and not to dream. She calls Mona that evening at seven, the time Moira has assigned. But Moira tells her Mona can't come to the phone. She's very "emotional" at the moment. "Not to worry," she adds. "It's all good. She's starting to deal with the consequences of her actions."

"Tell her I love her," Erica says. She, too, has a lot to learn. Like how to live without fear.

At home, she calls friends she's lost touch with. Deirdre, who she met at the town park when their daughters were toddlers, becoming friends through the years of school, sports, plays, birthday parties, play dates. Emily and Mona had been best friends when they were little, then drifted apart in middle school, but Erica and Deirdre have stayed, intermittently, in touch. They go to a movie and then to a local diner, where Erica bursts into tears about the dog who died in the movie. But she knows she's really crying from a terrible envy. Because Deirdre's Emily is the perfect daughter, polite, high-achieving, cheerful. Her adolescent rebellion had consisted of letting a guy take her top off behind the high school at a dance and getting caught by her father, who'd come to pick her up. After that, she'd resumed her perfection. You'd have to torture Erica before she'd admit it, but she secretly hates Emily.

"Ah, I'm so, so sorry you've had to go through all this," Deirdre, a truly nice woman, says at one point, reaching across the table to take Erica's hand. She must know Erica's tears are not about a dead dog. "All this" meaning losing John and gaining a drug addict for a daughter. Erica would kind of like to bite her old friend Deirdre's hand, even though she knows Deirdre has her own problems. Money is short and she has that shiftless brother she's always getting out of trouble. But Erica is still stuck in that navel-gazing stage of grief where the tribulations of others are not pertinent. And also, she is at her worst around mothers with satisfactory children.

"Remember that time," Deirdre kindly says, trying to divert her weepy, dazed friend, "when the girls picked dandelions in the grass and brought them inside to play with on my new couch?"

"Yeah, and they made the pollen stains worse by rubbing dishwashing liquid on it?" Erica sniffs.

"While we were sitting out on the deck, merrily gossiping."

"You were pretty pissed off," Erica remembers.

"Have you ever tried to get dandelion stains off powder-blue upholstery? But they were good girls. *Are* good girls. Mona's such a talented person, Erica. You can be proud of her. Will be."

Erica is unable to speak. Everyone in town has to know she has a daughter in rehab for heroin addiction. Thank God they're in a back booth, where she can't be seen blubbering.

"I'm a mess, Deirdre," she confesses. *Big revelation*, she

thinks. "But at least now that Mona's getting the right help, I'm going to start living my own life." Which, this year, means no Christmas tree, no parties. She's just going to paint.

As Mona's time in West Palm Beach accumulates, Erica keeps expecting to feel different. She'll wake up one morning, and the thick knots of fear and anxiety will have been smoothed out. She'll be emotionally Botoxed. Except it doesn't happen. She doesn't feel better. It's like she keeps slipping back down into a well. What if Mona leaves the Grove and forgets what she needs to remember?

Things get done, people are seen. She spends time in her studio, fiddling mostly, but she's there. And, of course, she walks the dog. Every afternoon, up and down the hill, rain or shine. She gets interested in listening to music again, in making meals. She has friends over for dinner. Gradually spends more time in the studio.

"Ronnie! Is this a good time to talk?"

"It is. I just got home from work."

"How's the home?" Ronnie has a new job at a retirement center as the activities director, and she loves it. *To each*, Erica thinks, *her own*, as she listens to the latest about the over-eighty set. Well, half-listens.

"What's going on with you?" Ronnie eventually asks.

"Well, I quit therapy—counseling, I mean. She's fine with it, by the way. And I'm *really* fine with it. I just don't want to sit there in her office with the knickknacks and the Dollar Store next door, going over the same old crap anymore."

"So, let's make a plan. Celebrate! I always celebrate when I leave therapy."

"I can come up to Connecticut. I'll bring the dog so Emma has a playmate."

"Let's look at our calendars."

LAUGHING AT LIFE

Erica's in an enormous cathedral with a sky-high vaulted ceiling. The ground begins to tremble and she falls to her knees. Bits of plaster crash down around her, and the building shakes, but she can't see a way out. Then she's awake and realizes she is safe.

Another year has gone by. The third Christmas without John arrives. When the richly embossed invitation to Ned and Tony's Christmas bash arrives the first week of December, Erica takes a deep breath and RSVPs for two. Because this year, Mona will be home for a long weekend from college and has specifically asked about the party.

"Really? I thought you'd be over that. Them."

"Are you kidding? Those guys are such hoots, and I love that house."

"But there probably won't be anyone even close to your age there," Erica says, trying to disguise her pleasure.

"That's the point! I love being around you old Boomers! It's like watching a play. And I'll get to wear my new red dress. Well, vintage new. Plus you and Dad never stayed that long because of all the drinking, so we can leave when it gets boring."

"You remember that?" She and John had taken Mona to Ned and Tony's several times when she was little and they couldn't find a babysitter.

"Oh, bring her, we *love* kids," Ned had drawled. And, the last time, when she was what . . . thirteen? Erica suspected she'd been smoking down in the basement with Tony and his trains. The two of them had been laughing hysterically at his train set, so, come to think of it. It had probably been more than tobacco.

"It wasn't that we didn't have a good time," Erica clarifies. "You know me, I am not great at long social interactions. John would have stayed."

"I remember. He would be playing the piano."

Erica sighs, remembering again how John had been the bon vivant, a three-drinks-at-the-party man, four at the very most. The kind of drinker she had aspired to be, but never achieved, all those heedless years ago.

Mona's living now in a tiny studio in the wilds of Brooklyn, doing well at college since her stint at the Grove. Her recovery group is full of kids her age, most of them apparently in the arts or IT. Mona has a job as a waitress on weekends at a "vintage" diner where she makes big tips. She's been clean for over a year.

"You don't think it will be a problem, being around people who are drinking at Ned and Tony's?" Erica has to say this and also, "And, please, not the red dress—it's a postage stamp."

Mona, who doesn't exercise regularly or eat properly, has a perfect figure. Middle-aged straight men will be licking their chops at the party. Erica can't help routinely pining for the cute little girl in the puffy party dress; letting go is often like untangling an endless knot, she finds.

"Dude! Sorry: Mom! Control issues? I'll wear what I want, OK? Also, I'm going to a meeting before the party. And I'll bake Christmas cookies for Tony and Ned. Sugar cookies with icing!"

"Oh. Well, they'll love that. So we'll go late and leave early?"

"After the food and before they're trashed," Mona translates.

"Dad got trashed there once."

"He did not."

"Well, you drove home, and he sat there reciting Shakespeare with that goofy smile."

"He was . . . tipsy." Of course, kids remember everything.

The night of Ned and Tony's party, it starts to snow: made-to-order, fat, lazy flakes. Their 1700s manor house glistens in the moonlight, the fairy lights twinkle around their perfect picket fence. Inside the hall is a fat tree covered in red-velvet bows, a pile of guests' gifts underneath. Air kisses, busy bar in the corner of the dining room, waiters with trays of prawns and cheese balls. A perfectly decorated, Revolutionary War–era house with nattily turned-out Ned, complete with a scarlet bow tie, waiting to greet guests at the door. A high-profile tax attorney in the city, Ned is a stickler for protocol. He demands and gets perfection in all he surveys, except for bad-boy Tony, once handsome and now collapsed like a soufflé and probably quaffing vodka tonics or playing with his trains in the basement.

"Erica. And dear *Mona*." Ned turns his large face to Erica, and she air-kisses his cheek. As always, he reminds her of a huge, basking lizard, not quite to be trusted.

"So, where's Tony? I baked you guys some cookies," Mona says, holding them out.

"Clever girl, I mean *woman*, and who knew you were a baker, Mona dear? Give them to Charles in the kitchen, would you? We'll have them for dessert."

Mona dashes away, shedding her parka, and, yes, she's quite the youngest person there, with her red dress and green-tipped hair.

"Where is Tony?"

"We had a fight. He's in the basement. He's in such a *mood*."

Which probably means that Tony's been boozing it up again. AA is, for him, a revolving door.

"Erica, I need to talk to you about him." *Oh hell.* Ned continues to think she has answers for Tony the train wreck, just because she's in the program. She's helped find him two rehabs, she's gathered lists of meetings, she's talked programs with Tony, who tends to yell his objections back at her. She's saved for the moment from having to hear about his latest fall from grace by the arrival of a slew of guests and goes off to get a ginger ale before plunging into one of the buzzing, already buzzed, groups.

Mona is already laughing away in the middle of another group. Unlike her mother, she loves parties, and tonight she loves being sober. When, presently, she hears a familiar, full laugh—Mom's— her shoulders loosen. *Thank God, Mom is enjoying herself for once.* Her worries for Erica, who she views as mournful and too isolated, can temporarily recede. And, lately, Erica has been showing signs of life: that guy Ben she went out with for a while. Though it fizzled out, Mona approves of the idea. Although the thought of old people with sex lives is best left alone. Better to think about that new show Mom is getting ready for: *The Bad Dream Notebook.* And those art classes she's doing for poor, little, Guatemalan kids. She dispenses with worrying about Mom.

She glances over at Erica, who's with Ginger and a bunch of random people. They're working on their drug of choice, alcohol, with that silly look already starting. Some of them go outside— in the snow!—from time to time. Duh! Boomers blowing weed, how funny is that?

Tony has reappeared. He's currently sprawled on the love-seat in the TV nook with one of the little dogs on his lap. The man is wasted; what else is new? However, Mona likes Tony. She likes his fantasy train set and his habit of blurting out uncomfortable half-truths. With him is that gaunt woman, Natalie something, an heiress who lives up the road, who matches Tony in the fucked-up department. Tony calls her his girlfriend, which makes Mona giggle. Why does he do that? Pretend he's straight when he's living with Ned? Or OK, maybe he's bi, but who cares? Dude: not *her* generation. She waves at Tony and snatches two mammoth shrimp a cute waiter (who is probably also gay) is offering on a silver tray. Well . . . maybe he's not; he's looking down her dress. Ha-ha. Ya never know. Out of the corner of her eye, she sees Tony lurch to his feet. Poor old Tony, in and out of the program. Ned keeps sending him to "spas," but Mona could tell him that as long as Tony's on marijuana maintenance and fixed for life—a Kept Man—it ain't gonna work. Plus Tony always thinks no one knows he's pounding it down.

Mona shivers. It's the loneliest place in the world, she knows, being an active alcoholic or drug addict. She had come to realize in rehab that she was a hound for all substances—even booze, which she'd always discounted, of course, because it's legal. Those times in high school when she swilled booze, she was always the first one throwing up and stumbling around; hence, her nickname Puka. Well, good luck, Tony, old man. She drifts away, looking for the cute waiter with the shrimp.

"Erica *Mason*, the lovely Erica!" Tony turns his cheek for a perfunctory kiss, holding aloft an ever-present cigarette. "You know Natalie Tremain, of course? We were just talking about Timmy's mad lover getting out of prison next week."

"Can you believe it?" Natalie shrieks. "After burning their *house down*?"

"In a bipolar rage," adds a woman with a tight little mouth

whose name Erica can never remember. But she does remember that she has the handsomest husband there.

"He'd been drinking a lot, too," Tony, who's more than half in the bag already, supplies.

"Well, Sam probably won't do much time," Erica finds herself saying.

Natalie stares at her blankly.

"Because think about it. If Sam was a black guy who held up a Seven-Eleven he'd do serious time. Or be dead. But a middle-class white guy?"

Natalie drains her martini. "Oh dear, a history lesson."

The bartender opportunely appears with wine.

"Can you get me a ginger ale?" Erica asks.

"You and me both, Erica." Tony smirks as the waiter goes off. Each time he resumes drinking, everybody wonders if this time Ned will throw him out. But he never does. "Cheers," he says, proffering what is clearly not ginger ale.

When Erica is released, she heads for the noisy crowd in the smoke-filled living room; Ned has given up banning cigarettes, which he hates, because of Tony and a surprisingly large minority of the others. The windows overlook the pristine winter scene, drifts of snow capping the stone walls like cream lit by discreet spots. *A Wonderful Life* outside, *Whose Afraid of Virginia Woolf?* inside, she thinks. Seeing Ginger again, in the black tent that is her holiday dress, animated as she always is in a tight, laughing cluster of her political pals who are, no doubt, raking over the town gossip, too—Erica opts for the thick arm of a chair near the fire.

"Hello, Peter."

Ginger's husband raises his head from the nearby, matching chair, reminding her of a big, old dog. "Hey, Erica." Peter, a guy who makes infrequent conversation, consisting of wry, often cutting remarks, is the precise opposite of Ginger. Right now, it's soothing to be near him, like a warm blanket.

After a few minutes with the warm blanket, though, Erica is ready again for the Ginger crowd: Gretchen from up the road; that old Broadway actor, still handsome in a roué kind of way; the actor's hawk-eyed wife; the high-strung copyeditor; and a sprinkling of others she doesn't know. There was a time when Erica would have cared that they don't seem interested in her. They're all political animals, not an artist in the bunch save the ancient actor, so it's hard going. Well, let them prattle on about the county supervisor who thinks she's a Dolly Parton clone, the fracas over the water bill, whatever. They're already more than a bit shit-faced, too.

Not surprisingly, they hone in on poor Timmy and the now-imprisoned Sam. Ginger, unsurprisingly, leads the chorus. "Can you imagine? Threw out all his furniture, like he was Hercules, *and* slashed his paintings, then forced Timmy out into the *snow, bleeding,* and lit the match!"

"And he only got three years? Black kids with pot get longer than that," Erica says, thinking she has just said that, more or less, hasn't she? But she feels compelled to point it out, even though this is a stoutly liberal crowd, because, to her it's the point.

Nobody else, however, seems interested in the inequality of the law, feasting as they are on high drama. "And Timmy wants to take him back when he gets out?" the high-strung copyeditor exclaims.

All of a sudden, Erica becomes impatient. Timmy Lord is a nice man, one of those boyishly good-looking gay men who never seem to show their age. She says, "Timmy and Sam both have a drinking problem (*avoid using the* "a" *word around civilians*) and, until they deal with that, they're going to keep self-destructing. In my opinion."

Ginger, who only drinks too much at parties, bats this away. "Oh, he's always made terrible choices."

That's circular logic, Erica wants to point out, but doesn't. Being a bore about alcoholism is not high on anyone's list, even her own. And speaking of bored, Erica is beginning to feel cornered. Why has she come here again? Isn't every year the same? *Well, yes, that's the point,* she tells herself. *It's a tradition, and it's good for her*—AA-speak again—"*to break the isolation.*" As she often does when feeling trapped, Erica begins mentally painting: Ginger, square and handsome. Usually in laborer's clothes for her landscaping business, tonight she wears the real pearls of her inheritance with her plus-size black dress. Ginger's been a fixture in Erica's life since they met in the pasta aisle of the, then, only grocery story in town, more than a quarter-century ago. And Erica both loves her and sometimes finds her highly opinionated self to be infuriating.

Erica takes a puff pastry from a proffered tray and drifts off to talk to Sondra, the county Democratic chair, for her sins. It's hard going, talking politics in the rising hilarity, but Sondra deftly extracts a promise from Erica to attend the next party function, which means coughing up a donation. Again, that will be "breaking the isolation."

"Well," they both say, duty done, and turn away. And, for a moment, Erica seems to catch sight of John's lovely head of thick, graying hair. Wearing his blue sweater and dress trousers, cradling a glass of red wine or a martini, talking animatedly to someone. At once, his ghost flits away, and she downs her ginger ale in a reflex action. They come and go, come and go, these sightings, inflicting her with a sense of amputation. Of the person she has lost and of the third party in the relationship, the marriage itself. Through some kind of alchemy it had taken on its own life. And it dies hard.

She has no time to process this. Ned, a small but important collector in the art world (Dalí prints, Mapplethorpe), approaches with a small, birdlike man in a tweed jacket.

"Erica, this is Mark Lerner. He runs the Slot Museum in Williamsburg? I told him about you. I told him he should give you a *show*," Ned drawls.

"Yes!" says Lerner, who clearly wants to be in Ned's good books. "Why don't you call me in the new year? Or, better yet, come see our new winter show and we can talk then?"

"Anti-Rauschenbergs! It's causing quite a stir," Ned purrs.

"I can't wait," she says and means it. She dislikes Rauschenberg. "Actually, I have been working on a new series, mostly paintings, also a few drawings, a collage, around a theme . . ." *Stop babbling.* Her face is burning.

"Well! That could possibly work for us," Lerner says, "because we're thinking of doing something on exurban artists next year."

Mona has circled in and hears the last bit. "*Oh my God!* My mom's project is *amazing*. I mean, not because she's my mom." A grimace. "It's about these bad dreams; they're these incredible, tiny, little stories packed with drama. There's a couple of good dreams thrown in, too."

"Mona." But Erica is smiling now.

"OK? So it's a *plan*. We'll definitely get together—not January, I'm in Berlin—but February? Call my office after New Year's." He proffers a card.

"Yes," she says, "I certainly will."

Just like that, it's become her world again.

"Oh my God, Gloria, you came!" Mark Lerner turns away to greet an overweight cabaret singer, prized in her tiny subset of the entertainment world.

Erica and Mona slip away and hover at the buffet table.

There are strawberries with cream and a cake and Mona's highly decorated cookies.

"I hear you made these yourself," Tony says, sidling up like an overstuffed cat and enunciating carefully.

"Yeah, my grandma's recipe."

"Oh, I *love* old-fashioned Christmas cookies." He wobbles as he scoops several from the tray.

Most of the guests are now at the repeating-themselves-laughing-at-their-own-jokes phase. Mona glances around with raised eyebrows. Stuffing a large bite of chocolate cake in her mouth—*Where does she put it?* Erica thinks, looking at her daughter's flat stomach—Mona says, "Mom, did you know they say if you eat a lot of sweets you won't want to drink or use?"

"Yes. That little tip saved me in the beginning."

"We should go now."

"You're right. Let's say goodbye to the guys."

"I'll wait here." At the dessert table. How does she do it, have such a sleek figure, a goal Erica has sought and failed to achieve for all of recent memory? And where can Ned be? She finally finds him in the kitchen, berating the cook–housekeeper, a young man with a spotty police record, hired in desperation when the previous cook–housekeeper disappeared with the estate truck one night and was never heard from again—this according to Ginger, who knows all.

"Oh Ned? We're leaving. And I wanted to say . . ."

Ned steers her out of the charged atmosphere into the den adjacent. "Why is the help always trouble?" he drawls. "First the truck, now this drinking on the job, and I can't possibly fire him until after the first. That reminds me, Tony and I are going to a spa in Cabo on January second. No booze, healthy food. Do you think I should book him into a rehab after that? I mean, he liked that place in Pennsylvania, and he was doing really well for a while, but he won't go back. There, anyway. I looked into a few around here. Golden Lomas is more for, you know, mental problems. His problem is booze. Well, marijuana, too, but that calms him down. And he's been off coke for years. I need a good, new, meat-and-potatoes booze place. You were so helpful with Pennsylvania. And whatever you did with Mona . . . she is looking *great*."

"That wasn't me, Ned. It was her. But I'll ask around. I can't, you know, promise you anything. But, off the top of my head, have you checked out Hilltop? It's old-school but pretty well thought of . . . Oh, I am sorry this is happening again."

"It is always happening. Anyway, enough about his woes. You and Mona both look fabulous—whatever you're doing, it works."

Poor Ned; poor, old owl; poor, old, high-functioning drunk himself. "Listen, I can't thank you enough for hooking me up with the Slot Museum guy."

Ned waves airily. "Oh that's a no-brainer. You need to spread your artist's wings beyond little Putnam County."

"All the way to Brooklyn! Again, many thanks. It was a lovely party. Mona says thank you, too—she's clearing out the desserts! Merry Christmas, Ned. And to Tony."

Who is, again, nowhere to be seen.

In the car, Mona starts giggling right away. "Seeing a bunch of old people getting trashed! It's Woody Allen, Mom!"

Erica shoots a look at her, shaking her head, but a laugh rises from some long-stored part of her gut.

"Tony's got the whole town now in miniature in the basement! The train station, the diner, The *El* . . . whatever-it-is . . . that Guatemalan bodega, the Q Lounge pool hall. He showed me the whole thing, smokin' a big, ol' blunt. He's so proud of his train set. Ah!"

They laugh most of the way home.

On Christmas Eve, renewing a family custom, Erica and Mona each open one present, saving the rest for the next day. Under the squat, little tree among the modest heap of gifts, Erica has tucked the letter she'd found in John's desk addressed to Mona, and this is what Mona selects to open on this night. The previous Christmas, determinedly off everything for three weeks, even cough syrup although she had a nasty lingering cold, Mona had spent at an AA party in West Palm. Though not as grim as it sounded—all her program buds were there, and everybody brought food and dessert—she'd cried when she went home and opened Mom's package. A year later, she feels incredibly better, if not yet well. (She has long talks with program people about emotional sobriety and serenity.) This is the first time in memory she's earned the money for gifts, including a scarf and necklace for Mom from one of the vintage thrift shops she frequents. She already knows what Erica's big gift is—tickets to a play in the city the day after Christmas. And she has plans later in the week to have lunch with Misty and go out on an actual date with a guy from her Brooklyn recovery group. A first.

It had taken all of Erica's willpower not to open the letter from John, and, now, as Mona does, not to ask her what it says. Mona's head is bending over the paper like a drooping flower. Sensing drama, Dim, then Dimmer, have padded over to a watchful spot a few feet away. Dim approaches and delicately sniffs Mona's hand while Dimmer stares. *What does it say*? Has John castigated Mona for her bad behavior, for shunning him when he got sick? For that matter, when had he written it? When he found out he was going to die or was it before that? Was it during that last Christmas they were together when he'd rallied, in that strange way the dying often do? Three years ago!

"Mom." Her beautiful child's tear-stained face. "Here. You read it."

It is the last line that breaks Erica.

"And, no matter how we squabble today, I know I'll be the proud father someday who walks you down the aisle."

Mona and Erica and Dim and Dimmer and Casho crowd together on the rug on the cold floor. "I wanted to make him proud of me," Mona sobs. "But now I'll never have the chance."

But Erica tells her she will. She will!

She wakes up the next morning with the feeling that something is missing. Has she forgotten something important? Did she buy the ham for Christmas dinner? She stretches, yawns, not quite ready to leave her warm bed, but Dim and Dimmer are scaling the mountain of her side with their claws and Casho issues brisk "feed me" commands every two and a half seconds. Yet, she enjoys the daily ritual of the animals crouched over their bowls, the coffee on, the cool, winter light, and the furnace humming. While she's drinking her second coffee, it comes to her that she had been given a kind of status report from her unconscious this morning: no lurid dream imagery lingers; in fact, nothing does. She can't remember the last time she woke up without a bad review from her psyche.

Mona still sleeps later than Erica likes, but she has a lot of lost teenager-hood to make up for on the neurotransmitter front. And it's not as monstrously late as it used to be. By noon, she's downstairs clamoring for coffee and helps make the buttermilk-blueberry pancakes that John had always seen to. Showered and dressed, they meet again at the tree. It was the smallest one in the lot, but it's pretty and full for all that. They take turns opening their presents—books from Grandma, gourmet chocolates from

Claire. Erica has given Mona gift cards and some makeup from Sephora. Finally, Mona pulls out what she calls "your special gift." "But before you open it, I, uh, wanna tell you something. My sponsor says I need to make another amends to you."

Oh God, don't let it be a slip. "Can we wait on that and just enjoy our Christmas?" Erica unties the gold ribbon from a box, which she's sure will contain another book. Probably an art book. She begins releasing the taped flaps of red tissue paper, remembering as she does so how, when she and Claire were small, they'd ripped off wrapping paper and ribbons, annoying their dad. She smiles: that little box of a house where they grew up, never much money, the inexpensive gifts at Christmas. But who knew? It hadn't mattered, not to children who were loved, if imperfectly, often distractedly.

"Oh right: 'my house, my rules,'" Mona says tightly. "But I really need to say this. And, no offense, you really need to stop being a control freak, Mom."

Erica sets her half-unwrapped gift aside and stands up. It's back to this again! She wants her illusion of a peaceful, tiny family, just for today. None of the landmines, planted during their war on drugs, are to go off. But it seems she has stepped on one. "Me, a control freak? Right, like I've been able to control anything lately. And I don't want to know anything else about your frigging disease—I'm sick of it!"

Whoa, how is this happening? It's like she, Erica, has turned into Mona—the old Mona—doing what Mona did to her for years. Yes! She's storming off, escaping to her room. *At least I didn't slam the door,* she thinks, as she sinks onto her bed upstairs. *What is wrong with me? I am acting like a goddamn baby. We've been having a beautiful time, the party, the letter, the pancakes . . . This is my resentment, not hers. So get up, wash your face, and apologize.*

She gets up fifteen minutes later and goes downstairs where she finds Mona smoking a cigarette, the TV on.

"*Intervention*? On Christmas?"

"What now?" Mona snaps coolly as Erica settles beside her on the couch. But Erica sees that her hand is shaking as she taps ash onto a plate and clicks off the remote.

"Mona, there is no excuse for my blowup. None. I owe *you* an amend." Erica laughs weakly. "I freely admit I am damaged goods. You didn't deserve that . . . display. I am really sorry. And I really do want to know what you were going to say to me."

Mona sighs rather elaborately. But, Erica notices, her hand has stopped trembling. "I don't blame you for your outbursts, Mom. I get that I was a horrible teenager and a dope fiend, and I owe you more than I can ever repay."

"No, you don't owe me. You don't, Mona! It doesn't work that way. So, what is it?"

They sit there. They've been through so many discussions, arguments, rapprochements, that it's actually getting boring. Mona jumps up and gets the package. "Well, I violated your privacy. I know you hate me going through your stuff without your permission. And I did. I went through your sketchbooks."

Erica sighs. She had—angrily—instituted that rule after four-year-old Mona had gotten into her studio and crayoned all over some sketches. It was she, Erica, who had been careless and left the door unlocked, though. And scared the shit out of a four-year-old.

"Oh," she says, rather tightly. "Well, no harm done."

"You're not pissed at me?"

"No. Yeah, well, annoyed, to be honest. But it's not a big deal."

"Really? So, open the package."

Erica tears off the rest of the paper carelessly. She looks at her gift—it is indeed a book—then at Mona. "I'm practically speechless. This is amazing, Mona!" Slowly she turns the pages of Mona's new graphic novel: *The Mona Project.*

BAD DREAM NOTEBOOK II

"It was like, after I saw your drawings, I had to do my bad dreams, too." She sneaks a look at her mother. "I'd already started drawing cartoons and random stuff when I was using. I didn't only do drugs, you know. I didn't want to just do drugs. I'd sit in my room and draw this fantasy world."

"But I never saw any of this when I was, well, cleaning your room."

"Snooping, Mom. It was different for *you* to look at *my* stuff, I know. You were worried about what I was doing. Hey, but you never found half my stuff! Including my sketchpads, which I stashed in the linen closet under some old towels."

"Very clever."

They sit close together on the couch by the glittering tree and dive into *The Mona Project*. There isn't much of a plot as far as Erica can tell. In the first pages, Mona's imagination is more than a little undisciplined, protean, yet that gives it a raw, and often funny, edge, with a punkish heroine fighting her battles of the unconscious. A page where she is alone in a skating rink, bending and dipping in that exact shade of periwinkle-blue skating dress that Mona had ice-skated in every week at the Ice Arena. Erica, a clumsy skater, watched with wonder. Wonderful years! She turns the page. The same girl is skating, but now the ice bristles with sharp icicles, like knives ready to trap and wound her if she falls.

Dinner and a movie are forgotten. They end up making sandwiches from the ham Erica had planned for their celebratory dinner (along with roasted artichokes, scalloped potatoes, and salad, now abandoned for potato chips). Around the studio they prop up Mona's sketchbook and Erica's drawings, collages, and the two oil paintings that comprise her *Bad Dream Notebook*. The relaxed picnic atmosphere—paper plates, cushions, Mona smoking, coffee Mona has made, Italian roast so strong it feels illegal—is in sharp contrast with the angst of their art. Yet there is a sense of closeness, of being in this together.

"This one, I know it's, like, from a cheesy Hitchcock wannabe . . . but I had this dream over and over for a while." This being a fifties noir drawing of a young woman seen from behind with cropped, platinum hair, tiny shorts, and floppy T-shirt—Mona, in other words. She is running down a bleak, deserted street—past an overflowing trash can, past a rat; behind her is a shadowy figure in a long coat and—yes—John's broad-brimmed Italian hat. On the facing page, the cropped-hair girl turns, saucer-eyed, mouth open. "No!" says a speech balloon, and the murky figure of terror is reeling away, as if struck by lightning.

"It's good, Mona. Really good. The terror is there. You stood up to it! And you're a good draftsman—draftsperson."

Mona's cheeks are pink with pleasure, and she is at once younger and more grown-up than in recent years. *Oh, Mona, you can't imagine how much I love that you don't have drug zits anymore, no fresh track marks. You don't make those horrible, honking noises, and you have boobs now. If this doesn't last, I will still have this. That you came of age and shared this precious part of yourself with me.*

"So many of these dreams we've had, they're *ghoulish*." Mona taps two of Erica's pen-and-inks: the mummy feet sticking out of the kitchen drawer and the operating table with the snake emerging from the patient.

Erica is suddenly tired. "Yes, I agree. But they're real; they have power. After I dreamed about the surgery, I remembered seeing these weird, little pictures in markets when I was backpacking around South America. Tiny paintings of dentists yanking teeth out and surgeons removing bloody blobs. So that's . . ."

But the mood has changed. Erica can feel Mona drawing away. "But it's about *him*, not some random Latino street art homage. It's my dad!" She drops her head. "And it was so awful."

"Yes. It was."

"My sponsor says there's no way to avoid the pain."

"Not that I've been able to figure out."

"It sucks!"

"It does suck. But it has to be gone through and it will get better; believe me. Ronnie used to say, 'There's a light at the end of the tunnel.'"

"Oh great, another cornball AA saying. These stupid drawings!"

Erica says she's going to bed. She lies in the dark a long time, to the murmur of Mona's laptop across the hall.

"There's a happy dream you haven't seen yet," Erica says at breakfast the next day.

Mona puts her toast down. "I thought I'd seen them all. It's in that locked drawer, right?"

"Yes. An oil," Erica adds. "To keep it away from the cats." She takes a slurp of coffee. "I don't know if you remember when one of them heaved on a painting that wasn't quite dry?"

Mona snorts. "No, but they've always been pukers."

So, Erica thinks, *she seems to be in a better mood.* "Well, that's the reason it's there. And, I haven't seen the last pages of your book either."

"OK, yeah, so let's wrap it up."

In the studio, Mona sits rather formally in the wicker chair, waiting while Erica retrieves and unrolls the canvas.

"Ta-da!"

"Wow. It's really . . . impactful. But, uh, isn't it kind of racist? You know, not PC?"

They both study the painting: It's Erica as a black woman on stage in a cloche hat with a big feather and a red, Roaring Twenties, form-fitting gown, with a three-piece band of black musicians behind her. Her gloved arms are opened wide, her white-painted mouth, too. A smudged crowd can be seen in the foreground, reaching out to her. Emotion gleams like fire in Erica's eyes.

"This is *not racist!* It's a completely accurate dream. I was an African American singer. I had to channel Bessie Smith. I was terrified with stage fright, but I just got it together, somehow, and being on stage belting out the blues felt fantastic! I was moaning the blues. And the audience loved me!"

"OK, yeah, it's really good, but who knows about Bessie Smith? I mean, I do, because Dad had vinyl."

"Well, but, do you like it?"

Mona squints at the painting. "You get how scared she is, and there's a lot of power in there, too. It's different than the rest of your dreams; it's quirky, and it's about you getting past the fear? Right? Getting past the fear," she repeats. "I guess it's not racist," she adds after a moment. "Universalist?"

"Good, because if we have to start censoring our dreams, I'll kill myself. Kidding!"

"OK, my turn, I guess." Mona sets *The Mona Project* in her mother's lap and stands next to her chair. She flips to the last page. It is also, unlike the rest of the graphic novel, in color—flat-out, glorious Technicolor.

The protagonist, the girl with short, spiky, platinum hair, is standing beside a convertible. And not just any convertible—a fire-red Ferrari Spider, parked at an angle before an enormous tree. The tree is backlit by slashes and whorls of brilliant shades of orange, pink, red, yellow, and purple. A forest fire, or maybe a firework display, illuminates the astonishing architecture of the dozens of lifted, arched limbs and branches and leaves of the tree. It has to have taken many hours for Mona to have drawn this. And then—the platinum girl. In three-quarter profile, her face is almost completely visible but with just enough in shadow to add emotional ballast. Her eyes are shining; her smile is wide. But, like the faux Bessie Smith, there is something ambiguous in her expression besides happiness, something other than joy and wonder. It is, Erica decides, the faint dye of fear. Yes, she is sure of it; it is unmistakable. And it is appropriate.

"Yes!" she says, again and then again. And that is all, and, apparently, all she needs to say. She and Mona are hugging, and maybe both of them are crying a little—Erica is—but it's all good, she thinks.

On New Year's Day, Erica opens her bad dream sketchbook again. Mona has gone back to her tiny but bright studio in Brooklyn. In January, she'll start her second semester at the college. She got 3 A's and a B the first semester. She will have all manner of encounters with the unending cornucopia of personalities to be found in New York City. She is working through her grief. Clean and sober. The pages of the sketchbook make a satisfying crackle, these drafts of the artifacts of her pain and, occasionally, joy. She believes they have been necessary, an exorcism for her. Even in the most ghoulish of them, an end was achieved. And, afterwards, there was always a new, blank page. But she feels done with this particular dance now.

The day is bright, the sky the blue of a child's crayon, the earth cloaked in white. She has talked with Mona earlier in the day about the group show at the Slot Museum in Brooklyn in early summer (on the other side of the borough, like the other side of the moon), told her again she *will* move through her grief for her father, that he would be happy to see her living well now, that he always just wanted her to be happy. She has taken Casho out for his walk, and, when he turned to stare at her with blank bewilderment after sinking into a snowdrift, her laugh rang out in the clear, cold air. The good mood persists now, back at the house. John had loved snow; together they had cross country–skied on golf courses, down forest trails; they had bought little Mona little skis. Erica had thought they'd always be together, gliding through the blue-white of winter, warm from exertion on those trails.

When she goes to bed, she gets the little bottle of sleeping pills but she doesn't open it. She's going to try to get to sleep without it. And she does.

Six little girls and one little boy are diligently and inexpertly dunking their brushes in water, then into pools of colors, and filling paper with flowers and tigers and Mom and Dad and brothers and sisters. Esperanza, Sonia, Tania, Jimena, Maria, Isabel, and Gustavo, the lone boy. Jimena and Gustavo don't speak English yet, but Erica keeps Spanish to a minimum. Like all small children, they quickly, gleefully pick up a new language and especially love to shout back the English words for colors.

At snack time, she gives them apple juice and graham cracker cookies in the shape of bears. At the end of the class, they carry their pictures proudly home, following their small mothers or older siblings across the street and up the hill into the shabby village, past the tattered gray-black March snow and the faded old houses, home once to Irish and German and Italian immigrants who'd worked on the farms and the iron mines and the little factories—all gone

now. The houses are cut up into rooms for these latest of the immigrants, the Guatemalans. Erica likes the quiet of the art room when
the energetic children are gone, although they are not noisy like
American kids. If anything, they are too subdued, these children
of "illegals" who shadow their peasant parents. And Erica also likes
cleaning up the spills, rinsing the brushes, gathering the abandoned
papers. She keeps their best work on a shelf in a closet for the show
they'll have at the last class in May, for which she'll bake cupcakes
and invite their mothers.

She turns off the lights and locks the door. Time for lunch
and a few chores, a rest maybe, a few hours of work with her own
brushes and paints. *Bad Dream Notebook I and II* is on for June
at the Slot Museum. Mona and her many friends in the borough
of Brooklyn will ensure a good turnout. Erica has the stirrings
of an idea for a new series, which will be sketches of patients—
clients—she'd met at Wings of Hope and the Grove. The images
are still vague, fluttering around, but with enough of a kick to
demand attention. Whether they'll be her best yet, who can tell?

*A woman is driving a car down a shady lane. She rounds
a bend, and a mammoth tree rises up straight ahead,
lit from behind by fireworks or flames. Its labyrinth
of branches is clothed in a molten cerise. It's such a
spectacular display, so beautiful, that the woman forgets
to be afraid.*

ACKNOWLEDGMENTS

Writing *The Bad Dream Notebook* meant facing years of emotional pain—and release. As is always the case with fiction, it also meant discovery—of personal shortcomings but also strength, and, above all, the peculiar satisfaction of allowing characters to inhabit their world in ways often surprising to me, the author. Because it is fiction, my own experience soon became another ingredient in the story.

Maybe some writers can create novels on an emotional desert island. I can't. I have needed the support of those who are dear to me and of the extraordinary team at She Writes Press. My publisher, Brooke Warner, and editor, Cait Levin, are always available—indeed, they are carving out new ways to support and empower women writers. Thank you to all at She Writes. And thank you, above all, to my children: Tim, an amazing chef, raconteur, and endless enthusiast, and Katrina, screenwriter, adventurer, and power of example.

ABOUT THE AUTHOR

Linda Dahl is an award-winning author of seven previous books of both fiction and non-fiction. She writes about challenging personalities and difficult issues, reflecting her interests in the arts and addiction and recovery. She has two children, lots of animals and lives in an old farmhouse in upstate New York where she serves on several organizations to educate, prevent and help young people with potential or actual drug use dependency.

Author photo © Chris Loomis

SELECTED TITLES FROM SHE WRITES PRESS

She Writes Press is an independent publishing company founded to serve women writers everywhere. Visit us at www.shewritespress.com.

How to Grow an Addict by J.A. Wright. $16.95, 978-1-63152-991-7. Raised by an abusive father, a detached mother, and a loving aunt and uncle, Randall Grange is built for addiction. By twenty-three, she knows that together, pills and booze have the power to cure just about any problem she could possibly have . . . right?

The Velveteen Daughter by Laurel Davis Huber. $16.95, 978-1-63152-192-8. The first book to reveal the true story of the woman who wrote *The Velveteen Rabbit* and her daughter, a world-famous child prodigy artist, *The Velveteen Daughter* explores the consequences of early fame and the inability of a mother to save her daughter from herself.

Shelter Us by Laura Diamond. $16.95, 978-1-63152-970-2. Lawyer-turned-stay-at-home-mom Sarah Shaw is still struggling to find a steady happiness after the death of her infant daughter when she meets a young homeless mother and toddler she can't get out of her mind—and becomes determined to rescue them.

Stella Rose by Tammy Flanders Hetrick. $16.95, 978-1-63152-921-4. When her dying best friend asks her to take care of her sixteen-year-old daughter, Abby says yes—but as she grapples with raising a grieving teenager, she realizes she didn't know her best friend as well as she thought she did.

Cleans Up Nicely by Linda Dahl. $16.95, 978-1-938314-38-4. The story of one gifted young woman's path from self-destruction to self-knowledge, set in mid-1970s Manhattan.

Fire & Water by Betsy Graziani Fasbinder. $16.95, 978-1-938314-14-8. Kate Murphy has always played by the rules—but when she meets charismatic artist Jake Bloom, she's forced to navigate the treacherous territory of passionate love, friendship, and family devotion.